Chasing Galaxies

EVELYN LATRICE

Even when your legs ache and the stars feel out of your reach— keep running— keep Chasing Galaxies

Untitled

Editor: Imajinconsulting

Synopsis

At twenty-one, Noodle is done being America's little sweetheart. Once a beloved child star, she's now desperate to escape the glittering image forced upon her and discover who she is as a woman. Her ultimate dream? To pour her soul into music and finally sing on her own terms. But carving out a new identity is messy, especially under the relentless gaze of a public that refuses to let her grow up.

Bu, on the other hand, is six months out of prison and navigating a world that moved on without him. At twenty-five, he's rough around the edges and no-nonsense, determined to focus on starting a landscaping business and leaving his mistakes behind. Love is the last thing on his mind until he crosses paths with Noodle.

Despite their differences, an undeniable connection blooms between them. As they navigate their own struggles— Noodle fighting to reclaim her voice and Bu learning to trust himself in a free world, they find solace, understanding, and passion in each other. Together, they embark on a journey that's as unpredictable as it is beautiful, proving that sometimes, chasing galaxies means finding the courage to reach for the stars in each other.

Stop, in the name of love!

This is an interconnected standalone that can be read on its own but reading from the beginning makes the experience sweeter.
To The Moon
Beyond The Stars
Woke Up On Mars

1

SEPTEMBER

The music blasted beneath Noodle, the floor vibrating with every beat as Aku tipped the fancy bottle to her lips. It burned a path down her throat. Megan rapped about bad bitches, and for once, Noodle let herself believe she fit the description. Any other day, she'd argue against it, but tonight she was determined to lean all the way in.

Madison Heights, California, was just a suburban blip outside of Los Angeles, a place she'd called home for the past two years. But the club and neon lights had been unchartered waters for her. Her network was always watching and whispering, making it nearly impossible to let loose.

But tonight was different.

Butterflies rumbled in her stomach, but she didn't care. She'd flung herself into the first club she saw, refusing to let another birthday slip by uncelebrated, even if the thought of another year around the sun didn't exactly thrill her.

Hands high and hips rolling, Noodle moved to the beat, her body flowing effortlessly as the bass thumped beneath her heels. She felt alive. She felt weightless, like nothing and no one could touch her.

"Drive the muthafuckin' boat!" Aku yelled, her voice cutting through the loud music as she pushed the drink against Noodle's lips again. If her girl wanted to turn up, then she was going to make it a night to remember.

The clear liquid burned but Noodle welcomed it. It wasn't her first time having a drink—just her first time having a legal drink. "It's my birthday!" she shouted as if Aku didn't already know. There was an anxiousness in her chest, but she pushed it to the side because it was her day. Onlookers and naysayers be damned, Noodle was going to live it up.

They were in a section having the time of their lives. It was just the two of them, the way Noodle preferred it. Having too many people around never turned out well for her. She had too much at stake to take the chance.

Aku pushed her phone to her ear with her face scrunched up. She said a few words before hanging up.

"Who was that?" Noodle yelled over the thump of the music, still moving her body never missing a beat.

"Little Lunar worrisome ass," Aku said, looking towards the entrance of the club.

Noodle's eyes followed and a smile stretched across her face when she laid eyes on Lunar.

Horns and sirens blared through the club as the DJ announced him and Devin Port to the club, making everyone throw their hands in the air.

Unlike Noodle, Lunar had found his footing in the rap game. He was blowing up more and more every day with a sound the people loved, and a face women dreamed about.

Aku bumped her shoulder. "That nigga so fine," she said licking her lips watching Devin Port swagger his way over to their section behind Lunar, with Lunar's best friend Pimp following closely behind.

Noodle nodded because Aku wasn't lying. Anyone with eyes could see that three of the sexiest men alive had just walked in.

The women were all vying for their attention, some even being bold enough to reach out to grab a piece of them.

Devin and Pimp seemed unfazed while Lunar soaked it up, winking and blowing kisses at a few of them. Noodle snickered at how much swag he had.

When they made it to the section, Lunar trekked towards her.

"Happy birthday, little Noodle," Lunar's smooth, intoxicating tone shook her more than the loud music.

His dimpled smile almost made her weak in the knees.

Her arms went around him, inhaling his scent. Dressed in all black, he knew he looked good. The two of them had a weird, flirty relationship that never went beyond that. As kids they flirted but Noodle put him in the best friend zone when they became teens. That never stopped him from picking on her from time to time though.

"You came," she whispered with gratitude.

It had been months since the two of them laid eyes on one another in the physical form, but once they linked, time nor distance didn't matter. What they'd created in the studio with Luna kept them linked in the most beautiful ways.

"You know I wasn't gon' miss my favorite girl turning legal."

"Damn, that's the only cousin you see?" Aku rolled her neck, loving the idea of getting under her big cousin's skin.

Lunar was the first born out of the sibling's kids but he only had her by two years. It wasn't long before her loud cries were terrorizing the house when he was just a baby himself. The two of them had been close ever since.

"Noodle ain't my cousin." He smirked before pulling Aku in for a hug, never taking his eyes off Noodle whose eyes went everywhere but to him.

Seeing Pimp, Noodle smiled. "Hey, Pimp."

"Gotdamn, Noodle. Them people know you out?" Pimp hugged her tightly while looking down at her.

While Noodle was five-eight, Pimp and Lunar had to be about six-one —no taller than six-two.

Pimp was a cutie. He had long locs and peanut butter skin covered in tatts. His downturned eyes pulled people in, and his fun and charismatic personality left them begging for more.

Devin pushed up, passing her a box. "Happy birthday, Jay Jay," he spoke in a low tone but somehow Noodle still heard him over his song, which the DJ played. It felt like the whole club was rapping along word for word.

Devin Port was what some considered an OG in the rap game. He started when he was eighteen and quickly rose to fame. Now at twenty-eight, his success had him in people's top five.

Nervously, Noodle giggled while opening the box to reveal an icy Cuban link bracelet. She had only met him once, so the extravagant gift had her mouth on the floor. "You didn't have to get me anything," she blushed.

"Oh yes he did," Aku butted in, admiring the bracelet with a nod of approval.

"Lunar told me last minute about swinging through. If I had more time it would've been more thought out." Devin shrugged like it was no big deal, at least to him it wasn't.

Noodle bumped Aku's shoulder knowing her bestie was smitten already. "Well thank you."

"And what you got me?" she looked at Lunar.

He smirked, "You want it here in the club?" His thick brows and deep dimples teased her.

Noodle shook her head, dismissing him before the five of them settled into having a good time. They ordered more drinks, this time adding food because the way Lunar and Pimp had Noodle tossing back shots, she knew she was going to need something greasy to soak it all up.

The DJ had the club rockin', making sure to say Devin Port's name after every few songs. Then he turned the attention on Lunar. They were in California and Cali showed Lunar so much love being his stepdad, Maverick was from there.

The DJ spun one of Lunar's more West coast songs that held a super up-tempo beat.

Lunar loved the way the song hyped the crowd every time he heard it being played. It was vibey and reminded him of a time when he went in the studio just to have fun, so his hands went up in the air to rap along, while Noodle bent over and shook her ass to the beat, holding onto the rail.

"My bitch ride around them thangs! The thangs that make you think, not go bang," Aku rapped before her hand slapped Noodle's round ass to the beat. "With my bitch it's never hard to explain."

As the beat cut in and out with the bass drops, Noodle made her ass do the same. With his hands still in the air, Lunar stood behind Noodle leaving just enough space to respect the friend-zone she kept him in. That and it was always a good time fuckin' with her.

With a devilish grin, Noodle threw caution to the wind. She didn't care who was watching, didn't care about anything, except living her life the way she wanted. Her careless behavior was courtesy of the liquor but she was vowing to make the best of it, before the lashing she knew she'd get the next day. Without hesitation, she pressed herself into Lunar, her back flush against his chest, her body melting into the rhythm of the music. His hands instinctively found her waist, but she wasn't having it - she wanted control, and tonight…it was all hers.

She was happy, and felt free for the first time in years. Of course, she wished the rest of her family could've been there, but she understood everyone had hectic lives just like her. Outsiders admired the hustle of the family without knowing how much quality time was sacrificed, while they continued to build their legacy.

"Little Lunar, you better hold on," Noodle laughed when his eyes bulged at her showing her playfulness in public.

Noodle was so much more complex when it came to her personality. In public, she wore her armor well. Always poised, controlled, and untouchable...*always on.* No one besides family got to see her just relax, so Lunar was happy she was letting her hair down for her birthday.

"Show out!" Aku screamed, deciding to do her big one too. Placing both hands on the railing next to Noodle, she bent over to throw her ass in a circle on Pimp, making sure to catch Devin's eyes as she did.

Of course he was looking. Those brown eyes of his locked in on hers.

Aku was the nineties kind of fine. Her sleek bob and caramel skin matched her *it girl* persona, while the freckles dotted across her nose gave her an innocent, naive girl look which was so far from the truth.

He licked his lips with a slight angling of his head to watch her handful of ass bounce to the beat. Devin couldn't lie, Aku was fine as hell. That was where his feelings stopped though. At twenty-eight, he knew girls like Aku weren't ready for the shit he was ready for.

It wouldn't hurt to look though.

Lunar smiled big, making sure to keep his movements PG, but staying right by Noodle. His hand went to her waist. "Aye, pull your dress down," he leaned in to whisper in her ear.

The dress she wore was like a second skin, clinging to her body. It was a brown color that looked beautiful against her tawny skin but with one wrong move, her pussy would be exposed. And no matter how much Lunar like messing with her, he never wanted to cross the line with her. He loved her too much for that.

Noodle twisted towards him, her hand tapping his face lovingly. "Aww, Little Lunar you love me like a cousin."

His head fell back with a loud laugh. "No more drinks for you. But Happy birthday, Little Noodle. I hope this year brings you everything plus a whole lot more." Lunar kissed the side of her face sincerely.

She hoped her twenty-first year was better than the others

'cause Lord knows she was drowning and didn't even want to get out the bed most days.

―――――

Noodle chewed on her bottom lip as all eyes seemed to sear her skin. She picked at the lint on her overly worn sweatpants regretting her decision to show up like she'd just rolled out of bed, even if she'd just rolled out of bed.

Her head throbbed as vomit rumbled in her stomach.

One night of fun had turned into a throbbing headache and questions she preferred not to answer.

Marcus, the mouthpiece of KidVerse tapped his fat fingers against the oak wood table that housed the other ten set of eyes on her. When his eyes gazed into hers she gulped.

Qamar's voice rang in her ears, telling her, *'if you want to be an adult, demand your respect as one. Open your mouth and set fuckin' boundaries'*. "I'm here… what's up?" Noodle asked. Listening to the shakiness of her tone she knew the words didn't come out as confidently as she wanted.

"I mean, we're here because of you… the floor is yours," Marcus challenged, knowing she would fold like she always did. People pleasers always crumbled. "You went out… had a good time, I suspect." His eyes swept over her top knot, wrinkled t-shirt and dingy sweatpants. "There are some beautiful videos and photos of how wonderful your night was floating around."

"'cause people seem to be way too concerned with my life," she mumbled under her breath.

"What was that?" Marcus cupped his ear, teasingly. When she didn't repeat it, he continued. "I understand you're bored."

"I'm not bored… I'm tired! Tired of hiding who I am… who I'm becoming."

"That was what you signed up for when you became the network's perfect little princess." He sighed, hating this part of his job because over the years he had developed a soft spot for

Noodle. She was such a breath of fresh air. Always in the best of spirits and had the best attitude. As the years progressed, her smile stopped meeting her eyes and Marcus hated how child stars struggled once they got older. He took his concerns to the network but like most things, they didn't see a need to fix what they felt wasn't broken. In their eyes, it was a rite of passage.

Noodle licked her lips, allowing a few beats to pass before she found her words. "I'm a young adult now. I want more adult-like roles... I wanna make music that relates to where I am in life now... How I feel... Love... relationships... self-doubts."

"Sex?" Marcus' brows damn near touched his spray painted hairline which he thought no one knew wasn't real.

The confidence in her chest deflated. Noodle was drowning in a pool while everyone stood around watching, thinking she was swimming when in reality she was fighting to keep her head above water.

Sarah, who was supposed to be her assistant, but really worked for the network as a babysitter, chimed in. "I think Jacory isn't beat for this conversation right now. I mean, she looks exhausted."

You think? She thought but refrained from saying it out loud. When it came to confrontation, she avoided it like the plague.

"That's what happens when you shake your ass all night," Justin snapped. He worked on her team as well and they never got along. He felt like she was taking up a spot someone else would've been blessed to have.

"Justin!" Marcus fussed, giving him a look that read, *play with someone else.* "I might have something in the pipeline for you, Jay Jay."

Jay Jay was the name of the show the network created around her bubbly personality and doubled as her name on the show. Jay Jay came from a wealthy family where her parents were never home, leaving her with her aunt who was only twenty-five. To make the show even funnier, they lived on a ranch that sat on acres of land with animals creating a bunch of mischief for her to get into.

At first, Noodle thought working on set would be fun but after about a year she was able to see it for what it really was— a job.

Her eyes twinkled. "Really? An adult role?"

"More teenager-ish," Marcus shrugged, like his words didn't just knock the wind out of her.

It was shit like that, that really made Noodle's heart race and not in a good way.

"I'm grown now— shouldn't I be doing things that reflect that?" Noodle huffed, cutting her eyes at her management team like they'd lost their minds. "That includes, drinking, dancing, and sex if that's what I want to do with my life and my body!"

Any and everything she did got blown out of proportion and she was over it. A night out to celebrate her birthday seemed to make the headlines which got her hauled into the office earlier than she liked.

Then to make matters worse, they were insulting her, acting like they were giving her something, when all they did was spoon feed her bullshit. It was the side of the industry no one talked about...the side where the dreams of kids coming to fruition somehow turned into a nightmare.

Marcus clasped his hands together and rested them on the table. With his weight on it, the table creaked— the sound wouldn't have been noticed if the room hadn't grown so silent. "That may be true but to America you are still their sweetheart, and no one wants their reality shattered by the idea of you being an adult."

"Forget their reality! What about my life? I'm the one suffering. I just turned twenty-one, for Christ's sake." Noodle jabbed a finger into her chest with every word. "I just want to live life my own way."

"That's not doable right now, Jacory," Marcus squeezed his eyes shut. "Just go home, let me see what I can do."

Noodle didn't wait to hear anything else before she stormed out of the conference room. As she huffed and stomped down the hall, through the cubicle area, she regretted her choice to sign under the largest child network in the world. Luna tried to warn her, but she didn't listen. The regret pained her chest. How would she get out of the toxic cycle she found herself in? She didn't want to involve her family 'cause when it came to those damn Moonys, they played no games.

To make matters worse, KidVerse liked to pretend they loved her but none of them had even opened their mouths to wish her a happy birthday.

———

Noodle stormed through the front door of the penthouse, her heart still pounding, chest tight with the frustration that had been bubbling up all day. Her head throbbed in tune with the pounding of her feet against the hardwood floor.

The door slammed behind her, echoing throughout the empty space. She didn't care. She needed to be loud, to do something that matched the clamor in her head. With a sigh that carried the weight of everything she couldn't say, Noodle threw her jacket over the back of the couch, kicked off her shoes, and peeled the sweatpants that felt like a second skin off her legs. She didn't know what was worse— the fact that she had let herself be dragged into that meeting or the fact that she had shown up looking like a hot mess, barely making an effort to try and look "presentable."

"Girl, what happened to you?" A voice broke through the silence, a cool and sarcastic sound that Noodle knew all too well.

Aku was already sprawled out on the couch, scrolling through her phone, as though she had been expecting Noodle's dramatic entrance. Her presence was the comfort Noodle needed, even if she didn't want to admit it right now.

"Don't even start," Noodle muttered, slumping down beside

Aku on the couch. Her stomach churned as she leaned back, closing her eyes. The motion only made the nausea worse, and her head felt like a hundred jackhammers were at work.

Her body was screaming for sleep, but the fire in her chest wasn't going to let her rest.

Aku snorted, not missing a beat. "Don't start what? You look like someone dragged you through the mud and left you for dead. Is that how bad your meeting went?"

Noodle turned to her, eyes half-lidded, a mixture of exhaustion and something darker in them. "You have no idea."

"Oh, baby, I think I know. The whole world knows. Hell, I could probably get the tabloids to tell me what went down at your little *sit-down*." Aku raised an eyebrow, tossing her phone onto the coffee table. "Did they at least give you a cookie for making it through that circus? Or did they just use you as a punching bag?"

Noodle groaned and buried her face in her hands. "I'm so tired, Aku. I'm tired of all this shit. Like, I thought I had the power to change things, to make them see me, to grow up and be more than the princess they want me to be." Her voice cracked on the last word. She'd been holding that back all day, along with the tears that wanted to break free. "But instead, they want me to be the same. They don't even care about me anymore. They just care about how much money I can make for them, how long they can keep the image of 'sweet, innocent Jacory' intact. They want me to keep playing dress-up for them."

Aku didn't say anything right away. She let Noodle spill, knowing the words would come out sooner or later. She didn't rush her. She just kept her eyes steady on her, waiting for Noodle to finish unraveling.

Finally, Aku let out a deep breath. "So, what happened in there? You look like someone just told you that you're never gonna get out of the little princess box."

"Because that's what they told me," Noodle shot back bitterly. She pulled her knees up to her chest, wrapping her arms around them like a shield. "Marcus said I was their perfect little princess. That I was *still* a teenager to them... that no one wants to see me as an adult. They gave me this half-assed role in a show for a bunch of kids, and when I said I wanted more— wanted real music, real roles— he just laughed... like it was a joke."

"Now you know you can be a bit dramatic... did he really laugh?"

"Bitch, you know what I mean." Noodle rolled her eyes at Aku. They both knew that if Marcus could let her be who she wanted to be, he would. But just like her, he was on a tight leash too.

Aku shook her head, clicking her tongue. "That's what you get for signing with them. You're just a product to them, Noodle. I hate to say it, but you should've known better."

"I know," Noodle mumbled, staring at the floor, her fingers tightening around her knees. "I *know*. But I thought... I thought if I just kept pushing, kept trying, they'd see me. I thought I could still be myself in all of this, but I'm not Noodle anymore, Aku... not the Noodle I want to be. I'm a damn business venture to them, a means to an end. They don't care about who I really am."

Her words hit like a heavy weight in the room, and Aku didn't respond immediately. The silence stretched between them, as thick and as suffocating as the fog rolling in from the window.

Then, finally, Aku exhaled sharply, a sound that bordered between a laugh and a sigh. "So, what now, princess? You gonna keep fighting this fight? 'Cause I'm gonna be real with you, you're gonna have to either break free or you're gonna drown. And the last thing I need is for you to drown in a sea of plastic smiles and fake ass compliments."

Noodle's head dropped into her hands, and she let out a low laugh. Aku was funny without trying too hard. It was bitter, hollow, but it was something. "I feel like I'm drowning already," she muttered.

"You're drowning because you're letting them control the tide. You're letting them pull the strings and play puppet master, while you're out here getting your soul chipped away. And no one—not even them—can take that from you unless you let them." Aku's voice was quieter now, the usual biting humor replaced with something that sounded almost like concern.

Noodle's throat tightened, but she swallowed hard. "I just want to make music that matters, Aku. I wanna write songs that reflect where I am. I wanna explore love... and loss... just real life shit, but they won't let me do that. Every time I try to step outside the box, they push me back in. I'm suffocating... I just wanna be happy."

"Okay, well then let's stop pretending that you fit in the box, huh? Time to break out of that muthafucka. Ain't no reason for you to stay stuck in a little cage of everyone's expectations. It's *your* life, Noodle... not theirs."

Those words hit harder than any advice Noodle had gotten in that meeting. Her eyes shot up to meet Aku's. No matter how nerve wracking or annoying Aku could be, it was the little moments like this that reminded Noodle how she needed Aku more than she knew.

"How?" she asked, her voice small and fragile.

Aku smiled, leaning forward, that knowing glint returned to her eyes. "Bitch, if you can pull off half the shit I've seen you do on stage, you can *absolutely* break free from these fuck ass people. You've got more power than you think. But you've gotta want it, Noodle. You gotta want to take control of your life, and use what you have to get what you want."

Noodle stared at her for a long time, allowing her best friend's words to really sink in this time. She `knew what she had to do. She had to stop letting the world dictate who she was. She was ready for her own revolution.

"You right," Noodle said, her voice steadying... the pressure on her chest easing. "I'm done playing their game, done pretending to be someone I'm not. I'm going to do it my way, and if they don't like it, then... fuck 'em."

Aku grinned wide. "That's my favorite bitch. And if that don't work, you sick the family on them. We are loved, respected, and protected...you just gotta stop acting like you don't want to involve them."

Noodle stood up, a sense of quiet determination settling in her bones. It wasn't going to be easy and it wasn't going to happen overnight. But for the first time in a long time, she felt like she had a shot at something real.

"Come on," Aku said, standing up as well. "Let's go home. This town will suck you dry and leave you empty. Little Lunar caught a flight back this morning." She slid her arm around Noodle's shoulders, pulling her toward her room.

"Why you always sounding like an old auntie?" Noodle scrunched up her face. "But go home for what?"

"Because we ain't seen our people and they having a party for Bu this weekend... you know he just got out?"

She rolled her eyes. "I should've known your fast ass was trying to get somewhere where the niggas be."

Aku wagged her tongue. "Duh! Life is for the prowl... I gotta find my forever thing."

"You don't think you too young to be thinking about settling down?" Noodle never understood why Aku was so infatuated with marriage and kids. She'd been a lover girl for as long as Noodle could remember.

It probably had a lot to do with seeing her parents love on each other for years. Aku's parents had been in love long before she was even thought of.

Aku cut her eyes at Noodle. "How you want to sing about love and shit but scared to even look for it? Make it make sense..." She stood from the couch, placing her hands on her hips. "Go pack so we can catch a flight in the morning."

Noodle rolled her eyes, not in the mood to go back and forth with Aku. When it came to an argument, Aku was always up for it. The great debater Noodle, on the other hand, preferred to let people have it one time. She never had the energy to go tit for tat with anyone.

Her fear of arguments turning into something more, fueled her to stay to herself and out the way. Between that and always having a camera shoved in her face, it was all too much.

Plus, she'd love to see her family and lay eyes on her Esmeray and Belinay. She missed them so much.

2

"ES!" Noodle groaned, suddenly noticing her niece sitting on her bed like she was waiting for something. It was creepy.

Esmeray's body bounced with excitement. "Get up girl," she huffed, ready to get some time with her favorite person in the world.

"What time is it?"

"Time for you to get up," Es said, snuggling up under Noodle like she'd done since she was a little girl.

Their bond had been that way from the first day Es laid eyes on Noodle. Back then they were so young and innocent with Es always following behind Noodle, looking and waiting to copy everything she did.

"This why I don't be coming home... you so annoying," Noodle groaned again.

"And you're so old." Es rolled her eyes. "Happy birthday, Noodle."

A tired smile splayed across her face. "It was two days ago."

"Girl, don't be so technical. Now get up so we can do something."

"Do what, Es? And what time is it for real?"

"Like I said a few seconds ago, time for you to get up."

Noodle stretched her arms out. "Where is Belinay?" she asked about Es' little sister.

The two of them had the same father but different moms.

"With her mama."

"And where is your mama?"

"Which one?" Es asked.

Noodle's heart leaped. Knowing that Es was loved by her big sister and looked at Siasia as a mother would always warm her heart. Siasia was easy to love like that. Thinking about her sister, had Noodle rolling out of bed to lay eyes on her.

Her and Aku had gotten into Emerald City late and once she made it to her sister's house, she took her butt to bed knowing Aku was going to have her ripping and running all day getting ready for Bu's welcome home party.

"Eww!" Es scrunched up her nose at seeing Noodle in nothing but panties— no shirt, no bra.

"That's why you don't need to bring your worrisome ass in here bothering me. Es, you know I like to sleep naked."

"You need to start locking your door." Es continued, looking disgusted. "My titties bigger than yours," she commented, looking down at her own chest.

Noodle scoffed, "Barely... now get out!"

"Wait, nooo," she whined, giving her those puppy dog eyes that seemed to work on Noodle since she was a child.

Noodle laughed, giving Es a look over her shoulder. Es had inherited beautiful dark skin from her mom and slightly down-turned eyes from her dad. She could've been a model but with the hell Hollywood had taken Noodle through, she'd be damned if her baby was subjected to that too. It wasn't worth it, espe-cially not when she was the daughter of one of the best profes-sional soccer players in the world.

Qamar had been breaking records since he learned to kick a ball. Even when his college career took a turn for the worst, the greatness God had for him couldn't be stopped. So, Es didn't have to make any premature moves. She could allow her mind to wonder and her heart to ease into a career. That and she was only fifteen. The world could wait.

While Noodle handled her morning hygiene in the bathroom, Es sat on her bed— Indian style, blabbering about her teenage problems. Some boy at her school asked her out but clearly he already had a girlfriend. Es needed to know if she was wrong for still talking to him and even revealed she kissed him on the lips.

"With tongue?" Noodle jutted her head out the bathroom, glaring at Es. The sweetness and innocence she saw minutes ago disappeared.

Es rolled her head. "Girl, no… but what's wrong with that?"

"First of all, he ain't shit—"

"Why?"

"Second of all, don't be swapping spit with these dusty ass boys."

"His parents have money Noodle," Es combatted.

"And he still dusty. Trust me on this." Noodle splashed water over her face.

Es stood up, placing her hand on her hip. "How you know? You ain't never had a man, Noodle."

"Hmph," Noodle pursed her lips, seeing her little Es as the teen she had transformed into way too fast. "So you talkin' back cause some dusty little boy got you smelling yourself? Oh, I see what this is."

"I'm not," Es whined. "I'm just asking… you told me I got the right to ask questions."

"Now I regret it," Noodle mumbled. Flipping her long spiral curls into a ponytail, her eyes softened. "Look, Es, liking boys is okay, but it's doesn't have to be a girl's whole existence. He's already doing you wrong by entertaining you before he left that other situation. Don't be silly over your first crush. Tell his dusty ass that he has to come correct with you or don't come at all. And never be another girl's heartbreak willingly."

Es' energy calmed when Noodle pulled her into a tight hug. Like Noodle, Es had a little height to her, a trait she got from both of her parents, and they were almost at eye level with her now.

Barefooted, Noodle trekked out of her room, down the long hallway and into the kitchen where she got the surprise of her life. Like a kid, she took off, slamming into French. "French!" she yelled, hugging him tightly.

There had always been something about his hugs that almost always brought her to tears.

"Damn, Noodle, you can't miss me this much," French looked down at her, placing a kiss on her forehead,

Aku pretended to throw up in her mouth. "Noodle, that's my daddy... you know that right?"

"Don't do my sister," Siasia playfully pushed Aku, making sure to keep her eyes on her mama, Solar since she didn't play about her kids.

"Yea, you better keep one eye on me," Solar sipped from her coffee cup.

"When you got here?" Noodle asked, looking into his eyes.

"I been here a lil while."

Cutting her eyes at Es, she balled her face up. "That's why you came in there with your worrisome ass."

Es beamed proudly.

"She's the only one that can get you to come out," Siasia laughed, yanking her sister into her arms. "Happy Birthday, Noodle."

The love of her big sister would never fade. Noodle knew everything that she was, and was going to be, was because her sister carried her on her shoulders when she didn't have to. Blood couldn't make them any closer.

"Thank you, Sisi!" Noodle smothered Siasia with kisses.

"No thanks needed. Sometimes I think you forget how much you're loved, Noodle." Siasia pulled back to get a good look at her little sister. There was something in her eyes that broke Siasia's heart every time she looked into them. "You do know that right?"

"Yes." Noodle laughed nervously. "I'm okay."

"Leave her alone, mama," Qamar walked into the kitchen with a cake. His son, Qamar Jr ambled in with a few gift bags.

Noodle's face split into an excited grin, bright enough to light up the room. "Put the cake down so I can get on your back," she laughed.

"Don't start that shit, Noodle," Siasia fussed.

"I mean, as long as it ain't my daddy, let my bestie make it." Aku tucked herself into French's side.

Solar snickered, knowing her baby was serious. French was the one thing Noodle and Aku fought over. Aku felt it was already bad enough she had to share her daddy with Qamar and her brothers, but Noodle was where she drew the line.

Noodle waved Aku off, bouncing on her toes, ready to bombard Qamar with her love. She missed him. The last time she was home, he was out of the country for a soccer game. With him being in high demand, it was hard for their paths to cross. However, he never let her go too long without at least hearing his voice.

"Auntie," Qamar Jr called her name, wanting some of her love.

Opening her arms, she cooed at the sight of the perfect little brown boy created by the perfect brown parents. After Siasia had him, they decided that was enough. Qamar had two girls prior to them having QJ so Siasia felt her family was complete when she pushed out her baby boy.

That and her photography business took off. They agreed that three kids was enough even if only one came from the woman he gave his last name to.

"I'm sorry, baby... come here," Noodle squeezed him and just like Es, QJ had some height to him at only ten. "You gettin' so big."

"Mama said I'm getting musty," QJ blurted like it was no big deal, making everyone cackle.

"How did 'talk too much' get passed down thru DNA?" Solar asked no one in particular. "Y'all just like y'all daddy."

"Happy birthday, auntie," QJ kissed her cheek before pushing the bags in his arms over to her. "I picked out the purse."

"QJ!" Es fussed when QJ ruined one of the surprises. "Yea, you talk too da—"

"I wish you would," Siasia bucked her eyes at Es who was about to slip up and cuss. "You be letting her cuss, Noodle?"

"How I get in it?" Noodle raised her voice. "I just got here."

"But she do everything you do and anything you tell her she can do." Siasia reminded Noodle, as everyone nodded in agreement.

Kissing her teeth, Noodle blocked them out as she opened her gifts. Her family went all out for her. From jewelry to designer bags and shoes, she felt blessed, and it went beyond the material things. The love could be felt and it made going back to the west coast that much harder. Anytime she was in Emerald City, she never wanted to go back to Madison Heights.

Thoughts of hiding from the world with her family replayed over and over in her mind. But Noodle knew if she wanted to truly be the adult she claimed to KidVerse, she was going to have to figure her shit out on her own. The one good thing about it all was, her family would love her even if she failed.

It was evident from the way they showed up for her. A few were missing but she understood everyone's lives were so hectic now a days.

"Yea, wear that when we go to Sapphire City tonight," Aku said when Noodle slung the designer purse around her body while looking at herself in the massive mirror in the family room.

Siasia and Qamar's home was stunning inside and out.

French gave both of them a look. "The fuck y'all going to Sapphire for?"

"Cause we both twenty-one!" Aku sassed, yanking Noodle's arm for them to take off running together.

3

BU GRUNTED, leaning against the handle of the cart as he watched his little brother, Pimp, and Lunar toss bottles of every size and color into it like they were on a game show. Who even knew liquor stores had carts? Not Bu. And maybe that was because he'd spent the last four years behind bars, or maybe because he'd never been the type to try and buy out the whole damn store in one go.

Either way, the shit felt foreign.

"Y'all niggas tryin' to open a bar or something?" he muttered, but they didn't hear him over the clink of glass bottles and their loud debate about white versus brown and what Bu liked to drink, as if he wasn't standing right there.

"You cool?" Lunar slowed his stride to ask Bu, looking up from a bottle of something wrapped in gold dangling from his hand.

Bu pushed his glasses up on his nose, the slight pinch of the frames a constant reminder of a life he didn't choose. Before prison, he didn't even need glasses, but after years of reading nothing but smutty books, old novels, and letters under dim, flickering lights, his eyes weren't what they used to be.

Just one more thing incarceration had taken from him.

"I ain't really into celebrating jail," Bu said flatly, his voice low but carrying enough edge to let Lunar know exactly where he stood.

Lunar stopped, his lips pressing into a thin line as he nodded slowly, taking in the layers behind those words.

Meanwhile, Pimp was a blur of motion, stacking bottles like it was a sport, oblivious to the tension creeping up— swarming in the air like an annoying gnat no one likes. "Yo Bu, you drink whiskey now?" he called out, holding up a bottle of something dark with a smirk.

Bu didn't even glance his way. "Yea," he lied, the word clipped and cold, as Pimp kept going oblivious to any change in Bu's attitude. Bu wasn't about to explain how four years of counting down the minutes while sitting in a cell had taken the taste for celebration - or even escape, right out of him.

Lunar shifted on his feet, his usual easygoing energy tempered with something softer now. "It's not about celebrating *that*," he said carefully. "It's about celebrating *you*. You back now, Bu. We just tryna remind you that life's still sweet."

Bu let the words hang in the air, his gaze dropping to the cart overflowing with bottles, promising good times and blurred memories. Life didn't feel sweet. Not yet, anyway. Not when he was still trying to figure out how to fit into a world that had kept moving without him.

"Yea," he said after a few beats.

Lunar didn't press him, just slapped a hand on his shoulder before walking off.

Bu stood there for a moment, his hand tightening around the cart handle as he stared at the rows of bottles stretching out in front of him. Life might've been sweet for them, but for him? It still tasted uncertain and bitter.

More bitter than expensive whisky.

Lunar knew it was a lie, but nodded at his appreciation of Bu going along with Pimp's joy of having him home again.

Pimp carried guilt like a heavy chain against his chest,

weighing him down no matter how much Bu swore there was nothing to change. His brother had laid it all down, and even if Bu wouldn't have done it differently, Pimp felt like he owed him — owed him for the time he couldn't get back... for the sacrifices Bu had made. So, Pimp did what he could— he got the hell out of Sapphire City and moved in a way that would make his big brother proud. He hustled harder, grew sharper, and stacked his paper hoping to show his brother his sacrifice hadn't been in vain.

As they continued to stroll through the store, Pimp's eyes flicked to a man across the aisle, lingering just a second too long before he quickly cast his gaze forward.

Bu caught it. He didn't miss much these days. Not the way Pimp's shoulders stiffened slightly, or the way his jaw tightened like he was bracing for something.

Bu knew what that was, the instinct to suppress...to hide pieces of yourself before the world could pick them apart, and everything about the world now felt different. From the air itself - thick with smells he didn't quite recognize, to the quiet hesitancy in his brother's eyes when he walked past something or someone who sparked his interest.

Lunar saw it to. He'd seen it so much that maybe he looked at it as just another day with his best friend.

Pimp was trying to hide, but Bu had been reading him since they were kids. He saw it all.

As if knowing exactly what Pimp needed, Bu reached out and slapped the back of his shoulder, pulling him into a hug that was all warmth and unspoken truths.

His voice was steady, low, but full of a love that refused to bend. "I love every version of you," he said firmly, his arms tightening around Pimp for a while before letting him go. "Never walk on eggshells for muthafuckas... not even me."

Pimp froze for a split second, his breathing stalling as the words cracked something deep in his chest. Wetness coated his eyes, but he blinked hard and swallowed it down. No tears here.

He'd already melted into his big brother's arms in the middle of a liquor store— he didn't need to give the world the full show.

"'Preciate you, Bu," he mumbled, his voice rough as he straightened up and shoved his hands in his pockets.

Off to the side, Lunar watched the scene unfold, a small smile tugging at the corner of his lips. He knew exactly how much that moment meant to Pimp. While Bu was gone, Lunar had stepped in, doing his best to hold his best friend down in the ways he needed it most. He'd been there for the quiet moments when Pimp's world felt too heavy and for the affirmations Pimp didn't know how to ask for but so clearly craved.

The world had a way of tearing men like Pimp apart. A Black man— a thug, and gay. Everything that could be stacked against him was, and still, Pimp carried it all

without a complaint...without flinching.

He wore it like armor, but Lunar knew better. He saw the cracks beneath the surface, the places where Pimp's weight shifted just to keep himself upright.

Bu saw it too, in his own way.

Lunar loved him before the titles and he'd happily stand beside him when he decided to take a husband. If that was in the cards for Pimp.

Until then, both Lunar and Bu would remain by his side while Pimp navigated the cruel world.

"Now, who all gon' be at this party?" Bu asked, flipping the mood.

Pimp cheesed. "Nothing but the baddest for the realest nigga from The Jig."

Bu had been able to keep the celebration from happening for six months but Pimp had decided he was tired of waiting so, now Bu had to fully lean into being at a party he cared nothing about. For his baby brother, he would always fold.

———

The party was in full swing with music and grills going while everyone danced and smiled. Bu puffed on a blunt with his head on swivel. The Jig still felt the same, even with all the updates and futuristic designs, home was home. No amount of money being poured into it would change that for him.

They were all at the park with the gazebos decked out in red, paying homage to the other family Bu had claimed as his own. That red shit ran through him and he wasn't talking about blood.

Memories of what it all used to look like flooded his mind. Thoughts of his mama wanting him to kick a ball like Qamar brought a smile to his face. Bee, his mama, tried her hardest to keep him out the streets, God rest her soul. But that was hard to do when the lights didn't always work and Pimp needed new shoes. So like most black boys his age, Bu became the man of the house, making shit shake when his mama's job didn't pay enough to support two growing boys.

At twenty-two, Bu broke her heart and caught a charge. It should've been for murder but he was too good for them to pin that on him. Yet, not good enough to not get caught with a gun when they pulled him over. The streets knew what it was though. Bu did his bid without fret and walked out six months ago a free man. No papers— nothing but a record that would keep him from finding a job to support himself legally.

No matter how hard his next moves would turn out to be, Bu was going to find his footing and show the world how much magic really came out of the Jig.

"Hey Bu," Amy twisted over to him, her voice extra syrupy and her words slow from the lean she sipped on.

Amy had blonde hair and wide hips from the three kids she'd pushed out back to back. She was still fine though.

He nodded his head in greeting, never one to say too much.

"You still mean as hell, huh?"

That made him chuckle. Was this how girls approached men now? Although a hood baby, Bee taught him manners and how to be a gentleman when it was time. "I'm just chillin'."

"Mind if I chill with you?" Amy asked, but took it upon herself to sit next to him, her strong perfume almost choking him.

"It's a party, you good."

"Are *you* good?" Lust danced in her eyes.

Bu knew the look all too well. He'd been getting it since he walked down the street for the first time when he got out. The girls damn near threw themselves at him, praying he would catch it. If he'd been a slave to thinking with his dick, he would've, but shit was different for him now. He had goals and the wrong woman coming into his life could derail it all.

Bu wasn't going to let that happen. He gave women just enough, making sure to keep the special shit close to his chest.

Bee always preached to him about knowing when he found the right woman. Said some shit about his heart switching up— changing directions or something like that.

He studied the side of Amy's sand colored skin. The blonde hair looked good on her. Her face was cute with an edge to it that hinted she was no little princess that needed saving. She was a fuckin' siren looking for her next victim.

He couldn't lie and pretend that his dick didn't stir around her, because it did. He was a man that hadn't felt the warmth of a woman in years so instinct was kicking in.

Her eyes cast down like she could see the affects her over-bearing perfume and cute face caused. "You still over on Jodh-pur?" she asked, mentioning the street his mama raised them on.

He still lived there but didn't want too much traffic at his door. It was why his celebration was being held at the park. At the same time, he couldn't bitch up on a woman like Amy. She talked plenty shit and couldn't hold water. Bu didn't need the hood feeling like he was ducking anything. "Yea, I'm still over there."

"Noodle!" Bu turned towards his brother who had his arms in the air, yelling across the field.

His eyes followed.

Two burly men parted like the red sea, and Noodle appeared with a big smile on her face with Aku beside her.

Amy snapped her fingers. "You heard me?"

Bu glared at her like she'd lost her mind. "Don't ever snap at me."

Amy swallowed hard. "My bad. I asked if you wanted me to come through tonight?"

"I'll let you know." Bu's tone was dismissive. He was over the conversation with Amy and wanted to smoke his blunt in peace.

Just as Amy went to get up, Noodle and Aku sashayed over to him.

Aku rested her weight on one side with her arms over her chest. "Get up and give me a hug, Bu."

Smiling, he did like he was told. "Man, Aku ain't a little girl no more."

"You always act like you so much older than us...we in the same generation, boy."

"I ain't no boy, Aku."

Aku stepped back to take him in. "You right— you ain't a little boy anymore. You look good, Bu."

"You don't look too bad yourself."

"Puhlease... I'm fine as hell," Aku fanned her hand down her body teasingly. "You probably don't remember my cousin, Noodle. You know she was working when we were kids."

Noodle's chubby cheeks puffed her eyes closed as she smiled. "Hey Bu."

His chest beat a different tune when he inhaled her coconutty scent. Her hair was long and curly in its natural state and her tawny skin was blemish and makeup free.

Noodle's lashes fluttered as he ogled her it wasn't in a weird way. It did something to her too. Licking her lips, Noodle put a little more space between them.

"I know you," Amy made her presence known. "Jay Jay?"

Noodle's eyes darted to her security prompting them to move in between them.

Amy kissed her teeth, waving her hand. "I ain't even on that... I'm here to have a good time."

Noodle had heard that so many times before but she had no choice but to believe the pretty girl since Noodle did want to enjoy her night.

Bu wanted to get Noodle out of there but it wasn't his place and he barely knew her. His chest was doing that weird shit Bee talked about.

Aku sliced through the awkward tension. "Come on, Noodle let's get some food and drinks."

Noodle nodded in agreement. Already feeling naked when she took her eyes off Bu.

Aku linked their arms together as she walked them over to where Lunar and Pimp were seated with a table full of girls in their face. Lunar was loved in The Jig and felt good not having his security for a change. Noodle didn't want hers neither but Qamar and Siasia weren't having that. French's opinion put the nail in the coffin. So there she was standing out like a sore thumb with two burly men dressed in black, flanking her, keeping just enough distance but not too much.

———

She felt him... smelled him too.

"This ground feels sacred." Noodle ran her hand across the air like it was solid ground. "Feels freeing... feels like love."

She'd ducked off into the night and was sitting on a rock, away from the rowdy party that brought out more people than Lunar and Pimp anticipated. So far there hadn't been any incidents but her security kept their eyes on everything and everyone moving.

Bu huffed a laugh. "That's the Moony effect. They say once you're loved by one, you become attached to Lunar."

"That makes sense." She smiled thinking about Qamar's love. It had been the best thing that happened to her after Siasia.

Bu stared off into the night sky, inhaling the night air. He'd been home for a little over six months and freedom never felt better. It was the quiet that calmed him when he went to bed at night and being able to move on his own accord that made waking up that much better. Noodle glanced up at him, drinking in how much he'd grown in the best ways possible. He was more chiseled, his face more defined and his skin was as clear as a baby's bottom. But the thickness of his neck created a yearning in her she'd never felt before.

Bu had smooth chestnut skin that soaked up the light of the moon and stars in the sky. His low-cut Caesar looked luscious with waves that spiraled around his head. Even his close shaved facial hair seemed to be well moisturized.

Dressed down in jean shorts, a designer shirt and retro Jordans, the swag and confidence oozed off him.

"Take a picture, it'll last longer," he laughed, calling her out.

Embarrassed, she turned her head. "Why you ain't over there enjoying your party? The girls are happy to have you home."

He smirked. "They just want some fresh out dick."

Bumps prickled her skin as thoughts of his dick crossed her mind. "So which one you taking home?" Noodle turned towards the full swing of people laughing and the girls that kept looking in their direction, waiting for Bu to return to see what type of time he was on. "I think the one with the blonde hair... she looks like a good time."

"Oh yea?" His brows rose excitedly.

"Mhmmm." She nodded. "Or the one with the braids. She smelled good." Her eyes went to the phone in her hand, checking her notifications.

Bu only snorted. "Why you over here?"

"Just wanted to breathe... it's only a matter of time before some random people with cameras show up."

"What you mean?"

Noodle's shoulders sank. "I was spotted." Pushing her phone towards him, she showed the image someone at the party posted on ig after she'd only been there an hour. The way people seemed to be infatuated with her trying to live a regular life needed to be studied. It was sick and nasty work. There was nowhere in the world that she felt safe and free to just be the twenty-one year old she was. Life as a child star had ruined that.

Just as she pulled her phone back, a few random cars pulled up with people who didn't belong in the Jig hopping out.

"Jacory," Fink, one of her security guards alerted her. "You staying or leaving?" he asked, moving in closer to her.

Both of her guards flanked her, ready to do whatever she told them the next move was. Over the years, the two men grew to love her like a little sister and wanted to protect her at all costs. They knew what her life had become which, meant they knew the anxiety she lived with.

Noodle looked up at Bu. "Guess it's time for me to go." Her smile didn't meet her eyes.

Bu looked at the people walking through the park. They were looking for someone... looking for her. "You ready to go home or you want a little more time to enjoy your night?" His deep voice was velvety smooth and so appealing.

Mischief danced in her eyes. "If I say I want to stay, then what?"

Bu held his hand out for her to take. He looked at her security. "Y'all know how to run?"

Noodle was confused but placed her hand in his anyway.

"Run!" Bu yelled, yanking her off the rock and they took off into the small tree-line.

Noodle followed him, laughing her ass off while her heart beat out of her chest with excitement. Looking back, she noticed Fink and Ben were right behind her.

"Jacory!" A photographer yelled, snapping his camera as he called her name.

The sound of their feet hitting the ground with old leaves

crumbling beneath their feet. She was in heels and didn't even think about falling or how silly she looked. Bu held onto her hand as he maneuvered through the bushes on the walking path created by people in the neighborhood.

They ran between a few houses before they made it to his.

Out of breath, Noodle doubled over. "This your house?" she asked after slowing her breathing down and looking up at where they were.

"Yea, come on." Bu grabbed her hand again, fishing through his pocket for the keys. Once he pushed the door open, he guided her in, the cool air hitting them in the face. September in Sapphire City was hot and humid.

Fink and Ben followed them in, shutting the door and looking around protectively, one heading to the back and one remaining up front.

Noodle stood in the living room looking around, taking it all in. It was quaint and modest, maybe about 1200 square feet.

The living room had a small couch in the middle but it was clean and led to a small open concept kitchen with an island that sat two. The floors were dark maple wood, or vinyl planks, she wasn't sure. It was nice though and made her wonder how he already had this nice place if he'd just gotten out.

Bu must've read her mind because he explained it. "Pimp kept the house for when I came home."

Satisfied with his answer, she smiled. "Can I take my shoes off?"

"You cannot come up in here asking weird as shit like that… take your shoes off if you want Noodle and sit down." He went to the kitchen which was only five steps from the door. "You want something to drink?"

"I do!" Fink announced, looking out the window to see if they'd been followed.

She snickered. "What you got?"

"Whatever you want, baby."

Eyes doubling, Noodle's skin flushed red when she saw Fink smirk at her reaction. "Uh, tequila?"

She could hear Bu moving around in the kitchen. She smelled him too— woodsy with a hint of brown sugar. It was a unique scent but it fit the man he presented himself as.

"Let me get a water," Fink called out.

"All I got is tap," Bu responded, not a bit ashamed.

For four years, he'd quenched his thirst with tap water and survived. He'd be damned if he started spending unnecessary money on bottled. The world had him fucked up if they thought so.

Fink kissed his teeth but accepted the cup when Bu came back into the living room. "Thanks."

"Aye!" He called out to Ben who was posted up towards the back of the house. "You want somethin' to drink?"

"I'm good!" Ben shouted as if the house was big enough to have a reason to shout.

Going back into the kitchen, Bu twisted the top of the tequila. He had stolen a few bottles of the liquor they got for his party to keep at his house. "I ain't got no juice."

"That's fine," Noodle said, her eyes still bouncing around the room. She jumped when he handed her the glass.

"Noodle drinking tequila straight…who would've thought."

With a lopsided grin, Noodle tapped her glass on the rinky-dink table before tossing the large glass of liquid down her throat. It burned, she thought. "This industry'll do that to you."

"Damn." Bu narrowed his eyes, angling his head at her. "You good?"

"I will be… as soon as this tequila warms my skin."

"You smoke?" Bu asked, flicking the lighter to spark his awaiting blunt. Since being back home, he had to admit the weed seemed better than he remembered. It was smooth but super potent and did what it needed to do.

Noodle nodded.

"What don't you do?" Bu mumbled, pulling the bag of weed

from the side of the couch, he grabbed a backwoods from the little drawer in the coffee table.

Noodle eyed him breaking the blunt down. The way his lips swiped over it had her yearning. "Have fun."

"Huh?" Bu asked, sprinkling the weed into the cigar.

"You asked what I don't do... I don't have fun. The world doesn't want me to have fun. So hurry up and pass me the weed."

Bu laughed loud. His chest shook, making him almost drop the weed. "You funny, Noodle."

"I'm serious." She laughed at how intense she could be sometimes.

If Aku was there she'd be digging her bony elbow into Noodle's side begging her to be cool.

Her almond eyes burned a hole into the side of his face, watching his every move. The way his temples flexed when he flicked fire across the blunt to seal it. The way his glasses slid down when he got up to clean up his mess. Every little thing he did, she watched him do it, trying to figure out why she was so caught up in it.

"You wanna watch a movie or something? Listen to some music?" Bu asked after he flopped back down on the couch, inhaling the smoke with no hands.

"Just pass the weed, Bu." Noodle crossed her legs, burying herself into the corner of his couch.

"With them pretty ass lips?" Even with a distorted voice from blowing out smoke, Noodle loved the sound of it.

Her tawny skin blushed. "I mean that's what they make lipstick and shit for."

"So, you round here wearing lipstick?"

"No!" She laughed. "I'm just saying, I will if I have to... you know when I get older."

"If you take care of yourself now, you ain't gotta worry about over doing it when you're older. Com'ere," his drawl lulled her to him. With his legs slightly gaped, he guided her between them.

Noodle wasn't a stranger to men flirting with her, but she'd be lying if she didn't admit Bu intimidated her. He seemed so confident and rugged.

Bu also seemed like a grown *man*, and she'd never had a man before.

When his large hand touched the back of her knee, she almost buckled. He smirked. "Here," he directed, twisting the blunt around to blow her a gun. "Keep your eyes open, for me."

Noodle blinked back and nodded, coaching her heart to slow down before she fainted. As the smoke exhaled from his brown lips, she sucked it back into her mouth, making sure to hold it before exhaling.

After a few more puffs, Bu tapped the back of her knee which became her new favorite spot. "Sit down for me."

The way he spoke to her was like a demand, but his smooth, southern jumble of words made it sound too sweet to be anything but a mere suggestion.

"How old are you?" Noodle just had to know. She remembered him as being Pimp's older brother, so she always felt he wasn't that much older than them, but his presence said otherwise.

"Why?"

I need to know if you're too old before I throw this pussy at you, she thought. Noodle kept her high and liquid courage thoughts inside. "I'm making conversation… getting to know you," she shrugged.

"I'm not the type of nigga you need to get to know, baby." Bu stood from his seat to grab a bag of chips once the munchies hit him.

He came back, sitting the bag in the small space he made sure to keep between them.

"Tell me about you," He laughed, half expecting her to answer.

4

BU SAT BACK, bobbing his head while sipping on his drink. Even in glasses, he looked like the nigga that would pull the trigger. His aura gave 'fuck around and find out' vibes.

Grinning like a kid in a candy store, Noodle plopped down beside him with all the energy of someone who couldn't stay still if they tried. The space between them was so narrow it barely existed, her thigh brushing his. As the cushion shifted beneath her from the force of her landing, a warm gust stirred, carrying that brown sugar scent of his that was quickly becoming her favorite thing.

It wrapped around her like an embrace, making her breath hitch just enough for her to wonder if he noticed.

They'd smoked and were listening to music off the smart TV in the living room just vibing out. Bu was high as hell while Noodle seemed to be a mixture of both drunk and high.

"You having a good time?" she asked, hating the words once they left her lips. "I mean... how have you been, I haven't seen you in years?"

Bu smiled, happy Noodle's pretty ass remembered who he was. She'd always been easy on the eyes and always been out of his league. Bu tended to pursue the more 'around the way' girls.

Not industry girls like her who had been taught to sit with their backs straight, be polite, and to keep a smile on their faces.

Noodle's tawny colored skin was blemish free. Her natural jet black curls swirled down her back along with the swoops that framed her heart-shaped face perfectly. She wore no makeup but her plush lips were glossed to perfection and her slim body had enough meat in all the right places.

His head bobbed. "It's cool... better than muthafuckas telling you what to do all day." He leaned in closer to her so she could hear him over the music.

As if she could taste him on her lips, she swiped her tongue across them.

"Been out six months now."

"So, how are you liking the free world?"

Bu paused, to look at her before the most beautiful smile stretched across his face. "Yo! You wild."

She snickered along with him. "I'm just saying... you seemed intense... the few times I did see you."

"I am." The two word reply held so much weight. "Felt like I had the world's problems on my shoulders... that shit'll make anyone stop smiling. Why you don't smile, though?"

His question almost sobered her up. Sucking in air, Noodle stared at a blank space on the bare walls. "How you gon' smile when you're drowning?" The sweet inflection of her tone dropped, showing how deep the reply had come from the pits of her soul.

A simple question shouldn't feel so deep and so open, but it did. It was something no one else had ever asked before and seeing that he didn't know her from a random person on the street and, it was too damn invasive for her to answer. But Noodle wasn't a rude person. No, she was a people pleaser and cared too much about other's opinion of her.

Instead of taking him deeper, she took the heat off by introducing something else more interesting.

"I've never had an orgasm!" Noodle blurted, her eyes expanding with her tone, feeling stupid seconds later.

Bu rubbed his forehead, confused.

"Earlier, you asked what I don't do... I don't have orgasms." Feeling the warmth in her body and the confusion in her head, Noodle seemed to have no barriers between them. As long as he didn't ask why her smile didn't meet her eyes.

"Um, I'm gon' step outside," Fink's voiced reminded her that they weren't alone. "Come on, Ben."

Ben's massive body made its way to the front and out the door. Leaving the two of them alone.

Bu felt her face go through a swirl of emotions while his dick jumped. He wanted to promise her a night full of pleasure where he was one hundred percent sure she'd have too many orgasms to count.

He couldn't do that though.

Noodle wasn't Amy. Noodle was more than that, more special than any girl he'd ever stuck his dick in.

Jacory was out of his league.

"Say something, Bu." Noodle begged, her sweet voice not helping the ache of his dick.

The feel of her phone vibrating in her pocket pulled her from the moment. It was Aku calling. "Hello?" she answered it on speaker.

"Jacory! Where the hell you went?" Aku asked, the sound of the party still going on in the background.

"She left with that nigga Bu," Noodle heard Lunar slur. It sounded like they were having a good time.

And as good as their time might be, she knew it wasn't better than soaking in Bu.

Noodle's eyes widened when she realized Bu was locked into their conversation too. Embarrassment jolted through her, tightening her throat at the unreadable expression on his face. Her fingers twitched, gripping the phone with regret.

"Aww, Lunar you still got that little crush on Noodle?" Bu playfully taunted, laughter in his voice.

Aku gasped. "Noodle! You over there throwing pussy at Bu?"

Noodle felt even more embarrassment as she watched Bu's eyes twinkle with something in them... something that said if she was throwing pussy he was catching it,

possibly with his mouth by the way he licked his lips.

"I'm hanging up 'cause all y'all doing too much," she sneered at Bu, making his head fall back with even more laughter. "I'm at his house. Don't come over here now, just in case someone is still looking for me. When y'all ready to leave, you can come 'round here to get me."

Before she could hang up, Lunar hollered into the phone. "Bu, you need to come to me like a man... you better marry her if you round the—"

Noodle hung up abruptly before he could finish.

"Why you hang up, I wanted to hear what my boy had to say." Bu rested his head on the back of the couch that playfulness still in his voice tinged with a hint of grogginess.

He was tired but didn't want to end his night with Noodle. Being in her presence was nice. She had an intriguing personality that hinted maybe she wasn't so innocent after all.

"I need another drink," she hummed, leaning back, and plopping her bare feet on the table while some song played on the TV.

Bu's attention went to her hot pink painted toes. Thoughts of licking them while giving her back to back orgasms played in his head like a movie. "You a virgin?" he asked, relaxed like he wasn't on the edge of his seat waiting for her answer.

"Why?"

"I'm just asking since you said you never had an orgasm."

"Women can have sex with a hundred men and never really experience pure unadulterated pleasure."

"Shit, I don't know nothin' about that. I'm a pleaser."

Butterflies fluttered to her center. She wanted to be bold and ask him to show her, but KidVerse hadn't taught her how to be a woman in the public relations and etiquette classes they shoved her in when she was twelve.

They didn't explain the art of seduction or how to get anything you wanted from a man. So, Noodle sat with her mouth and legs clamped together, counting how many times her pussy thumped per minute.

"Don't go mute on me now, Jacory." A flash of humor crossed his face.

Noodle angled her head towards him, her neck lax and her eyes low. "This was fun."

"You ready to leave me?" Bu gazed over at her.

The way he said it, Noodle never wanted to leave him. But life had to go on. She had shit to do and he probably did too. Plus, she was getting so wrapped up in him, when her life wasn't built in the way to fall for a man... even temporarily.

"Yea, I want to catch Luna tomorrow and she be on the move," Noodle said, standing to her feet while sending a message to Aku telling her to bring the truck around there.

Aku must've been just as ready to go as her because Noodle glanced out the window, noticed the truck lights and heard her talking to Fink outside.

Bu stood, pulling his jean shorts up with him so they didn't sag too much. "Don't be a stranger," he teased, as they both drug their feet to the front door. The house wasn't big enough for it to take them the amount of time it did to get to the door.

Noodle faced him with those innocent almond eyes.

His dark eyes outlined her plump lips. Bu fought his urge to touch them, losing before the battle could fully begin.

Noodle shuttered as his calloused thumb swiped across her top lip before trailing its heat to her bottom— searing her skin, branding her like an exclusive private club that kept its traditions a secret.

Perfect teeth peeked out through the thin parting of her lips. "Bu," Noodle whined.

"I know, baby... have a good night." Bu reached around her to pull the door open. "Do me a favor, Jacory."

"What?" Her eyes widened, ready to do whatever he asked.

"Smile tomorrow." He looked into her eyes. "And if I was a betta nigga, I'd give you all the nuts your body could stand."

———

The morning sun peeked through the thin curtains Pimp swore he got a good deal on when he told Bu all about the updates to the house over the jail phone. Bu could admit, being locked up, everything sounded better but seeing shit in real time, either Pimp lied about the good deal or he'd been played. Whatever it was, he knew he needed to get some better ones.

Resting his forearm on over his face, thoughts of Noodle bombarded his brain and traveled down to his dick. Echoing the action, Bu rushed his hand into his boxer briefs. His front teeth sinking into his lip as he squeezed the base of his dick with just enough pressure.

Those almond eyes.

"Shit," he hissed, stroking himself at a slow pace. His memory of Noodle felt so real.

Small bell pepper nose.

He squeezed again.

Tiny waist with a nice juicy ass.

That syrupy sweet voice that he wanted to desperately hear be whispering naughty shit in his ear.

Bu wanted to hear her groaning and moaning while begging him to let her tap the fuck out. He wanted to fuck a smile onto her face because orgasms made you happy— giddy and ready to take on the day.

His slow strokes turned into fast, full length jacking off.

As the blood rushed to the tip of his mushroomed head, his

toes curled as his balls tightened. "Fuck!" Bu panted, his chest rising and falling rapidly.

The warm nut rested on his lower stomach— a reminder of what Noodle's presence did to him. He was willing to bet she had no clue what those fluttering lashes did to the most unsuspecting men.

The release was long overdue but would never compare to the real thing. Allowing his heart rate to return to normal, he just lay there thinking. He'd spent so much of his time locked away that all he could do was think. Focusing on anything outside of that would do more harm than good, so Bu kept his mind in a positive place— devising a dream so when he was marked a free man, he'd be prepared and willing to live it.

Begrudgingly, Bu made his way to the bathroom, turning the shower on while he stared at his blurry reflection in the mirror. He didn't even feel the same without his glasses on.

Bu studied every detail of his face. His eyes looked brighter and his feet walked lighter. He couldn't say he was one hundred percent happy, but he was well on his way to a brighter future or to happier days.

As the small bathroom fogged up, he knew it was time to jump in the shower to get his day started. Just as he removed his underwear, he heard someone knocking on the front door. "The fuck?" He grabbed a towel to wrap around his lower half, padding to the front of the house.

A few more knocks hit the door before he could get to it. Pulling it open, he squinted at the unexpected guest.

"Good morning," Amy twirled her finger around her blonde curls, thirst dripping off her.

He felt like a hoe by the way she ogled him as he stood there in nothing but a towel. Bu twisted the towel tighter around his waist. "What's up?" His brows rose, looking down the block at the slow traffic going up and down the neighborhood street.

"That's what I came by to see... what's up with you?"

Swiping his hand down his face, Bu surmised he didn't have

time for Amy. He was already on a deadline and needed to be somewhere. "I don't have time for this, Amy. You need something?"

Shocked at his blasé attitude, she pushed her hip out. "Oh, I was just coming to make sure you slept good last night and to help you get your day started."

"Bye, Amy," Bu stepped back to close the door, leaving her dumbfounded and red in the face.

Like he said, he didn't have time for her bullshit. Looking over at the wall clock, he measured how much time he had to get dressed and make it to the car dealership. Six months without a car was long enough. It was officially time for him to put one foot in front of the other and make those dreams he'd conjured up come true.

5

NOODLE SPUN around in the office chair, listening to Luna wrap up her call. She'd been there for well over two hours and had yet to talk to her big sister.

Luna no longer actively sung but was still a big household name. Her first album took the world by storm, solidifying her voice and brand for years to come. Along with being the wife of the highest paid quarterback, she left her mark by doing features and writing amazing songs for other artists.

"I really need to get in there to do a sound check," Luna pressed. Her big curls bouncing every time she spoke.

Based on the nature of the last few phone calls Luna took, Noodle knew they were all in regard to Javen's retirement. After 17 years, he was finally hanging up his cleats. He would be going out on a high and considered the greatest of all time. He'd brought too many championships home to Emerald City and the city was ready to throw a parade in his honor.

Luna wasn't letting them half step her man. She was calling in all kinds of favors and making sure she did her biggest one for him. He deserved it, after the way he held her down when they were only kids and when she lost her twin. Luna would never be able to repay him for all the love he'd poured into her over the last few decades, nor would she ever stop trying.

Luna had to be one of the prettiest people Noodle had ever seen. The way she carried herself - Noodle could only aspire to hold a fraction of it.

She looked at Luna the way Es looked at her with... admiration... inspiration. All the things black mamas wanted their little black girls to look up to, but

none of the traits, Noodle felt she possessed. She was a pushover, way too calm, never ready to go to war about her. When a line was drawn, Noodle stayed on whatever side they told her to stay on.

She felt weak.

Noodle stopped spinning when her head grew an ache and her belly flipped. To busy herself, she pulled out her phone. Her days of carelessly scrolling social media had become few and far between. It was like the wild wild west for celebrities like her. People were opinionated and judgmental, creating false narratives.

With all the fame, no one ever talked about people building you up just to tear you back down. It hurt more when they looked like you.

Still, with nothing better do to, she swiped— liking things her family posted and stopping when she saw an image of Pimp, Lunar, and Bu from the party last night.

Drinking Bu in, Noodle liked what she saw. With his hands clasped handsomely in front of him, a red scarf hanging from his back pocket, and his feet slightly ajar making her think about him being a pleaser.

"He grew up to be so cute," Luna said, leaning over Noodle's shoulder, her voice breaking the spell.

Noodle jumped, her finger darting to darken the screen of her phone. "Who?" she asked, her eyes instinctively following Luna's line of vision.

"Bu." Luna breezed around her, sliding into the other chair parked in front of the mixing board.

The two of them were nestled in Luna's home studio, a cozy creative haven that had morphed into her office. It was Luna's sanctuary, the place where she handled all things music related and beyond.

When she needed to be found, her children and husband knew where to go. Ever since Luna designed the personal studio, she'd been in love with the energy it gave her every time she stepped foot inside.

"You like him?" Luna's marbled eyes stared into Noodle's, ready to catch her in a lie.

Of course she looked away. "I don't know that man like that."

"Jacory, please." Luna kissed her teeth.

"I'm for real," Noodle raised her voice, still not looking at Luna.

Her eyes wandered lazily around the studio. It still looked the same from the first time Luna brought her down there. Stars on the walls with a moon mural on the back wall. The booth was etched into the wall in the shape of a moon keeping up with the whole *to the moon* theme. Plaques, awards, and images of the people she loved the most also lined the walls. Noodle smiled at the picture of her and Little Lunar with microphones in their hands at French and Solar's wedding. Her eyes misted when she noticed an off guard capture of her on the floor with her little notebook in front of her. Her lips were poked out, a clear indication that she was in deep thought.

"That's one of my favorites." Luna's eyes crinkled sightly, her lips curling into a smile that held her deep-rooted love for the little girl before her.

When Noodle was just ten, after having lost the only parents she knew, Luna found her curled up in the corner at Qamar's house with her little notebook writing songs, afraid of showing true emotions in an effort not to make her big sister sad.

It had to be the saddest thing Luna had ever seen.

The way her heart almost leaped from her chest wanting to save the pretty little girl from a life that mirrored hers - walking around carrying everyone else's emotions while keeping your own bottled up. Luna took Noodle under her wing until Noodle decided to sign to KidVerse.

Luna begged and pleaded with Qamar and Siasia not to let her do it.

Noodle's pleas mirrored Luna's but for the opposite reason.

Siasia's desire to support her sister's dream allowed Noodle to make an adult decision far too young, but Siasia was barely an adult herself. Discernment hadn't quite reached her frontal lobe.

"I should've listened to you," Noodle whispered, still locked in on her younger self framed on the wall.

"Don't do that, Noodle." Luna rolled closer to her, placing her hand on hers. "Life is for learning. You gotta do it wrong to learn how to do it right."

"I don't want to let y'all down." Noodle sniffled, her angelic face breaking Luna's heart. "Don't want to let myself down... I thought I knew what I wanted but now, I just want to be happy."

"And what does happiness look like to you?"

The question seemed to be playing on a loop lately.

"Music..."

"Then let's make the best shit the world has ever heard."

"What about—" Noodle's eyes traveled to the door that seemed to creak open, halting her words in her throat. "You called him?"

"Stop actin' like you don't like seeing me, princess," Qamar smiled, calling her by the name he'd given her the first day they met. It was a *yes* day where no one was able to say *no*. The rules had been set moreso for Siasia because she had a hard time accepting Qamar's affection for her but it extended to Noodle too.

Eleven years felt so far in the past.

Her frame seemed small as she nestled into his embrace.

They all gave the best hugs. It was so comforting. Just like going to church and swearing the pastor was speaking directly to you, the Moonys hugs made you feel loved, seen, and heard… *like they were just for you.*

"This some kind of intervention?" Noodle bounced her eyes between him and Luna. "So lay it on me," she rolled her eyes, leaning back in the chair.

She was ready to get to the nitty gritty. There was no need to beat around the bush when Noodle knew Qamar was here for a reason.

"Nah, princess, you lay it on me. I ain't here to fuss or judge. I'm here to check on you and see what I need to do to fix this for you?"

He'd seen the blogs and had gone back and forth with Siasia when she was ready to rip into every person that had something negative to say about her little sister. Qamar had even seen the tears swell in Siasia's eyes when she cried about Noodle shutting her out and keeping them at bay.

"Tell me what you need." His voice had always been so soothing. Qamar talked to her in the same manner he would talk to his kids— stern but full of love. When it came to Noodle, Qamar gave her more leeway when it came to being stubborn and wanting to figure life out alone. He could relate because his inner battles had almost cost him his career when he was fighting to find his footing.

A blank stare coated her face as she studied Qamar.

His brown skin had a natural sheen to it, and his locs looked fresh along with his lineup. Qamar's body was buff from his daily workout and him playing professional soccer.

Noodle smiled when she saw her name tattooed on his arm along with the names of his daughters and son. Of course, her big sister Siasia's name had been inked across his neck showing his love and devotion for her too. It reminded her of the mural on her back of the beach and moon shining across its waters. As much as he loved her, she loved him ten times over.

"I'm okay, Qamar."

"I ain't convinced… tell me the real? The network ain't playing fair?"

Luna sat quietly allowing him to get through to Noodle.

"I signed a contract," she sighed knowing she was lawfully obligated to fulfill the paperwork she signed on the dotted line.

"All shit I can make go away." He was so unperturbed, she believed he would do anything to make it go away.

The thing about Noodle was, no matter how much he'd changed her life, no matter how much he'd poured into her, there was still a longing to figure it out on her own. She wanted no lifeline - didn't want to get anyone else mixed up in her mess because going against KidVerse was no small feat. They were very powerful in Hollywood and could do things that would crumble the ones she loved so much.

Wrapping her arms around him, she let out an exaggerated huff, her head resting against his chest. "I know, and I love you so much for always looking out for me," she said, her voice soft but firm. Her words carried a mix of gratitude and quiet defiance. "Just let me do this one alone. If it gets too tough, I promise I'll let you know."

He sighed, his hands settling on her forehead, his thumb rubbing against her brows. The tension in his eyes told her everything he hadn't said yet. Qamar was willing to search beyond the stars for Noodle's happiness. But before he could argue his stance, before he could declare how devoted he was to her as a brother, Luna's voice cut through.

"It's already too tough, Noodle," Luna said, her tone sharper than usual. She stepped forward, hands on her hips, her usual calm replaced with a rare edge of irritation. "I don't like it, and if you really want to be set free, you gotta let us do what we do. You think I don't have a little pull? I am The Moonlight," she popped her shit. Another rare occurrence.

"Luna, not now." Qamar cut his eyes at her like he used to do when they were kids.

Noodle tried to stifle a nervous chuckle, but it slipped out, her lips curling into a sheepish smile.

Luna, sweet Luna, always the steady one, rarely showed anger or even a flicker of frustration. She worked too hard, kept her head down too much to let the world's weight make her lose her cool. But right now? Right now, Luna's eyes had a fire in them. This Luna was putting her cape on for Noodle like she'd done for her blood brother and sister. Always the first into the fire—it was just in her, not on her.

Qamar, with his brown eyes, glared at her. "Why?"

"Why what?" Noodle stepped out of his embrace.

"What happened that you don't want us to find out if we can help you?"

Her finger massaged the thickness in her throat. "Nothing, happened... why are you mad that I want to be responsible and do things the right way?"

With tight lips and the look of a father on his face, Qamar's eyes dared Noodle to keep playing with him. He was at his wits end with her, and those tears swelling in her eyes weren't going to calm him.

Noodle couldn't ignore the sudden heat in the room - the kind that came when someone you loved cared so deeply, they'd be willing to fight battles you didn't even know you needed help with.

Luna, always the voice of reason, stood between them. "Noodle, this conversation isn't about whether or not you need our help, it is only a courtesy to inform you that we are getting you out of there."

————

A few hours with Luna and Qamar turned out to be just what she needed. The missing pep in her step returned. That feeling probably wouldn't stay long once she was back in Madison

Heights but for now the smell of The Jig had her belly swarming with beautifully nervous energy.

A sheen of angst covered her as she sat in the backseat of the truck after riding for two hours.

The new and unique feeling had city limit sign of The Emerald City in her rearview with no reason as to why she was there.

He wasn't even her type.

Did she even have a type?

If she did, he would fit the description of the right one for Noodle, but not what the world expected Jacory to choose. He'd done something so profound that now he was the only image aesthetically pleasing to her eyes and her mind because she was intrigued.

"You gon' get out or just sit there staring like a weirdo?" Ben tossed over his shoulder from the driver's seat, a smirk pulling at his lips.

Noodle's shoulders sagged, her head tipping back against the headrest as if the truck ceiling might whisper the answers she couldn't figure out herself. "Do women even do this?" she finally asked, her voice tinged with desperation as she turned to study their faces. "Or am I just thirsty?"

"You're definitely thirsty," Fink laughed from the passenger seat, his grin wide as he glanced at her dramatics. She groaned, sliding down the seat until she was nearly in the footwell, her arms flopping like she was fainting from dehydration.

"But," Fink added, drawing out the word teasingly, "two things can be true, Noodle. Women *do* approach men."

"How would *you* feel if a woman approached you?"

Fink let the question marinate for a few beats, tapping his fingers on the doorlike he was trying to think of the right way to put it. Finally, he shrugged. "Honestly? I don't think I'm secure enough in my manhood to let it go further than casual hookups," he admitted. "When I think of women, I think of... I dunno – dainty, a little helpless, maybe. I want to be her knight in shining armor, you feel me?"

Noodle sat up, slowly, her face scrunching in disbelief like she'd just heard the most absurd thing in the world. "You for real?" she asked, though her tone already said she knew he was.

She loved Fink - adored him really, but his stance hit her like a slap across the face. Sexist didn't even begin to cover it. The idea of him seeing women as these fragile little damsels who couldn't fight their own battles made her stomach churn. Yeah, she might feel like she was drowning sometimes, like she was clawing for the surface and never quite breaking through, but she didn't need anyone to save her. She'd been pulling herself out of her own messes for a long time and she was used to it.

Sure, it was cute in theory— the idea of some man swooping in, being all protective and strong, had its fairytale charm. But the reality? It was messy, suffocating, and rooted in a whole lot of outdated shit she didn't have the patience for, even if it sounded like her sister's story or the story Aku claimed would be hers.

Her teeth caught her bottom lip as she gnawed on it, holding back all the words she wanted to throw at him. Standards? Expectations? What Fink wanted in a woman? None of it mattered to her because, honestly, his whole perspective made her feel like cussing him clean out. Noodle was pissed at herself for even asking.

From the passenger seat, Fink chuckled, breaking through the growing tension. "Should've kept your mouth shut," he said, amusement dancing in his tone as he shook his head.

Fink exhaled hard, dragging a hand down his face like he could wipe away the awkwardness. The thing was, he *knew* he should've stopped talking. He also knew how Noodle worked— how the little things he said or did had the power to shape her outlook, the way she saw herself and the world. She was still figuring herself out, still pliable in a way that made him want to be more careful. He *should've* made him more careful.

"I didn't mean it like that, Noodle," he started, glancing back at her.

But the way she folded her arms and gave him a pointed side-eye told him she wasn't trying to hear it.

The air in the truck was heavy now. Fink shifted in his seat, Ben tapped the door handle, and Noodle just stared out the window, her jaw tight as her mind worked overtime.

Why was she there? Looking at the quaint little house with the new pickup truck parked in the small driveway, she sighed. How did she end up here?

"Whatever," she finally muttered, her voice low and clipped. She wasn't about to let his opinion derail her entire night. But one thing was clear— she didn't need saving, not by him, not by anyone and definitely not by Bu.

And there he was again, forcing his way into her mind without her permission.

"Are you getting out?" Ben asked for the second time. "I'm not rushing you... just don't want you all in your head."

"If you like him, let that nigga know." Fink watched her face loosen out of the corner of his eye. Like he knew it would, her whole face changed based on what he'd just told her.

Noodle wanted to please everyone and that came at never fully pleasing herself.

"So I should get out?" Noodle inquired, her eyes darting between the two of them.

Ben was about to tell her that was up to her, but Fink stopped him with a simple 'yes'.

_6_

BU STOOD at the small kitchen island, its surface barely big enough to hold the chaos he'd spread out. His notebook was flipped open, pen balancing on the edge, and bank statements were scattered like puzzle pieces waiting to fit together. His hand moved with purpose, jotting down every detail of his plan. The first step was already checked off— a brand-new work truck parked out front, gleaming like a symbol of everything he was building from the ground up and he felt proud and accomplished.

Playing in the background, were a few of Lunar's unfinished songs he wanted Bu's opinion on. When it came to music, Bu was all in. The way he heard music was artistically inclined. Where some loved the beat or the lyrics, it was the deeper dive on the instrumental placement that intrigued him, and the voice of the artist could make or break the song for him. A slow smile danced across his face thinking about Lunar playing songs through the jail receiver. Back then it was choppy and grainy.

A light tap at the door was almost missed over the sound of Lunar's crisp voice rapping about the naysayers.

Bu became annoyed thinking it was Amy's ass shooting another shot. He had the mind to pay it no attention and go back to what he was doing until the volume of the light knocks turned up a few notches.

In nothing but sweats and socks, Bu padded to the front door ready to cuss Amy out. Snatching the door open, before he could get a single word out, *her* curly hair and pretty face snapped his mouth shut.

With her lips twisted to the side goofily, Noodle said, "hey."

That unique beating of his chest Bee warned him about returned as her coconut scent wafted though the air.

Bu fought hard to keep his schoolboy grin at bay. With Noodle standing in front of him dressed down and fresh faced, it was hard to do.

On the other side of the spectrum, Noodle had to stop herself from drooling. Bu with no shirt on was too much. His body was cut up and his chest was inked with a meaningful art probably telling of life's mysterious stories. All she knew was she wanted to study them like bible study and learn them word from word.

Her eyes scanned the old English letters that spelled out The Jig across his chest. Fuck being in the jig, she wanted to be The Jig— sprawled across his chest like she belonged there.

The two of them just stood there, drinking each other in, until Bu motioned for her to come inside.

"You busy?" she inquired, observing the chaos of things spread across the island. Swinging around, she caught him ogling her. Heat coated her face.

"Not really. What you got going on?"

"I can't just stop by to see you?"

His brow dipped as he went to straighten up his mess. "You can but I don't understand why. I thought you'd be back in Madison Heights by now."

"I probably should be." Noodle looked down, twiddling with her thumbs.

Bu came around the island, lifting her chin. "You can be anywhere you want to be, baby. Remember that."

Chill bumps coated her bare arms and her pebbled nipples pushed against the thin fabric of her fitted babydoll tank top.

"What you doing in The Jig, Noodle?" Bu's deep tenor held so much sex appeal and authority.

"Can I be honest?" Her soft voice brushed against the air nervously. Lunar's distinctive voice threw off her train of thought. "Is that Lunar?" she asked, her mouth slightly ajar and her ear towards the sound to get a better listen.

Bu, leaned against the counter. "Yea but back to you being honest…"

"Umm, this isn't released…is this unreleased?" Noodle was too caught up in the music to focus on Bu.

Angling his head, Bu watched her. He could see her mouth moving but no sound came out. Looked like she was counting something out too. When her head began to nod with the music, he knew exactly what she was doing.

"Snare," he blurted.

Noodle turned to him, her almond-shaped eyes narrowing with curiosity beneath her perfectly arched brows. "Huh?"

"You trying to figure out what that unique sound is that doesn't seem to fit and somehow sounds the best… it's a snare."

Noodle's lips parted slightly, then curved into a slow grin, nodding in understanding. "Something needs to hit right there," she murmured, pointing to the beat as if she could reach in and fix it herself. "Lunar's gotta say something that makes that snare stand out. A line that's dope as hell but still lets the beat breathe, you feel me?"

Bu leaned back, nodding as if the idea had already taken root in his mind. You know your shit."

"What you thought I was just a KidVerse kid?" Noodle cheesed. She loved how people seemed to underestimate her real talent. Yes, she could act her ass off and give little kids catchy songs but her talent went beyond that.

She laughed, but the fire in her chest burned hotter. There it was again— the assumption people always made. That she was just some cutesy entertainer for kids, good for catchy hooks and bubbly TV appearances. They had no idea.

Yes, she could act circles around anyone, and yes, she had a gift for crafting songs that kids couldn't stop singing, but her talent was deeper than all that.

There was a time when music had been her lifeline— the one thing keeping her from drowning in everything life threw at her. She'd clutched it like a secret, hated how the world never saw the full scope of what she could do. Music wasn't just a skill— it was her survival, the way she stitched herself back together when the pieces didn't fit.

It was why she woke up with melodies humming in her veins, why she stayed up until her eyes burned, scribbling words on scraps of paper that no one else would ever see. When life yanked her by the hair, dragging her through hell, leaving her bruised and broken, music had been the only thing that consistently soothed her— the only thing that never left her behind.

Just thinking about it now… about the nights she poured her heart into lyrics no one cared to hear— had a lump rising in her throat. Tears stung her eyes, but she blinked them away, unwilling to let them fall.

Music was her truth, her voice, her reason.

Bu watched her for a second longer. He observed the way her gaze softened before she locked it down, grinning at him again like none of those thoughts had ever crossed her mind.

"Ride with me." His request was impromptu and yet it felt so normal.

Noodle's eyes sparkled with laughter. "What? Ride with you where?"

"Do you trust me?" Those glasses should've made him look corny but with no shirt, tatts covering his chest and that red flag hanging from his back pocket, he was anything but corny.

"Teach me to trust you," Noodle challenged, confused at where those words came from. She didn't talk like that. She sounded like a dainty, submissive girl vying for Fink's attention because that was the kind of girl he liked.

That sexy ass smile— slow and deliberate had to be crafted just for her, because there was no way God had allowed him to smile like that for other women. God was a jokester, but he wouldn't play her like that.

"I'll teach you any and everything, baby." Bu licked his lips before disappearing into the back of the house to grab a shirt and his keys.

———

Noodle never got the pleasure of spending much time in Sapphire City so she could never appreciate how much things had changed over the years. She'd taken a walk down memory lane plenty of times with Qamar and the family but photos and stories couldn't do the city justice.

Bu on the other hand, came home feeling like the city had morphed into something completely different from what he was used too. The roads didn't have as many potholes, the buildings were new and the old ones had been updated.

Downtown Sapphire City was beautiful as the sun set and the lights danced like stars in the night.

The temperature was still hot and humid but the a/c in his brand new truck blew snow balls. Having Noodle riding shotgun with him felt good. She made sure to inspect the car giving praise on how luxuriously it was for a pickup truck.

Fink and Ben followed behind them in the SUV.

"It's so nice down here," Noodle said, looking out the windows admiring the black businesses and couples holding hands while walking.

"I remember when people from the Jig didn't come down here. It felt so stuffy and out of our league. Now, we frequent it like everyone else." Bu's observation warmed his heart knowing life kept going for those on the outside. It was all he had to look forward to because how sucky would it be if he came home to everything being the same?

"How long were you in jail?"

"Four years."

Noodle gulped, hoping her face didn't give away her shock.

Bu snorted. "I'm cool now though."

"You got a girlfriend?"

"Why?" he asked, pulling into the perfect parking spot that had another open spot for Fink and Ben to park too. That had been one of the rules they laid out for Bu when it came to riding with Noodle in his car.

"I need to know if she'll like me sitting in your new car before her."

"How you know she ain't already been in here?" Bu kept his face straight.

Noodle's eyes bucked. "So you do have a girlfriend?" Her hand slapped against her face with a groan.

He laughed. And boy was it full of flavor. How did a laugh turn her on? "I'm single, baby...but you should've seen your face."

Her legs clamped together at him calling her baby. It was something about the way it slid from his mouth like an Olympic ice skater—low effort but just so damn right. "Do you call all of them baby?"

"No." Bu smirked. "You don't like me calling you that?"

Did she? Noodle wasn't sure. Maybe she would like it, if he didn't use the pet name on everyone and reserved it specially for her. "Depends," she shrugged, still wrapped up in him.

"Depends on what?"

"If you call anyone else that."

"If I did... I won't do it anymore," he declared his dark eyes locked in on her.

Noodle's bottom lip poked out. "You won't call me baby anymore?"

"I won't call *them* baby anymore... come on."

Floating somewhere in the galaxy, Noodle forgot all about them pulling up to an unknown location. Her eyes scanned the red brick building with multiple storefronts. When her eyes read the sign right in front of them, she looked at him, shocked. "The music factory?"

She'd always wanted to go there. She'd heard so many people had been discovered in The Music Factory since it was started and owned by Luna's best friend, Loyal who was one of the greatest R&B singers of their time.

Noodle had been around him and his family for years but she'd never been to his establishment.

"Do I have to sing?" She fluttered those lashes at him.

"Hell yea, baby."

"Ugh!" she pouted. "Some of the best singers come through here."

"I know, that's why I brought you." Bu studied her side profile. "You scared?"

"Sometimes, I tell myself I ain't good enough," Noodle revealed, looking straight ahead at the illuminated sign that got brighter and brighter as the sun set deeper into the sky.

Adjusting his body towards her, Bu licked his lips. "How you a loser in your own imagination? I just want to see you smile and I think I figured out the one thing that'll keep a smile on your pretty ass face."

Little did Bu know, his presence was slowly changing the ranking of things she loved in her heart. Music had always been first but maybe there was room for something else.

She watched him get out the car, stopping to say a few words to Fink and Ben before he pulled her door open with a cheeky smile that had his eyes tight behind his glasses.

Noodle had never thought glasses were sexy until Bu walked into her line of vision. Now, she only wanted a hood nigga in glasses that carried a red flag.

Fink and Ben flanked her, staying close as her hand clutched

Bu's in a death grip. When they stepped inside, the low hum of music and the scent of fried food and weed hit her all at once. A few heads turned, eyes widening in recognition. Noodle felt her stomach churn, her nerves bubbling like a shaken soda. She knew what a single photo or a careless whisper could do to their night, and to her carefully constructed image.

Bu squeezed her hand, his dark, steady eyes catching hers in an intense stare. The silent promise in them calmed the storm inside her, if only for a moment. She exhaled, letting him take the lead as they weaved through the tables.

The Music Factory was a seat-yourself kind of place, with mismatched chairs and a low-lit, intimate vibe. Bu found them a spot tucked to the side, away from the main crowd but close enough to feel the thrum of energy from the stage. A man stood under the soft glow of a single spotlight, crooning about *Summer Rain*. The melody felt familiar. It was a song she believed she'd heard Cynthia listening too. Cynthia had been on her mind a lot lately. Noodle made a mental note to look the singer up later. His voice had a way of wrapping around the room like velvet.

"You good, baby?" Bu leaned in close, his voice low and warm, his hand finding her thigh.

Her pulse jumped. When his tongue swiped over his bottom lip, her legs trembled slightly, a reaction she prayed he didn't notice. "Do they have drinks?" she asked, her voice tinged with the nerves she was trying to shake. She was desperate for something to take the edge off. Nervous about being spotted, getting on stage, and being so close to him.

Bu's eyes sparkled, a smirk curling the corners of his lips. "You ain't no alcoholic, is you?"

She rolled her eyes but couldn't hold back the grin tugging at her face. "And if I am?" Noodle wanted to scream out all the reasons it would be okay for her to overindulge in liquor. It was almost expected for kid actors to have a nasty vice.

"Then I definitely ain't getting your wanna-be-grown ass nothing to drink."

Noodle smirked, her voice sharpening just a touch. "You know I'm perfectly capable of getting my own drink, right? I've made it all my adult life without waiting for some boy to get things for me. You understand that, don't you?" Her words were firm, but the playful curve of her plush, pink lips softened the bite.

Bu's arm draped over the back of her chair, pulling her closer with an easy strength that left no room for argument. His deep voice dropped lower, just for her. "You know you ain't never been with a man, right? If I say you ain't drinking, I dare you to order one, baby."

Her breath hitched, and for a split second, she wasn't sure if she wanted to challenge him or let herself sink into the intoxicating way he looked at her— like the whole room could disappear and he'd still only see her.

"Can I get a drink?" she asked. Hating herself for how easily she submitted to him. Aku would be proud.

A gleam filled his eyes like he was more prepared for her to challenge him. When she didn't, his dick jumped. Having her pretty ass asking for permission wasn't on his bingo card of things that made his dick ache. Bu kept his eyes on hers, as his hand went up in the air to wave the bartender over. "What you getting, baby?"

Noodle cheesed hard. "Strawberry lemon drop."

"Let me get a whisky and some wings... see what they want," he pointed to Ben and Fink.

Bu cussed himself in his head seeing that Noodle was learning the key to getting whatever she wanted out of him. That pretty little mouth of hers was going to be the death of him. He could feel it.

Bu pulled the pre-rolled blunt out of some gold case in his pocket that looked like it keep the blunt from breaking. Noodle's eyes brightened. He chuckled as he flicked the fire over the end, inhaling deeply before exhaling.

"Com'ere," he said, getting in her face. "Open up."

Eagerly, Noodle formed an o with her lips ready to accept the smoke that had been in his mouth first. After smoking with Bu, she didn't want to do it any other way. It was like his mouth was the filter and inhaling weed any other way seemed beneath her now. Maybe that was his plan all along. Noodle wasn't sure and couldn't care less.

Her chest swelled before she blew the smoke out. A goofy grin spread across her face making Bu grin proudly.

Fink and Ben sat behind them loving the way Bu was with Noodle. They'd never seen her be so free. It was long overdue.

The bartender slid their order onto the table, and they dove in. Between bites of wings and fries, Noodle waved down the bartender for three more drinks. But only after shooting a quick look at Bu. His small nod of approval was all she needed, though his smirk told her he knew she wasn't about to push her luck.

The vibe in the room was warm, as people took the stage to rap or belt out their favorite songs. Some were good enough to turn heads, others had the crowd laughing or cheering just for trying. It was chill, a judgment-free zone, but none of that eased the weight in her chest when Bu leaned over, his voice soft but firm. "You're up next."

Noodle gulped hard, clutching her drink like it was the last lifeline on a sinking ship. He wasn't backing down— she could tell by the quiet determination in his face. He wasn't doing this to embarrass her. He wasn't trying to be mean. He just saw something in her that she was too scared to admit to herself.

She bit her lip, her heart thundering in her chest. Disappointing others had always been her greatest fear, but this? Standing up there in front of strangers with nothing but her voice? That fear felt bigger than the room, bigger than her.

Some wouldn't understand that since she was on a hit show and to those people she'd say, 'you do it and see how different it is.'

But Bu's gaze stayed steady, grounding her in a way she

didn't think possible. He wasn't going to let her hide from herself, not tonight.

———

Her heart pounded in her chest, sweat forming at her hair line ruining any attempt at looking cute on stage. It had been years since Noodle had been on a stage. For the last eleven years, her life had been centered around a set.

Looking around the medium-sized room, she forced a smile on her face. The blue lights were dim and a smokey scent was in the air from the weed people puffed on, her and Bu included. She thought the euphoric feeling would take the edge off.

"You got this, baby." Bu cupped his hands around his mouth drawing a few laughs from people at him cheering for her like she wasn't Jay Jay from KidVerse.

Noodle smiled, knowing he was trying to loosen her up. His words replayed in her mind. *'How you a loser in your own imagination?'* No one had ever broken self-inflicting fear down for her like that.

All the fear in her body was of her own doing. Noodle knew she had what it took to be everything she wanted to be. Her voice was top tier. Her song writing abilities, award winning. All of that and she still felt like she was at the bottom. It was time to change the narrative.

Stepping up to the mic, Noodle coated her lips before swallowing the excess. "First I want to thank you all for having me here tonight."

The crowd hooted and hollered with their phones out, ready to capture it all.

"This isn't an original song but I think you'll like it." She was talking to everyone but her eyes focused in on Bu.

Like the subtle and chill man he was, he nodded before tossing his glass in the air to her.

"You ready?" she twisted to the band, facing forward when they nodded.

The guitarist played.

"I believe in you and me. I believe that we will be..." Noodle's voice slid over the room like silk, her tone low and dripping with sensuality.

Bu straightened in his seat, his usual cool slipping for a moment as he took her in. Around him, women swayed their hands in the air or leaned into their men, mouthing the lyrics with a little too much feeling. But his focus stayed locked on her. Sliding his glasses down the bridge of his nose, he let his gaze trail her unapologetically—from the subtle peak of her hardened nipples beneath her fitted top to her pretty toes resting in designer slides. Both of them were dressed down and comfortable, but somehow she made simple look good.

"And like the river finds the sea... I was lost, now I'm free," she hit the note like a mini Whitney, her presence on stage shifting into something untouchable, untamed. She was a different person up there.

Bu couldn't take his eyes off her.

Her eyes were low, maybe from the weed, or maybe from how deeply she felt the words. She wasn't just performing, she was *living* the music, breathing life into it. The air around her crackled with energy as she held the room in the palm of her hand. Noodle was a natural-born star without even trying.

Her voice dipped effortlessly into the chorus - sultry and smooth. "When all the chips are down, baby. I will always be around."

She continued to serenade him, effortlessly singing the words. "I will always let you in boy, to places no one's ever been."

It wasn't just a song. It felt like a confession, and the way she sang it made it feel personal, like it was meant for him and only him.

Bu felt heat rise in his chest as her gaze swept briefly over him, her lips curling into a knowing smile before she pointed the mic toward the crowd, giving them the go ahead to sing the chorus with her.

Her body heated in bliss. Her head went to the sky and her body swayed to the small percussions of the song.

Bu didn't just watch her—he *felt* her. Every note... Every sway... Every laugh. She was electric, and the rest of the room may as well not have existed, because in that moment, all he saw was her...all he wanted was her.

The smile he put on her face, he could get lost in for the rest of his life. If he'd known God had her waiting for him on the outside, he wouldn't have decided to ride out his full bid. He would've acted right and paroled out after sixteen months.

The song ended, and he just had to touch her. Meeting her at the stage, he smiled down at her with a goofy smile.

"Hey," Noodle giggled, feeling the high of her night at its peak. "Thank you... my Buuuu," she sung to him playfully.

Bu looked over at Fink and Ben who nodded that it was best they go ahead and head out. They'd been at The Music Factory long enough.

———

A storm must've been brewing based on the way the wind was blowing.

When they stepped outside, Noodle begged for them to just chill before getting in the car. She said it felt too good to not bask in God's gift to them.

Bu was slowly learning that a singing Noodle was a happier Noodle. She smiled harder, dreamed deeper, felt freer, and looked prettier with the wind whipping her hair over her face.

"You said you was going to be honest," Bu reminded her of the conversation they never got to dive into at his house.

Noodle swayed beside him. "Bu, I'm tipsy...you gotta be more detailed on what you're talking about." Her body was on fire and she felt so good. The humid air kissed her already glowing skin, making her beauty stand out even more.

"I asked you what you was doing in the Jig."

"Oh that," Noodle hiccupped, twirling towards him— drinking him in because he was the only drink that could quench her current thirst. She tried to trick her brain by tossing back liquor. It didn't work.

Glossy eyes stared down at her... waiting. The smell of weed mixed with brown sugar made her body shiver.

Noodle's dainty hand lay against his face. "You are something special," she hummed, almost drowned out by the music inside the club.

If Bu could blush, his skin would flush crimson. "Noodle," his lips twitched.

"It ain't so much about being in the Jig...I wanted to see you. I wanted to be near Bu," she confessed, thanks to the liquid courage and the R&B song crooning from the inside of the club.

Bu lifted her in his arms faster than she could blink. Hemming her up against the wall, his lips pressed into hers, but Noodle was greedy.

She pushed her tongue into his mouth to explore.

Bu's hands roamed her body. Inhaling her natural scent from her legs being wrapped around him, he almost lost all control when she started to hump her pussy into him. The pliable fabric of her sweatpants was a recipe for disaster.

"Hmmm," Noodle moaned, trying her best to get in his skin hoping he could put out the fire burning inside of her.

"Baby," Bu spoke with his lips still on her. "Are you a virgin?"

"I'll be whatever you want me to be." Noodle was too hot to have coherent thoughts. All she wanted to do was him.

He chuckled a little, his hands cupping her ass, his knuckles scraping against the brick of the building. Her ass fit perfectly in his hands like it was made to go there. Freeing one hand, he pushed her wild hair from her face and just stared.

Noodle's chest bounced up and down, her eyes begging him to put his lips back on her. "Bu," she whined, ready to throw a fit. Something that was so out of her element. Noodle didn't pout or complain and she damn sure didn't throw fits with men.

The flash of a camera pulled her back into reality. Panic set in. "Bu… put me down."

His face balled up. His brows dipping while he looked her upside the head. The hell did she mean put her down?

Her hands pushed into his chest as more flashes almost blinded her. "Bu, you gotta put me down."

Fink and Ben rushed towards her, creating a wall around the two of them. Fink held his large hand out to block the camera lens.

"Hey! Don't touch my shit," the frail and thin man fussed continuing his exploiting of her.

Anger set in. Noodle read Bu's expression. It concerned her but she needed to get out of the compromising position with him before things really got bad. "Just—"

"Put you down… I know," he grunted through his teeth. Doing as she asked, Bu started to walk away.

"Bu," Noodle whispered yelled. Her eyes going from the photographer back to Bu whose back was to her. "Wait… Bu."

Spinning around with anger etched into his handsome face, Bu grilled her. "Go back to Madison Heights, Noodle. I got too much on my plate… this too much, baby." His hands went up in the air, letting her know exactly he meant.

So damn mad, he needed to do something— anything to express it. Bu snatched the photographer's camera and smashed it to the ground.

"The hell?!" the photographer looked at the ground in disbelief with his arms flying into the air. "You're going to pay for that!"

"Fuck you!" Bu spit at the man's feet. "Sue me, bitch ass nigga."

As he got in the truck, he felt played. Thoughts of how far

out of his league Noodle was, ran rampant in his mind. Like he'd told Amy, he was trying to accomplish too much to be running behind pussy.

But Noodle made his heart do shit his mama told him would happen when he found a good thing. Still, he had to keep his eyes on the prize and let her do the same.

7

HER HEELS ECHOED SHARPLY against the high-gloss floors, the sound slicing through the sterile silence like a reminder of the cold, impersonal space. The marble shimmered almost too brightly, its polished surface more of a slip hazard than any design triumph. The building itself always felt like it was holding its breath. Or maybe it was Noodle who held her breath every time she had to show her face there.

Noodle was back in Madison Heights, California and she was already regretting it. The video of her singing at The Music Factory went viral and now KidVerse needed to have a talk with her again. She didn't know if it was about that or the bullshit script they'd sent her.

Of course, her character was a teenager and for the first time, Noodle said *no*. The no came with a sense of power she never felt before. So, she walked into the building, her head held high.

People rushed by in a blur of suits and briefcases, eyes fixed straight ahead, barely sparing a glance as they slid past one another, too busy to speak.

The lobby, however, was a different world. With the network geared toward kids, the space was constantly full of hopeful parents and their wide-eyed children, all clinging to the fragile hope that *this* audition would be the one that launched them into stardom. Children fidgeted nervously, clutching their headshots, while their parents' whispered prayers under their breath. Their eyes darted around as if looking for the magic formula to make it all happen.

Noodle kept her head down not wanting to be seen or bombarded with questions and picture requests. If she had it her way, she'd tell all the parents to run and never look back but even she knew her thoughts came with a smidge of privilege that her found family afforded her. Because had the opportunity presented itself when she was still in Lynn Beach living in a trailer, she would sign away her soul on the dotted line.

She inhaled sharply as she stepped off the elevator.

The fifth floor was a vast contrast to the lobby. The smiles kinda met their eyes up there. Whether joy or sympathy - they smiled.

Noodle nodded with tight lips at those that greeted her as she switched her way into the big conference room. There were five rooms on the fifth floor. The biggest room was reserved for their top earners— the kids that held rank in the world. A false rank, but rank, nonetheless.

Her meeting was in the first room.

"Noodle," Marcus greeted and held his arms out to pull her into a hug.

"This better be good," she whispered to him before pulling away. Her eyes went around the room. They were all seated and waiting for her to get there. She was a little late, but she was there.

This time she dressed up, showing them she meant business. When she got the email, she had no idea what she would be stepping into but knew she desperately wanted them to see and treat her as an adult.

"It will be," he smiled enthusiastically.

After much consideration, Marcus went to his bosses asking

them to meet her halfway. It took a a bit of negotiating but he believed he had an opportunity that would be of interest to her.

Noodle nodded, taking her seat, making sure to keep a seat between her and each person on either side her. Resting her hands on the table, she straightened her back before looking up at Marcus who stood by the presentation board.

"Did you look over that script we had delivered to you a couple days ago?"

"Mhmmm and I feel the same way about it as I did about the ones before."

"And what is that? You know how this goes... you email us feedback when we send you scripts for consideration," Marcus reminded her.

She kissed her teeth. "It's not really *consideration* though is it?"

Before Marcus could respond, the door was pushed open, letting in a gush of a sophisticated floral scent that filled the room. "I think you're in the wrong room, dear."

"Elle." The perfectly dressed woman asserted.

"What?" Marcus rested his hands on his round belly. His perfectly tucked dress shirt made his out of shape body stand out even more and the fitted slacks didn't help neither.

Elle pulled the chair out to take a seat right next to Noodle. "My name is Elle. I am Ms. Jacory Hunter's attorney." She looked to the right, past Noodle at the assistant KidVerse assigned to Noodle. "You're fired," she said, without cracking her facial.

"What is going on? I have no knowledge of a new attorney for Jacory." Marcus looked around the room for answers but everyone was just as stumped. When his eyes landed on Noodle, she shrugged with a smirk on her face. She knew who Elle was, and it didn't take long for her to figure out who sent her. No matter how much she claimed to be able to handle KidVerse on her own, Qamar and Luna had sent in the big dogs because the attorney she'd been using for years clearly never had her best interest at heart.

Elle pulled paperwork out of her designer briefcase, her bob being the main character—swinging with every little movement she made. A black woman dressed to the nines, highly educated and no nonsense— it was a beautiful sight.

"Sign right here, Noodle." Elle pointed at the line, handing Noodle her pen.

Elle was an attorney turned family friend so Noodle knew she could trust her. She knew Qamar had sent Elle even after Noodle told him to let her handle it. It was a testament to the love he had for her...the love the whole family had for her. Noodle knew it but sometimes she forgot. Sometimes she felt less than, because she didn't share their bloodline. However, none of that was needed when it came to the family God had blessed her with. Signing her name on that line proved it.

"Now…" Elle looked around the room once Noodle was officially her client. Tucking her hand inside her briefcase again, she pulled out a thicker stack of papers. "This is a contract to terminate the current contract you have with my client."

Marcus laughed, tossing his head back as if he was at a comedy show. "This is KidVerse, honey… we don't scare easily."

It was Elle's turn to laugh boisterously. Her almond eyes turned into slits. "And I'm not to be played with. I will have y'all so sewed up in court… with all kinds of junctions and sanctions while I pick through every contract with a fine tooth comb." Her heels clacked as she stood up and walked around the room. "And I won't stop there. I will get every ex-employee and any current ones, who are fed up of your shady tactics, to attest to the working conditions and the predatory practices of a network that claims to be kid friendly and family oriented." She leaned in to whisper to Marcus. "And my shit goes beyond the courtroom, ask around about me and how I've made friends with some of the most powerful people this world has ever seen."

He swallowed. "That's not how this works."

"Maybe not but it's how this is going to go." Elle sashayed back over to the stack of papers near me. "Have your people sign the damn paperwork! And don't call my client, call me from now on."

————

Noodle lay across her bed, scrolling down her social media page bored out of her mind. Aku was out on the town as usual, so Noodle was home alone and all she wanted to do was curl up in bed and watch Whitney Houston movies.

Seeing an image of Pimp on her feed, she clicked on his page just to be nosey. She'd seen him recently, since him and Lunar were in Madison Heights wrapping up Lunar's new album.

The first pinned photo on his page was of Bu standing in front of his new pickup truck holding a bottle of champagne. Under the post, Pimp congratulated his big brother on stepping out on faith and starting his landscaping business. Noodle's mind went to the pile of papers on the kitchen counter and she felt horrible because not one time did she inquire about his life and what he had going on,

Bu was tagged, so she clicked on his page, clicking follow immediately.

There wasn't much there besides the same picture on Pimp's page and one picture of him that looked like it was a candid shot. His chest was bare, and his jeans slightly hung off his waist. There was also a gun tightly tucked in the waistband with that red flag hanging down.

He was so sexy to her. And clearly other girls felt the same.

Noodle's nose scrunched up when she read the thirsty comments. Some telling him how fine he was, while others promised to welcome him home the proper way.

Her front teeth sank into her lip as she contemplated whether or not to leave her own comment. Always one to follow her first mind, Noodle clicked the heart eye emoji before sliding over into his direct messages to congratulate him.

Bowl-o-Noodles: Congrats and I'm such a horrible friend.

It didn't take long, maybe a couple seconds before her phone dinged with a notification.

BigBu: I appreciate that, baby. We friends?

She sucked in a breath because reading his words were like hearing his deep voice say *baby*.

Her legs shook in anticipation, wondering what she should say next. Flirting wasn't her strong suit because for most of her life, Noodle had placed work before boys. Now, she'd found someone that made her heart skip beats and she was at a loss for words. But Bu wasn't a boy she never talked to before, he was a man that made her want to stumble over her words just to get a little of his time. She jumped when her notifications went off again.

"Shit!" she hissed when the phone fell onto her face. The pain didn't stop her from rushing to see what he had to say.

BigBu: The way you seemed ashamed when the cameras came out, I didn't know we were like that.
    Bowl-o-Noodles: I'm sorry
    BigBu: It's all good, baby.

· · ·

She swooned at that word again. How was his impression on her so deep, so fast that she swore she could hear his thick hood accent calling her baby. Too quickly for her to gather her thoughts to respond, Bu sent another message.

BigBu: Shoot me your number, baby.

Noodle didn't waste a second before sending him her number.

After that, she closed the app without checking any of her other notifications. Noodle had over two million followers, whether there because they genuinely liked her or to stir up shit, she always had hundreds of notifications in her mentions.

The sound of her phone ringing had her hand darting towards it. The number on the screen wasn't saved which meant it had to be Bu. Noodle squealed, kicking her feet in the air while laying on her back.

"Hello?"

"This how you answer the phone for all your lil boy toys?" Bu's baritone vibrated in her ears.

Noodle giggled. "I don't think I've ever had a boy toy... is that what you are?" she twirled her finger around a strand of hair.

Bu grunted, "Stop playing with me."

"You started it," she snorted, her hand slapping against her mouth when the god awful noise came out.

"Wow," he dragged the word out making her laugh harder with embarrassment. "What you got going on over there?"

"Nothing really."

"I see you back in Madison Heights. What all you be doing out there?"

Noodle pondered over his question. Most of her time was spent at KidVerse or doing something they'd commissioned her to do. When she wasn't walking a red carpet or recording some kid friendly pop song, she was in the house. Saying that out loud sounded so boring and lame though. Times like this, she needed Aku to coach her on the art of flirting. "Honestly?"

"All I want is for you to be honest."

Chewing on her lip, she confessed, "watching movies."

"By yourself?" Bu inquired over the light noise in his background.

"Do you watch movies, Bu?"

"Not really." Silence filled the line. "I'll do that shit with you though."

Her mouth opened wide, silently screaming like she'd just been asked to prom by her crush. Once she was settled, she went back to their conversation. "What are you doing now?"

"Fuckin' with this social media shit, trying to put up a ad to hire some workers." He sounded frustrated.

"For the yard business?"

"Yard business?" he chuckled.

She cackled. "That's what it is right?"

"Yea, but landscaping sounds more professional, you know?"

She did know, and she nodded as if he could see her.

Noodle fully understood moving in a way that made people respect you. She'd been taught the art of perception her whole career. So, Bu preferring landscaping over yard business was understood.

"I didn't mean it like that."

"I know, baby. I'm just fuckin' with you." Bu cleared his throat. "Congratulations are in order for you too. I heard KidVerse fired you."

"Is that what the story is?" Noodle had seen the headlines.

There was so much discourse online about her getting dropped. Some gave praise, knowing she was so much more than some kid shit, while others thought she fumbled the biggest bag she would ever get. The way no labels wanted to take meetings with her, she didn't know how she truly felt about it all.

Leaving KidVerse didn't stop the million and one thought

pieces on her. If anything, it added to the theories about her doing drugs and being at wild parties like all the other child stars.

Everyone had something to say. No one used their common sense to figure out why most child stars spiraled once they became adults. Yes, some didn't know what to do with their newfound freedom while others had been mentally stifled and adulting seemed to come with too much responsibility for them to handle.

"Don't worry about what the story is…figure out what the story is going to be." Bu's words came with a hint of wisdom. He seemed so prolific, dropping gems without trying. His mind worked that way. If life hadn't taught him anything else, it taught him that the story was never over.

"When you become the author of your story, you can write until you say it's the end. But even then, a well written story stands the test of time and never truly dies or ends." He adds.

Noodle sat up, leaning her back against the headboard. "What should my story be?" her tone was low. She held her breath waiting for him to answer her.

"That ain't for me to tell you. What are your dreams? You got any goals?"

Noodle honestly didn't know anymore and that was sad to say. She'd been content with others telling her what to do and where to be. The freedom she craved didn't seem as free as she expected. "I don't know," she whispered. "Is that a deal breaker for you?"

Bu sighed. "Baby, what I do or don't want, ain't got nothing to do with you. Never let a nigga like me get close to you. You're precious… a jewel, and right now my hands to rough to handle something so delicate. So deal breaker or not, I'm not on your level anyway."

Noodle wanted to yell and scream at him for diminishing who he was. As far as she was concerned, he was probably the best man for a girl like her. He was humble and hardworking.

His spirit was easy and airy. Plus, he wasn't pretentious like the men she encountered in Hollywood.

"I think you're my speed." A smile split her face, butterflies fluttering in her belly at how corny she sounded.

He laughed and had they not been on the phone, she would've seen his brown skin flush with color. "You been hanging in the Jig too much, baby."

"Come see me." Noodle blurted. "Let me show you my world, Bu."

Thick silence fogged the line. Noodle, stopped breathing, eyes wide open, waiting for him to let her down easy.

Listening to her sweet voice, he'd never tell her no. Whatever she wanted, Bu was more than willing to give it to her, even if he knew he wasn't the best nigga for her. He wouldn't look good on her arm. Hollywood and red carpets weren't welcoming a nigga like him— a nigga with a gun charge that should've been murder.

"Let me move some shit around and I'm there, baby."

8

IF THE EARLY bird gets the worm, then what does the nigga that never went to sleep get?

Bu splashed water on his face for the fifth time and still felt tired. All night phone conversations weren't the best idea when he needed to have his feet on the floor early. Listening to her soft voice pulled him into her bubble more with each word. When she talked, he listened to every jumbled mess of thoughts in her mind that seemed to spill effortlessly.

Within one conversation, he surmised that Noodle wasn't as naive as he thought, but she'd been deprived of free thinking, and she was smart and articulate.

While Bu often struggled to pronounce words correctly, her vernacular was like that of a private school kid attendee—proper enunciation never sounded so sexy. But every now and then her time in Lynn Beach showed up, reminding him that there was more to her than meets the eye.

Thoughts of her were the only thing that kept his eyes open.

After taking a shower, brushing his teeth, and washing his face, he was ready to get his day started. There was so much he needed to get done if he was going to make it to Madison Heights within the next few days.

Once he was fully dressed in jeans, a shirt and crisp sneakers, he grabbed his keys and left home. Just as he stepped off the elevated porch, Ms. Linda waved him over to her.

"Bethune!" she called his name.

"Good morning," he responded once he was in her yard.

Her thin lips were pursed. "When you got that new truck?"

He snorted a laugh, knowing when she called him over it was to be nosey or gossip about the comings and goings of the neighborhood.

Stuffing his hands in his pockets, he smiled. "I bought it a few days ago. This your first time seeing it?"

"Un uh," she said shaking her head. "My first time seeing you, since you got it." Her weary eyes trailed over to his all black Ford F-150 Raptor.

It was a beauty with the black rims and the slight lift. Bu was proud of it especially since he was able to pay for it with cash.

His tattooed hand slid down the nape of his neck. "Trying to get this business off the ground...been busy Ms. Linda. You've been good though?"

"Yea, they cut my stamps by twenty dollars cause they raised my social security by 40... ain't that some shit? Them greedy bastards ain't givin' me nothing but seventy-seven dollars a month well shit, fifty-seven now." Anyway, that ain't what I called you over here for." She looked down the street both ways before giving Bu those tired eyes. "That truck must cost a lot because I seen some young boys snooping 'round here the other night. It was 'bout four in the morning, but you know my old bones be up by then."

Bu tilted his head, listening intently to what nosey Linda was saying. The Jig, although it had been spruced up and had more resources, was still the hood. That aside, he had no knowledge of the young boys jackin' cars. It was all news to him.

"They probably just wanted to look at it... you know how we get when we see something new," Bu reasoned, laughter in his voice.

Ms. Linda snorted. "If you say so. That's why I got them cameras…" her head nodded towards one of the cameras. "Can't trust your own."

Bu's eyes went to the cameras on the corner of Linda's small home. When he first got out, he thought it was weird that one of them faced his house directly. But after a few days, he decided not to make a big deal out of it. Ms. Linda was harmless and his days of illegal activities were long behind him.

"Let me let you get on with your day. Bee would be so happy you done lost weight… thought you was gon' be on that million pound show, chile."

Bu laughed with a thickness in his throat because his mama would've had all kinds of jokes about him losing weight. She never got to see the more fit version of her oldest boy because after a year and half down the road, his mama left this earth. Before then, he forbade her from visiting him. Now, he would give anything to see her one last time… show her how her oldest baby had transformed into a man.

———

Bu sat in his car, the engine off, but the keys still dangling from the ignition. The silence settled around him, thick and heavy, as he leaned back against the headrest and closed his eyes for a moment. The day replayed itself in his mind like a slideshow leaving him both drained and a little proud.

He'd started the morning at FedEx, standing at the self-service station, fumbling with the printer until the business cards and flyers finally came out right. Good thing he was born in the 21st century and when it came to technology not much had changed over the four years he was gone. From there, he hit up every local spot with a job board, stapling and pinning his "Now Hiring" posters next to ads for babysitters and garage sales.

The home improvement store was the last stop. He spent a good hour walking through the aisles, sizing up riding lawnmowers trying to figure out which one he was going to get. Now he was back at home ready to call it a night before doubt lingered in his mind too long.

He exhaled slowly, gripping the steering wheel like it might hold him steady. It wasn't just about starting the business, it was about proving to himself that he could. It was about making Bee proud because he knew she was up there watching his every move.

With a deep inhale, exhale, he climbed out of the truck making sure to look up and down the street. No matter how legit he had been, sometimes the reaper came for what had already been promised to him and in his past life, Bu had made an enemy or two.

Bu dragged his feet across the threshold, the weight of the day clinging to him like wet cement. Each step felt heavier than the last, his legs protesting with a dull ache that spread through his entire body. His eyes burned— dry and tired, as if every ounce of energy he had left, had been squeezed out hours ago. He'd been in the streets since seven-thirty that morning, and now, with the sun long gone and the neighborhood steeped in quiet - all he wanted was the comfort of his bed. Even food felt like too much effort.

The faint hum of the refrigerator buzzed from the kitchen as he passed by, unbothered by the thought of a missed meal. His focus was singular-- a shower and sleep. Tugging his shirt over his head, Bu let it fall to the floor without a second thought.

His thumb swiped across his phone screen, checking for missed calls or texts. Pimp had hit him up, but aside from that, his notifications were silent.

His mind wandered to Noodle. What was she doing? He could picture her curled up on her couch, eyes glued to a screen — because she was afraid of living.

He wondered if she was happy, now that she was stepping into the freedom she'd been chasing. He prayed she'd find something more than the life that had been scripted for her. Something real.

The urge to call her tugged at him, but he let it pass. Not tonight. His body was shutting down, and he didn't have another night of late-night conversations in him— not if he wanted to be worth anything tomorrow. With a heavy sigh, Bu hit the shower, the thought of her lingering like the faint scent of fresh rain on a pavement -

a scent he hadn't smelled since being home.

Sapphire News said some shit about it being a drought with them having had no rain in weeks.

Inhaling a deep breath, his mind played tricks on him as that coconut scent, he loved more than the rain, engulfed him. Bu's dick stirred, thinking about his calloused hands cuffing her plush ass that night after The Music Factory.

That crazy shit his heart did whenever he was around her happened

He couldn't get Noodle off his mind no matter how hard he tried but he also didn't have the energy to call her. Instead, he sent a message to Lunar telling him to get her out the house and in the studio. He knew his request would be accepted because Lunar respected him and knew Noodle needed to get out of that bubble, she was always in. Once Lunar responded back letting him know he was on his way to drag her out the bed, Bu felt content and could finally shower and go to bed.

After he scrolled down her social media page like the creep she made him, his eyes finally got too tired for him to keep open and he went to sleep.

9

"HELLO?" Noodle answered her phone, her tone low and groggy.

"Good morning, Jacory," Jackie greeted.

Desperate to see what time it was, Noodle pulled the phone from her ear. "It's six in the morning here."

"Still morning… did your daddy not teach you manners?" Jackie sounded like she was smoking a cigarette.

"Good morning, Jackie."

"Will I ever be mom?"

No! She wanted to scream. The only mother she acknowledged was Cynthia and she was dead. Maybe if Jackie would've tried harder to have a relationship with her or not let her daddy take her to his wife, then maybe she'd be mom. But she didn't say that. It was too harsh even if it was true.

Noodle didn't say anything.

Couldn't say anything because there was just so much that had transpired between the two of them. Jackie liked to pretend things didn't happen when Noodle was old enough to remember — like her signing over her child for money.

Jackie kissed her teeth. "I've been praying for you. How have you been?"

If Jackie had been praying, Noodle wondered what for because life had been turning her upside down. Every other day, she was in the media with speculation on why and how KidVerse dropped her as if her dropping them was too farfetched.

"I've been good. You?"

"Wishing I could spend some time with you. How are we going to get to better place if you ain't trying?"

"I work, you know that. I ain't easily accessible."

"But you got time to be seen pouring liquor down your throat? Or with your cousin who always at somebody party living it up? You make time for what you want to make time for, Jacory," Jackie's word held no venom. It was true. Noodle did make time for what she wanted to make time for and her mama wasn't on that very, short list.

Noodle groaned again, her eyes straining as she shut them tight. "Jackie, it's six in the morning."

"Well okay," Jackie voice held sorrow. "I'll let you go. If you ever make a stop in Lynn Beach, I'd love for you to come to my church... can't keep praying for you if you won't at least show your face in the Lord's house."

Noodle just listened. It was comical to her how over the last eleven years her mama gave her life to God. After twenty-one years of not being a present parent in Noodle's life, Jackie wanted to get right with the Lord.

She snorted to herself. "I'll let you know if I make it there."

"Have a good day, Jacory," Stacy whispered as they ended the call.

Noodle's arms and legs went wild as she fought the air, tangling herself in the sheets. Her heart was so big. She felt bad about handling her mama that way. Her heart was fragile when it came to that subject. Maybe her life would've been different had Jackie kept her. Maybe it would've been worse. One thing she knew was, she wouldn't have Siasia had Jackie not allowed Stacy to take their daughter home to another woman. Noodle felt good about getting Siasia out of the whole fucked up ordeal. But then why was her heart so bruised?

Rolling over to her side, she decided to get a little more sleep. When it came to sleep, Noodle was going to get it. She knew a bed hated to see her coming.

"Jacory!" Lunar burst through her room door. He marched over to shake her leg. "Get yo' ass up."

"Nooo," she whined wanting a few more hours of sleep.

Aku yawned, walking into her room before climbing in the bed with her. "If I gotta get up, so do you, Noodle Doodle." She snuggled into Noodle's side.

Noodle pulled the cover over their heads. "If we lay still, he'll go away," she whispered.

"No the fuck I ain't. Get up! Both of y'all. We got shit to do."

When his boy hit him telling him to get Noodle out the house, he did just that. He wasn't able to do it the night before because he got caught up, but showed up bright and early once he was done.

Aku snickered, her eyes looking over Noodle's face. "Are you happy?" she asked.

"Why you ask that?" Noodle smiled shyly, looking over her best friend too.

Aku was beautiful and Noodle loved the freckles that coated her nose. Her beautiful, tanned skin always seemed to have a natural glow like she was always happy. She'd never seen her girl not smiling or just enjoying life. It was something she envied, but never enough to want to dim Aku's light.

"I want you to be happy. I want the world to meet the real Noodle, the one who'll give a stranger the shirt off her back... the girl who loves everyone but sometimes she neglects herself. Are you happy, Noodle?"

Tired , Noodle shrugged. "I think I am... I want to be."

"Then be... my little Noodle Doodle." Aku tapped her round nose like a Disney princess.

"I'm still waiting," Lunar reminded. He could hear them whispering, unable to make out what they were saying.

Seeing the two of them under the covers brought joy to his heart and reminded him of when they did that as kids. Anytime Noodle was sad, Aku would crawl under the covers with her and if Aku wasn't available, he'd be the fill in. There had even been times when Noodle would pull Pimp into her happy den as she'd liked to call it.

Aku emerged from under the covers, glaring at Lunar. "But why I gotta get up,?"

"Because our girl needs our support while she goes into the studio," Lunar informed them. "And this shit is a family business."

Noodle's head popped out from under the covers, fear in her eyes. "Wait...what?"

"He said you going to the studio." A crooked grin tugged at the corner of Aku's mouth.

"And you too," Luna pointed to remind her that she was going too.

If they were going to take it all to the next level, it had to be a family affair. He had seen how their parents did it as a unit—feeding each other's dreams, holding each other accountable. If the three of them were going to carve out their own path, it had to be together. He'd heard the lessons of his father. It was how Big Lunar created the dreams inside of his people. It was only right that he did the same.

His hand went to his chest, as a pain of not knowing the greatest man alive, all while walking around with his heart in his chest shot through him.

"Get up, Jacory," he smirked, knowing Noodle was close to cussing him out if he didn't stop with her government name.

"I don't want to go to the studio," she pouted.

"My boy Bu sent me."

Aku cheesed hard, shaking her shoulders. "Bu?! Get up bitch, yo' man said get yo' ass in. the studio."

Noodle blushed, knowing even 2000 miles away, he still thought of her. With an extra pep in her step, she got out the bed making Lunar and Aku crack up. To add a little more pizazz, she switched her hips.

"Stop playing with me, Noodle," Lunar said squinting his eyes into slits. "I'm already salty you got my boy falling in love. I thought it was going to be you and me," he played like his heart hurt.

"Oh, please," Aku waved him off. "That's our cousin/auntie."

Lunar shook his head because he really did love Noodle. She would always have a soft spot in his heart.

———

Noodle sucked, and she was frustrated.

Lunar was too but tried to hide it.

Aku just sat on the couch with her leg bouncing and her eyes darting across the room.

"I can't get it right." Noodle snatched the headphones from her ears, marching out of the booth.

"You overthinking it," Lunar sighed. He knew she was in her head bad.

"Maybe I don't got it no more." She plopped down beside Noodle on the couch.

Aku cut her eyes to her. "Or maybe you need to feel it more

"What that mean?"

Lunar slapped his hand on his forehead knowing they were about to argue. It had been that way. Noodle watched her words while Aku's spilled like an overflowing sink. Knowing how this could end, he plopped down in the spinning office chair.

"You're not dumb, Noodle. You know what I mean," Aku didn't even look up from her phone.

Noodle snatched it. "I'm talking to you."

"You 'bout to be on the floor… the fuck wrong with you?"

"You! You got a lot to say but then don't be saying shit!" Noodle fumed.

Lunar's eyes grew in size at Noodle cussing. She hardly did that or even raised her voice but they all knew there was a beast inside of Noodle waiting to break free.

"Noodle, please," Aku waved her off. "I ain't saying nothing Lunar ain't thinking."

"Don't put me in it," Lunar chimed in.

Noodle's eyes darted to him. "Say what you need to say, Little Lunar."

"Oh, it's Little Lunar now?" He nodded, amused. "You got it, Jacory, cause I ain't 'bout to go back and forth with you. Like I said, you all in your head. Your voice is top tier. You can really sing but you let them people get in your head. They got you second guessing shit. You feel it in the pits of your stomach, let that shit out."

Noodle stood with her fists by her side, fuming, but unable to say a word 'cause they were right.

"But when I say it, you ready to fight," Aku mumbled before snatching her phone back from Noodle. "Tell that nigga Bu to come get you right."

Lunar jumped up when Noodle charged at her.

"Aku, stop playing with me cause you know I'm really like that."

"And so the fuck am I." Aku pounded her chest. "Let her go, Lunar."

"Nah, we family, sit the fuck down." He huffed bear hugging Noodle. She was small but strong as hell. He remembered the two of them fighting as kids. It was funny then. Now, there was too much love to allow them to take it there."

"Ouuu, you better be glad I love you," Noodle hissed, knowing she didn't really want to fight her bestest friend in the whole wide world. Besides, she knew French would be so disappointed in them if they did. He'd taught them to love each other and fight the world.

"Okay, Lunar, you holding her too tight. Let her go," Aku fussed at him.

"And this why I don't be getting in y'all shit." He let Noodle go. "Just..." he pinched the bridge of his nose thinking. "Just go home and listen to my verse... write something from your heart and we'll come back when you ready."

———

A month later

"Look at that nigga standing up there like he don't belong," Pimp joked as they pulled up on Bu waiting in arrivals at the airport.

He was dressed down in sweats, a t-shirt, and designer slides with socks. Nothing too extravagant but his basic attire made him stick out like a sore thumb at the Madison Heights airport.

Lunar laughed because Pimp was right. Everyone coming and going from Madison Heights Airport dressed up like they were going to the Met gala. On the rare occasion someone tried to wear something more fitting for travel, you better believe it was going to be designer.

Pimp laid on the horn drawing attention to the black SUV he'd taken the liberty of driving for the day.

Lunar stuck half of his body out the passenger window, arms in the air, yelling, "what's up baby?!"

Bu frowned before grabbing his luggage, pulling it to the truck. "Y'all doing too much... the fuck?"

"We missed you too," Lunar laughed when Bu slammed the backdoor after getting in.

Bu didn't respond, instead he smacked his baby brother in the back of the head. "Bro, you 'bout to have them people calling the law on us with all that blowing."

"The fuck you hot with me for and not him?" Pimp rubbed the back of his head.

"'Cause I know y'all late because of your can't get out of bed ass and you the one blowing that fuckin' horn like you lost your mind. Who raised your ass?"

"The same crazy ass woman that raised you." Pimp dodged the next swat just in time.

"Your flight was good?" Lunar turned to ask Bu.

Bu cleaned his glasses off with the end of his shirt. "Man, it was a flight… ain't that special." nothin' special 'bout it .

"I'm just being nice, nigga."

"Don't," Bu grunted. "The weather out here good already. What's the move?"

Pimp merged into traffic. "Lunar wants to stop and see his granny in LA. It ain't too far."

"Cool," Bu nodded, settling into his seat. "You hittin' the studio tonight?"

"Hell yea…"

"Nigga lives in the studio."

"And you be right there living with me," Lunar jested.

It was true. Lunar and Pimp were best friends and loved being in each other's presence. It was like Lunar was able to bring a piece of home with him everywhere he went. It helped since Pimp had been his business partner through it all. He'd even produced a few songs on his last mixtape. So when it came to getting money, Lunar was always going to put his friend in the mix.

As kids, they'd met from Lunar going back to Sapphire City with his family anytime they had toy drives or anything to do with their hometown. The two of them kicked it hard after Lunar saw Pimp fighting a group of neighborhood kids. They've been close ever since with Lunar's mama, Tiny making sure to include Pimp in all family gatherings and vacations.

Pimp couldn't refute the claims so he didn't say anything as he continued to drive. Cali traffic was horrible any day of the week. Even with Madison Heights being a smaller city outside of the city limits, traffic there was just as hectic and made getting to LA a much longer drive.

"Let me hear something while y'all riding in this hoe in silence," Bu grunted.

"You need some pussy or something? You done got off the plane in a horrible mood," Pimp put on his best professional voice he could muster causing him and Lunar to crack the hell up.

Bu opened one eye—too tired to open both of them up. "Nigga you don't know the half."

"What's up? Everything good?" Pimp's playful banter ceased the moment he felt his big brother was battling something.

Lunar peered over at Pimp.

"Ain't nothing I can't handle."

Over the last month, Bu had been trying to get his business going and it had turned out to be harder than he expected. So far he had a few clients doing residential yards but he was spread thin being as though he hadn't found any help. None of the niggas in his neighborhood wanted to do manual labor. They approached it like it was lame or some shit. He wasn't sweating it knowing, what was for him, was for him.

"Why you gotta handle everything by yourself though?"

Bu shrugged. "Just used to it being that way. I'm good though bro… I promise."

"Like niggas don't be lying on promises and shit," Pimp mumbled, his shoulders growing ridged.

Lunar kept his comments to himself. If he didn't learn anything else from his own family, he knew to stay out of people's family business unless they came to you directly. He knew Pimp and Bu had a unique relationship. While Pimp spent a lot of his time in Jade City or Emerald City with Lunar, Bu stayed in Sapphire City making shit shake as he liked to say.

A few beats passed before Bu was asking again. "Play something, damn!"

Lunar laughed as he went to his phone to find one song he was the most proud of. It was an ode to love— in the eyes of his mama. Losing love, finding love, and embracing love.

The beat of Lunar's track hummed softly through the speakers, a smooth blend of deep bass and keys, the kind of sound that made you feel like you were being gently rocked in a boat, cruising through a moonlit night. The melody was soulful, but there was a rawness to it that kept it grounded— *his* story woven into the music. Lunar's voice came through, deep and steady, a touch of raspiness in the way he crooned the hook.

'Momma lost love, but she found it again,
In the arms of a man who never left her side,
She held on tight, she never let it slip,
Through the tears, through the fight, through the pain in her ribs…'

Lunar's words swirled around the SUV, his soul pouring into every line. It was a song about his mama, a tribute to the love she'd lost and found, the resilience of her heart. It wasn't just a love song, it was a whole story, layered with the grief and hope that came from living and loving in this world. Lunar's fingers drummed softly on the door, each beat a testament to the woman who'd raised him, to the woman who had given everything for him and still found room to love again.

Pimp's head nodded more, his eyes on the road but clearly feeling the song like he hadn't heard it before. But Bu, always the harder critic, was quiet. Too quiet.

As the song faded out, Lunar turned to Bu to gauge where his head was at when it came to the song.

Finally, Bu broke the silence. His gaze sharp, the glint of his experience clear. "Yo, that's a fire track, no doubt. But—" he tapped the seat with his fingers, "it's missing something. You need a voice. A female voice, man… to really bring the thing to life. You know, something to complement that melody. A hook with some soul. Like…I'm thinking somebody that'll make it pop. That's what it needs. Somebody who can belt it out with you, pull the heartstrings."

Lunar let the words hang in the air for a moment. He'd been working on this song for weeks, tweaking it, rearranging the lyrics, perfecting the vibe. And Bu's suggestion hit him right in the chest. It was exactly what he'd been missing but hadn't been able to see— *her* voice. Someone to carry the weight of the love, the hurt, the joy.

"Yeah…you might be right," Lunar finally said, his voice low but thoughtful. "I just needed to hear it from someone else." He leaned back in the seat, letting the song play out in his head again, imagining what it would sound like with the right voice filling in the spaces. There was only one voice he could even imagine on the track. With a smirk on his face, he let the music replay in his mind on a loop while his heart skipped a few beats just thinking about doing music with her again.

Noodle was the ying to his yang. They'd started music together as kids with Luna being the meister of it all. Times down in Luna's basement filled his memory bank, keeping him rooted in how it all came to be.

Bu knew what voice needed to be on the track but Lunar had told him of her mishap in the studio the other day. He'd been so busy with getting things rolling for his business that he hadn't spoken to her to check her about letting the world get in her head.

"Bu you good for something, bro," Pimp smiled loving to get under his brother's skin.

The traffic was jammed pack, making them get to Lunar's granny's house a little later than he wanted. It wasn't like he had anything on the schedule but he did want to hit the studio before the night ended. As they pulled up, he noticed his aunt's car parked in the driveway along with a few niggas hanging outside. He already knew who it was and had no issues getting out the car.

"Aye, who that?" Bu ran his tongue across his teeth, seeing the Hispanic men dressed in nothing but red. A few of them even had guns tucked in their waistbands.

"Them his people." Pimp turned the car off before facing his brother. "It's cool, bro... I would never walk you into some shit that ain't safe."

Bu nodded. "You got that for me, though?"

"Always, got you, big bro... under the seat."

Once the *thing* was stuffed into Bu's pants, he pulled his shirt down with the two of them getting out the car trekking behind Lunar.

"Nephew!" One of the men shouted with his arms up in the air ready to embrace Lunar.

Lunar's smiled, pulling the stocky man into a hug. "Tio Bobby."

He went down the line embracing the others with a smile on his face. Pimp and Bu stood back just waiting for the next move. Pimp was familiar with them but didn't want to make Bu feel uncomfortable while also drawing a line in the sand.

Bobby sized Bu up. "¿Él contigo sobrino?"

"Yea." Lunar didn't hesitate to answer, knowing how shit could go left at any given time.

Bobby was married to Lunar's stepdad's sister and he'd spent many summers in LA seeing shit he probably shouldn't have seen. It was like God knew the path Lunar would take, making him multifaceted in all walks of life. The silver spoon had been in his mouth but his people never let him forget what it meant to be black in all walks of life.

Bu looked between Bobby and the rest of the men standing around sizing him up. Four years locked away didn't help his PTSD. Sucking his teeth, he stepped up, making sure his brother was behind him. There was no issue with showing respect because he'd been taught that a long time ago. But the funny thing about respect was, it had to be given before he ever dished that shit out.

Bobby stuck his hand out, his index and thumb making a circle while the other fingers stood straight creating a b.

Seeing that, Bu smiled and returned the gesture.

The breath Pimp held, seeped out but his chest still rattled from the exchange.

"Brother," Bobby laughed, pulling Bu into him like he'd done Lunar seconds before.

Bu nodded before showing love to the others.

Just as they were about to start smoking, Vitta pushed the front door open. Maverick did right by his mama. Her home was grand and lavish, boasting five bedrooms that were all mini master suites with their own sitting areas and bathrooms. The only thing missing from the bedrooms were kitchens.

"That's my grandbaby?" she squealed as if she didn't know he was coming. Anytime Lunar came close to LA, he made sure to stop at his granny's house. Maverick wasn't his biological father but he'd been there since he was a jit still in diapers. When Maverick fell in love with Tiny, he also fell in love with her son. The love extended to Vitta and Vashon who was next out the door along with her children.

"What's up granny?" Lunar asked, hugging her tightly since it had been a few months since he last saw her.

Vashon eased herself between them to hug on her nephew with her kids greeting him as well with jokes and play fighting.

"Damn, y'all gon' ignore me?" Pimp held his arms out, making Vitta laugh before hugging and kissing him on his cheek. "This my big brother," he introduced Bu.

Vitta slapped his hand down. "Baby I don't do no damn handshake...you save that shit for Bobby and them. Give me a damn hug," she sassed, invading Bu's personal space.

Bu laughed but hugged her 'cause he wouldn't dare go against his elders. He was from the south and had been raised by a true southern woman. His mama didn't play that.

"Come on in. I made tacos," Vitta shooed them into her house.

As soon as they stepped inside, the aroma of Vitta's food attacked their noses reminding them they hadn't eaten anything all day.

Like always, Vitta's house was clean with everything in its place. On the walls were images of her family and all the people she loved. Of course her grandbabies filled most of the frames and that included Lunar. If you didn't know Lunar's story you would believe he'd come from Maverick nuts like his little brother Monday. The amount of love Lunar received from Maverick and his family was something he'd never be able to repay.

"Tacos?" Bu eased beside him to ask under his breath. In Sapphire City, people's grannies were frying chicken on a random day, not having a full spread of Mexican food. He couldn't lie though, the shit smelled good as hell, making his stomach rumble at the thought of digging in.

With a laugh and a head nod, Lunar placed his hand on Bu's shoulder since they were the same height. "Nigga, 'bout to be the best taco you ever had... better ask Pimp's ugly ass." His eyes went to Pimp who was talking to Vashon's son, Bobby Jr. The two of them were always super cool whenever Pimp came to L.A.

Bu made a mental note to keep an eye on shit because Bobby Jr was big Bobby's son, and shit like that was what almost costed him a murder charge.

Once Bu was done eating, he walked outside where Bobby had invited him to smoke one with him. He could tell the old head wanted to get a feel for him. He wasn't worried nor would he ever back down, so he eased over to the group as they leaned against souped up old school cars.

"This muthafucka nice," Bu nodded at the red 1970 Oldsmobile convertible with the butter interior. On instinct his hands rubbed together when Bobby invited him over to check it out. He whistled lowly at how nice the ride was.

Bobby laughed, passing him the blunt. Bu shook his head. "No disrespect but I don't smoke nothing I ain't seen rolled."

"I respect that, baby boy," the words rolled with a hint of an inner Spanish accent. Bobby directed his boy to pass Bu a big bag of weed and rolling paper.

"Paper?" Bu looked between the contents and Bobby.

With a strong nod, Bobby explained, "this weed is too good to water down with backwoods, baby boy."

Bu shrugged, down to try it. It had been years since he smoked a joint. Even in prison they had someone sneaking in backwoods, but when in Rome. As soon as he opened the bag of exotic, he looked up at Bobby shocked.

"You see?" Bobby laughed with the others joining him. "No backwoods, baby boy. Take this to the head."

And to the head, Bu did.

It didn't take long for his eyes to hang low and his body to feel warm all over. They sat outside for hours just laughing and talking a whole lot of gang shit. Bu didn't get that too often since he kept his distance back in Sapphire City. He fully understood if he wanted to do shit differently, he had to actually do shit differently, but Bobby and his family seemed to be about their business. They gave him tips and tricks on business while also letting him know, Madison Heights was the perfect place to really get his landscaping business off the ground.

He ended his night at the suite Lunar and Pimp had rented for their stay in Madison Heights. It went from them just listening to music, to Bu looking up and there was a penthouse full of people. He wasn't tripping though.

10

NOODLE JOLTED awake at the sound of stumbling footsteps echoing through her house. Her heart thudded in her chest as she shot up in bed, ears straining to pick up more. It couldn't be Aku, she made it clear she wouldn't be home tonight. The photoshoot for that local designer came with a stay in some fancy hotel, leaving Noodle alone. And now, fear snaked its way through her body.

She threw off the covers, moving on instinct, her mind too scrambled to register the fact that she was wearing nothing but panties. Creeping toward her bedroom door, she eased it open, the hinges groaning slightly under her trembling fingers.

The hallway stretched out, dark and unusually quiet. She stepped forward, her bare feet brushing against the cool floor. Each step was careful, her weight shifting slowly as if the house itself could betray her with a creak.

"If she come out here and whoop your ass, I don't want to hear shit," a low voice muttered from somewhere up ahead.

She could hear snickering and more rummaging.

"I ain't scared," another voice shot back, cocky but quiet enough to send her pulse sin overdrive from fear.

Noodle couldn't make out the voices since her brain hadn't

gotten the memo to wake up fully yet. Her breath caught, panic clawing at her throat as she edged closer to the living room. The voices grew louder, but her mind couldn't make sense of them. *Who the hell is in my house?*

Noodle screamed, her knees buckling as fear took over. She hit the floor hard, the cold tile jarring her as she scrambled backward, her palms slipping against the smooth surface in her haste to get away.

"Wait, wait!" one of the voices called out, but Noodle's body didn't listen. Her survival instincts kicked in, every muscle tense, every nerve screaming for her to run.

"Damn," Lunar stood beside Bu, eyeing her small grape sized breasts.

Bu pushed him. "Nigga, get the fuck on," he grunted, extending his hand to help Noodle to her feet. "The fuck is your shirt at?"

Noodle snapped her arms around her chest. "I don't sleep in shirts."

"Then why the hell you come out the room like that?"

"To see who was breaking in my house."

Bu stared at her, his head cocked to the side. "And that makes sense to you?"

Looking everywhere but at him, Noodle just stood there nibbling on her lip.

Kissing his teeth, he pushed her back down the hall. "Come on."

Noodle's bare feet padded down the hall, those crazy butterflies rattling her even more. The idea of smelling him in her room sent electricity to her thumping pussy. If he told her to spread her legs, she would do it in point two seconds flat. He watched her ass jiggle in her boy short panties. But there was something on her back that caught his attention. Noodle had a tattoo on her back. It was down the middle where it could be hidden very easily since she didn't wear backless tops while at KidVerse. A beach with the moon shining bright over it. He wanted to know more about it, but first he needed her to put some damn clothes on.

Before she made it down the hall, she turned to ask, "how y'all get in here anyway? Lunar!" she yelled. "How you get in my house?"

Bu yanked her. "Shirt! Now!"

Lunar and Pimp snickered.

"I been seen her naked, Bu!" Lunar hollered, darting out the entrance of the hall when Bu gave him a menacing look.

Noodle huffed, pretending to have an attitude when in reality she was turned the hell on. As they stepped into her room, Bu closed the door while looking around. It was what he thought her room would look like. Warm and cozy with her coconut scent filling the space. He could tell the windows were massive but his Noodle had blackout curtains up. His heart grew sad thinking about her living her life in the dark.

Noodle emerged from the closet with a thin shirt on. Her nipples poked out.

"You cold?" Bu asked, licking his lips at her perky nipples begging to be licked. He was also high out of his mind which translated to horny.

Glaring at him, Noodle flopped on her bed, grilling him. "When did you get here?" she folded her arms with her legs crossed.

Lazily, he sat on the edge of her bed. "Earlier. We was chilling until them niggas got us kicked out the hotel."

"And y'all thought it was a good idea to crash my house?"

"You don't want me here?"

"I don't know, since I haven't talked to you in a few days."

"Something wrong with your phone?" he asked, leaning back with a deep sigh. His back hit the mattress, almost sinking in from how plush it was.

Noodle didn't respond, knowing the phone worked two ways. She was new to liking someone and didn't want to be too thirsty with calling him all the time. They didn't talk every day and hadn't had another long night of conversation but Bu did check in with her. She understood he was trying to work and didn't want to bother him.

"Don't get quiet now, baby," Bu yawned. "I'm high, hungry, and tired." He wanted to add horny but didn't want to scare his baby.

"I can order food."

"You don't know how to cook?"

She shook her head. Having him in her bed, she wanted to touch him so bad... wanted to straddle his lap to put the fire out that blazed between her legs.

His hand ran across her thigh leaving a trail of goosebumps. "My baby scared of the studio and don't know how to cook... what I'm gon' do with you."

"Teach me." She hunched her shoulders. "I'm sure you can teach me a lot," she hummed the last line.

His head twisted to look at her, searching her eyes for the blaze he knew was in them. Swiping his thick tongue across his lips, Bu's heart skipped a few beats. "Oh yea? Teach you what?"

"Whatever you think I need to know...teach me how not to be scared."

"You ain't scared, Noodle. You just be in that little head of yours overthinking shit."

Needing to get her mind off his dick, she grabbed her phone, typing away. "What you want to eat?"

"You ain't paying for whatever it is I'm 'bout to order." Bu had closed his eyes again.

The rise and fall of his chest seemed to put her in a trance. "You're my guest, it's only right."

"I'm a man... so it's all wrong. I can pay for my own food, baby."

"I know but what if I want to do stuff for you? Is it always gonna be wrong?" Noodle asked. In her mind, doing things for a man was no different than a man doing something for a woman. If the respect was there, she didn't see an issue.

Bu pondered over her question. "Nah it ain't, but let me wine and dine you first, baby."

That put a cheeky smile on her face. "Okay."

———————

Bu and Noodle had a spread on the floor in her room like a picnic. She was in bliss just being near him. Bu had a magnet-like pull on her from the night he walked up on her at his welcome home party.

Bu, his long legs stretched out in front of him, eyed Noodle as he took a bite of his burger. "You gotta get some food in here," he teased, his voice low and playful.

Noodle, chewing thoughtfully, shot him a side-eye. "Since you're the unwanted guest, maybe *you* should get the groceries," she quipped, swiping a fry off his plate without a second thought as if she didn't have her own.

Bu raised an eyebrow, unfazed by her boldness. "Unwanted, huh?" He wiped a smear of ketchup from the corner of her mouth, the motion slow and deliberate. His finger lingered a second longer than necessary before he sucked it clean, his eyes never leaving hers. "Am I really unwanted though?"

Noodle froze, her bite halfway to her mouth. She forced herself to focus on the wall behind him, anything to escape the intensity in his gaze. There was something about the way his eyes locked in on hers— intense and dark, like they could see through every defense she had. Or maybe it was his voice, smooth as silk, with an edge of mischief she couldn't quite shake. Whatever it was, she felt it like a strong pull in her chest.

She cleared her throat and swallowed, trying not to let him get to her, but damn— how could she not? His presence was overwhelming, like being caught in the pull of a magnetic storm. If she looked at him too long… let him have too much of her attention, she'd drown in him. And maybe… just maybe, she *wanted* to, but not today… not just yet.

Plus, she'd drowned enough for one day.

She glanced over at him, a small smirk playing at the corner of her lips, but it didn't quite hide the heat rising in her cheeks. "Definitely wanted."

He laughed. "You be trying to play me, baby." Bu crumbled his trash, stuffing it back into the bag.

Stretching his muscular arms over his head, he yawned. "I'm tired as hell now," he said, patting his stomach. "You ready for bed?"

"That's what I was doing before y'all broke into my house."

"You ain't gon' let that go, huh?"

"Nope." She popped her lips, cleaning up her mess before taking it all to the kitchen.

While she did that, Bu stood up so he could go sleep on the couch.

"Where you going?" Noodle asked when she met him at her door.

He looked into her eyes. "'Bout to go sleep on the couch... I'm tired baby."

"Ummm," she bit her lip, her heart pounding out her chest. "You can sleep in here. Aku will kill you if you sleep on the couch."

Bu thought it over, knowing damn well he wanted to get in that bed with her. "You sure?"

"Yes. You have clothes?"

"Yea, Noodle, why?" He laughed lightly.

"You smell like cheap perfume and need to take a shower." Noodle had tried her hardest not to think about what hoe he had in his face because she knew how Lunar got down and if they got kicked out, it was due to a room full of hoes.

Bu went to grab his things out of Lunar's truck. He and Pimp were in Aku's room since they probably knew she would blow a fuse if they slept on the couch. As he walked outside he noticed how different the streets were compared to his neighborhood. While it was pretty quiet, he noticed a few people out late walking their dogs. It was too late at night for people in the Jig to feel comfortable doing that, even with the new houses and lush greenery.

When he walked back in her room, he closed the door behind him, noticing Noodle in the bed propped up with her phone.

"I'm getting in the shower. You cool?" he asked, with his duffle bag tossed over his shoulder.

"Mhmmm," she hummed, pretending to pay him no attention. Once the bathroom door closed and she heard the shower start, she clicked on Aku's name.

"Noodle, why are you up? Did Lunar and them come in there making all that damn noise?" Aku sounded like she was asleep herself. With it being well past two in the morning, she understood it.

"First you could've warned me, but Bu is in my shower," she whispered, listening to make sure he wasn't coming out the bathroom.

"Ookkaay," Aku dragged out.

"I want him to do something to me... what am I supposed to do to let him know I want him to touch me or fuck me?" Noodle cringed, listening to herself talk. How had she turned into a horny teen?

She could hear Aku shifting, probably sitting up in shock. "You want him to fuck you? Who is this on my phone and what have you done with my bestie?"

Noodle snickered. "I'm serious... maybe not go all the way but... you know."

"Just tell him," Aku said, like it was just that easy. "Bu is a man, boo... you gotta tell him what you want and how far to go. He ain't got time to read your mind. Just say, hey, I want you to lick my coochie."

"Aku!" Noodle blushed. "Is that what you do?"

"Girl no. I'm a hand in your pants type girl," Aku cackled like it wasn't too early in the morning for all that.

Noodle got quiet thinking she heard Bu. Once she heard the

shower still going she continued. "Then why you telling me to do that?"

"Because, you need to be an adult and take things into your own hands but also be yourself. You ain't as bold as me but deep down inside you ain't as innocent as you let them people tell you, you are either. If you want him to touch you down below, you gotta tell him and I promise Bu will rock your world. Now, get off my phone and get some dick or something." Aku hung up before Noodle could respond.

Kicking her legs, she fake yelled with no sound coming out. Thinking long and hard about what she was going to do, her aching core reminded her that she wanted to feel something and wanted it to be Bu.

Bu stepped out of the bathroom, steam curling around his shoulders emphasizing just how godly he was in her eyes. His bare chest glistened under the soft glow of the lights in the room. He looked like something created personally by God himself— broad shoulders, sculpted arms, and a confidence in his stride that made the air feel heavier.

Her eyes ventured to the deep V, perfectly pointed down to a dick she just knew had to be heavy. It was the only thing that explained the weight sitting between her legs.

"This cool?" he asked, his voice low as his hand swept down his body, motioning to his loose sweatpants slung low on his hips.

Noodle swallowed hard, her throat suddenly dry as her body betrayed her, heat pooling at her center. Her nerves were firing on all cylinders, her heart racing. She tried to speak, to form some kind of response, but all she could manage was a quick nod with her lips slightly parted.

Bu raised an eyebrow, his dark eyes narrowing just enough to suggest he caught her reaction. A flicker of amusement played at the corner of his mouth, but he didn't say a word. Instead, he moved to her bed, pulling the covers back before easing in beside her, the mattress dipping under his weight. "I gotta get me one of these."

The chill in the room didn't seem to faze him. If anything, the cool air contrasted with the heat radiating off him.

Noodle sat frozen for a moment, her thoughts racing, her skin hypersensitive to his closeness. Her breath hitched when the faintest hint of his soap, clean and fresh, reached her nose, making her nerves flare up all over again.

Bu rolled over to his side, his back to her praying his dick went down. Being wrapped up in her sheets, smelling that scent of hers he loved so much, he was walking on thin ice knowing he was about to go crashing into the water any minute.

"Bu?" Noodle's voice cracked, he could hear the yearning behind the lusty whine of her calling his name. It sounded so damn needy.

"What's up, baby?"

"I need you to do something... my body is on fire," she moaned, her body twisting in heat.

He stopped breathing. For thirty seconds he didn't inhale or exhale, too shocked to do so. "Noodle," he said squeezing his eyes shut, fighting with himself on what to do next. He couldn't tell her *no* but didn't want to say *yes* either. Bu was truly between a rock and a hard place. His dick was the rock with Noodle being the hard place.

Softly, her hand touched his back, gliding up and down, when her voice dipped a few octaves, Bu lost it all. "Bu."

Bu twisted his body towards her. As he stared into her eyes, he looked for even a flicker of doubt. There wasn't an ounce of doubt in her eyes. Noodle was digging her feet in the sand. She was not so subtly telling him she was ready. But, no matter how sure he knew she was, Bu couldn't wrap his mind around it being him she wanted to be ready with.

She leaned forward to kiss him gently. "Please," she begged. That one word made all the blood in his body rush to the head of his dick.

Noodle's chest shook with anticipation, her eyes already rolling into the back of her head. "Please," she crooned again.

Bu licked her neck before sucking on it with pressure, heightening her senses. His lips trailed down her body, leaving kisses as he yanked her shirt over her head. Those pebbled nipples begged to be licked.

First, he placed gentle kisses on both before sucking them with equal attention. Then, he made his way down her body. Noodle was on pins and needles— ready to feel his mouth on her lower lips.

Impatiently, Bu tugged at the band of her panties, ripping them in half.

"Bu!" Noodle fussed. "Those cost forty dollars."

"I'll buy you more, baby," he said, inhaling her bald pussy deeply.

Even with tawny skin, her mound was a shade or two darker. "Twenty-five years on this earth and I ain't never had fine dining," he growled.

Noodle snickered, her body shaking from the heat of his breath against her thighs.

Joke time was over, because her mouth snapped shut when his thick tongue swiped across her throbbing clit. Like she was possessed, her back lifted off the bed and she tried to close her legs.

"Un-uh, baby. You want me to put this fire out, I gotta use my mouth," Bu said between each flick. "Open your legs for me."

"I—I can't," she stuttered, writhing under him.

Bu wasn't trying to hear any of that. Pushing her thighs back, he lapped up all the juices that leaked from her. One taste of her and he was a fiend. His tongue motion went from quick swipes to slow circles around her bud as it grew and hardened. "Baby, you taste so fuckin' good," he groaned, the vibration of his voice making her stomach clench.

Noodle tried to break free. "Bu! Please..." she yelled. "Oh my God!"

"Yea baby, give me that shit," he encouraged. "Let me suck another one out of you so you can take your ass to bed. Can I put you to sleep, baby?"

Noodle was having an out of body experience and if women were claiming they never orgasmed with a man, she wanted to have a meeting with them to figure out what the hell they were talking about. Because if what Bu was making her feel with his mouth wasn't an orgasm, then she prayed she never got one. The way he had her body convulsing, anything stronger would for sure put her in an early grave.

Like he promised, Bu sucked another orgasm out of her before standing back to see his work.

His face was soaked. He licked his lips not wanting to waste a drop of it. It was too damn good.

Noodle lay sprawled out, her chest panting and her legs aching from him having them pushed back to her shoulders. "Wait," she called out when she saw him trekking to the bathroom. Her eyes went to his dick straining against his sweats.

Bu looked down at her. "I need to handle this, baby."

"Let me," she was whispering but Bu heard her loud and clear.

Shaking his head, he took a step forward to the bathroom.

"Just come lay down with me, then…then you can handle that," Noodle smirked, her eyes blinking slowly.

Bu knew she was full of shit, but he just couldn't tell her no. "Are you a virgin?" he asked, leaning on top of her, placing delicate kisses on her soft lips.

Noodle bobbed her head, still trying to catch her breath. "But I want to do this, Bu."

Bu's face twisted. "Nah baby, you save this shit for someone better."

"I've been saving it… for someone like you…" she said because that was the only explanation she could give herself as to why her desire for sex had heightened since she met him. "You the only one. Don't tell me no."

Rolling off her, Bu laid on his back staring up at the ceiling. "Baby, I ain't good enough for no shit like this."

Noodle climbed on top of him. She reached her hand in his sweatpants, grabbing for his stiff dick that fought against his boxer briefs. "You the best." She snaked her tongue into his mouth, inching slowly down his girth once she had him free.

Bu hissed, his toes curling. "I'm not though, baby."

"Shh," she shushed him, fighting to keep a straight face due to the way his long and meaty dick stretched her entrance. She was still well lubricated from her own release but the pressure that sat in her stomach was painful.

His hands gripped her ass, stopping her after his mushroomed head broke through the first barrier. "Jacory, you don't have to do this." He looked in her eyes, needing her to understand he liked her regardless even when his mind told him to not taint her innocence.

That magic power of hers sucked him into her web again. "Please," she begged with those lashes fluttering and her forehead wrinkling. Noodle was new to sex but she'd been on a dance team growing up so she knew how to move her body. Like the skilled dancer she was, she rolled her belly with the tip of his dick still inside of her. "Baby."

Bu chewed his lip, his stomach knotting up as he tried to stop his dick from going deeper inside her. "Hold up, baby...damn," he blabbered incoherently.

Tears rolled down her face as she accepted more of him.

Bu reached up to wipe them, his muscles tensing the more he felt his dick inside of her. He needed to take control or she was really going to hurt herself. Thrusting his hip upwards, he flipped her over, landing on top of her.

"Bu!" she yelled when all of him pushed inside of her.

"I'm sorry," he soothed. "Just—" he couldn't finish his sentence and had to just lay there. His dick pulsed profusely.

Noodle's tears rolled down her face. She was in so much

pain, still she didn't regret any of it. Being under him felt so right. Under him, she felt the sun's warmth, the night's chill, and the ocean's waves. Life stood still as he gazed into her wet eyes. Sniffling, Noodle wrapped her arms around him as best she could because Bu was no slim nigga. "Let me feel you... I want to feel you." Her hips pushed up, needing him to go further.

"Shit," his face twisted as he inched deeper into the depths of her tightness. "It's been almost five years since I been inside something, baby." His deep voice whispered in her ear. Bu was fighting not to explode too soon. It was hard because Noodle fit him like a glove and those eyes looking at him for guidance had him ready to tap the hell out.

Noodle could hear the strain in his voice, unsure if he was in pain or if it felt good. For her, it hurt like hell. Bu's dick stretched her with little effort. The only joy she could find was the fact that it was him inside of her.

He tapped her thigh. "You gotta open up a little for me, baby.... If I nut too soon just know it'll be the only time I get mine before you get yours."

Noodle nodded, spreading her legs more. Him talking to her couldn't have been normal. At least Aku hadn't prepared her for this part of sex. The sound of his voice drove her delirious.

Bu pulled back a little before driving back into her. His walls slapped her ass and he started to give her more movement. Swirling his hips, he hit every crook and crevice inside of her yummy pussy.

Sweat dripped down his forehead onto her face and she wanted to shower in all of him.

"From this day on, I belong to you, baby."

"Okay," Noodle wiped her tears that flowed more from his declaration. Fear filled her. Love was scary and she didn't know if she had it to give him. Instead of expressing that, she just let him take her anyway he wanted her.

Bu fucked her all over the bed. When he tried to put her in

the tub to soak, she wanted more of him. Her sore pussy swallowing him whole— her body loving it the more he made love to her.

11

"BABY," Bu shook Noodle's shoulder, his voice low but insistent. "Bae... come on, get up."

Noodle groaned, yanking the covers over her head like a kid. "Bu, I just went to sleep... what time is it? And why is it so damn bright in here?" Her voice was muffled, thick with irritation. Between him waking her up, the sound of Lunar and Pimp clanging around in the kitchen, and the sun blazing through her room like it had a vengeance, she was already overstimulated before her day had even started.

The bed dipped as Bu sat down beside her, his weight making the mattress shift beneath her. "Noodle, it's almost twelve. You need to get yo' ass up."

"Okay," she mumbled. "But why is the sun in here?" Her voice pitched higher, making him think of all the whimpering she did earlier this morning when he was balls deep inside of her.

He followed her gaze— or what would've been her gaze if her head wasn't buried under the white sheets to the floor-to-ceiling windows across the room. They opened out onto a small balcony he wouldn't have even known existed if he hadn't pulled back the heavy curtains earlier. Now sunlight was spilling into the room unapologetically, as if it had every right.

Bu chuckled, thinking about the thin, dollar-store curtains he had hanging in his own room. They didn't block out anything. Not sunlight, or noise, not even a little privacy. But Noodle? Her shit had the kind of luxurious touches that could make someone forget the world outside, and it seemed like she had.

Her breathing was slowing again, growing shallower as she started to drift back

off. Bu shook his head, tapping the top of her head lightly. "Yo', Noodle, I'm serious. Don't go back to sleep. We got shit to do."

She shifted under the covers, barely responding, and he sighed.

She was too young to be this tired all the time... too young to let life pass her by like this, and yet, it didn't seem to bother her. Either she didn't realize what she was letting slip away, or she just didn't care.

He sat there for a moment, watching her breathing steady out, her beautiful face half-hidden by the blanket. A young woman like her, so full of talent, beauty, and potential should've had the world on its knees. But instead, she seemed content to stay in bed, letting the days blur together.

Another deep sigh emitted from him as he got under the covers with her. The thin sheet allowed for the sun to shine through giving him the perfect view of her. That round nose and those chipmunk cheeks kept his attention.

"Does sex make you weird, Bu?" Noodle asked, her eyes still closed. She could feel him watching her.

His chest shook from his small chuckle. Yanking on her curls, he gently pulled her closer to him. Bu didn't recognize himself with the way Noodle made him want to kiss on her. His heart did that weird shit but he had gotten used to it. Didn't mean he was all in, he just wasn't out neither. When he sexed her into oblivion, he knew he'd never not want to have her in his life. In what capacity, he wasn't sure because Noodle's world was complicated and she hadn't figured out how to block out the noise. All of that made her flighty. Bu had too much going on to deal with a girl like Noodle no matter how much Bee plagued his mind with hopeful thoughts of finding someone to love.

Before he laid eyes on her, the thought never crossed his mind. All he wanted to do when he got out was build his empire and watch his little brother live the life he deserved. Now, he saw the whole galaxy in Noodle's eyes when all she could see was black skies.

"Bu?"

"Yea, baby?"

She wet her lips before she continued. "You're in my happy den." Her smiled pushed her cheeks up and her eyes tight.

His mouth twisted. "the fuck is a happy den?"

"What we're in... when I was younger I used to hide in the closet when my mama and daddy fought. Then when I moved into a house that seemed so perfect, whenever I got sad, I'd just tuck my whole body under the sheets and started calling it my happy den."

Bu didn't say anything as she stared off into oblivion since he was the only other thing in her happy den besides herself.

"It's crazy how many times I made Aku and Lunar get in it with me."

"Why?" Bu asked, craving a deeper glimpse into what made Noodle tick.

For a split second, he saw the little girl she was trying so hard to hide. Forcing a smile on her face, Noodle confessed, "A happy house scared me."

Bu needed more. His arms circled around her bare back.

"Do you believe in love at first sight?" Bu's voice was low and rough, as his finger traced lazy hearts over the ink sprawled across her back. That tattoo always got him...left him staring like it held secrets he didn't know how to unlock.

Noodle shivered under his touch, her skin pebbling with chill bumps. She tilted her head to the side, her cheek pressing into the pillow. Did she believe in love? Her heart pounded against her ribs, uncertain. "Maybe... then again, probably not." She shrugged, her voice soft but heavy.

She paused, her thoughts flickering through her mind. "The woman who raised me as her own, believed in love... and it left her with black eyes and broken bones. My sister believes in love too." Her voice cracked, but she kept going, the words spilling out in a steady flow. "She's got a life most people only dream about because of it. Love built her a world of abundance."

Bu listened intently, seeing the façade of her foundation cracking.

Her throat tightened, the weight of it all settling on her chest. "I guess I should be happy... my chances are fifty-fifty, right?" She gave a bitter laugh, one that didn't quite reach her eyes. "So, I don't know. I'm just stuck somewhere in the middle."

Bu didn't answer right away, and the quiet between them felt thick, like it was pressing on them. His finger stopped moving, resting on her bare skin like he could ground her there. "Middle's not a bad place to start," he said finally, his voice softer now, like he knew she needed the gentleness. "Least it means you still got room to figure shit out."

Noodle didn't respond, but the corners of her lips quirked up, just slightly. For now, his touch and the quiet weight of his presence were enough.

But was it enough for him? Did Bu secretly want more, but was just afraid of putting himself out there with her? His heart told him he knew the answer but his brain told him to not get his hopes up, tread lightly.

————

A few hours later, Noodle and Bu showered, dressed and were on their way out the door. With Bu, she didn't really have to think so she didn't pay attention to anything until the glass doors slid open. Noodle cupped her mouth as she followed Bu outside. Her eyes grew big and her face flushed red. "Where did you get this from?" She grilled Bu playfully as he propped himself up against the car.

While she was asleep, Bu called in his first favor. There was no way, she was losing her virginity and not getting tricked out big time. Bobby had the red 1970 Oldsmobile convertible delivered with the backseat full of red roses. There were so many flowers, their petals covered the full interior. It cost him a grip too but he'd say it was money well spent.

"I know people, baby." He winked. "Com'ere." His arms expanded, ready to embrace her. Noodle had her phone out, capturing him in his dark denim jeans, a white shirt, red hat, and gold chains around his neck. Designer sneakers pulled his d-boy look together and that red flag hung from his back pocket as usual.

When she fell into him, he grabbed her phone, panning it over to them while he kissed all over her face. Noodle's cheeks hurt from smiling so hard. She couldn't wait to send the video to Aku and brag on her amazing first experience and how her man surprised her with a backseat full of flowers.

But he wasn't her man, she thought. Her smile fell.

"Get out your head, baby," Bu kissed the side of her head again.

Pushing her shoulders back, she nodded. "Where we going?"

A slow lazy smile tugged at his lips. "Just ride with me." He smiled, irresistibly and how could she say no to that?

Bu thought Noodle had him wrapped around her finger, not knowing her thoughts of him echoed his thoughts of her. If he was driving, she wanted to ride. Anything that he was involved in, she wanted to be involved in too. Their infatuation with one another wasn't one sided at all. It was reciprocated and duplicated though neither of them had a clue it was happening. The universe was shifting but they were so caught up in the right now, they couldn't feel the earth moving up under their feet.

Looking over to Noodle while she adjusted her seat, he typed in an address on his phone's gps since he had no idea where he was going or how to get there.

"I can't believe you got me all these flowers," Noodle said in awe, turning to glance at the colorful display of his appreciation in the backseat.

Bu revved the engine, drawing the attention of the neighborhood people walking by. "This is just the beginning baby," he laughed, taking off into traffic.

The wind from the car's acceleration left a trail of flowers behind them like they'd just gotten married. Noodle, feeling wild and free, tossed her arms in the air. The wind whipped through her fingers and goosebumps coated her skin.

As they drove through Madison Heights, people stared, took pictures, and women smiled wishing a man had gone all out for them like Bu had for Noodle. She felt so special in the passenger seat sitting next to her Bu. She couldn't keep up with the pitter patter of her heart and the wind did nothing to cool her warming skin. If this was even close to the feeling Aku longed for, then now Noodle understood it.

Glancing over at him, her teeth sunk into her lip at how fine he looked with one hand on the steering wheel and the other propped sexily on the door. His body slightly leaned toward the driver side door.

If he was a tall glass of anything, she wanted to drink it all down in one gulp.

When they pulled up to a red light, Noodle saw a group of teenaged girls snickering and giggling at the red car with the fine man and flowers floating from the back seat. Grabbing four roses, she reached out and handed one to each of the girls.

"Thank you," they gushed in unison, squealing as they inhaled the earthy scent of the roses.

Bu looked at her with admiration in his eyes. This was the version of her the world needed to see.

On their way to the shopping district, Noodle leaned out

the car at every stop sign and red light, handing out flowers with a smile so bright it seemed to soften the whole street— warm the world with the genuineness of her actions. What she couldn't pass out, she threw in the air and let float to the ground, where people eagerly snatched them up like little treasures. Even if they never made it to their destination, this thirty-minute ride was already cemented as one of the best moments of her life.

When Bu finally parallel parked on the bustling main street, he cut the engine and turned to her with a playful smirk. "You ready to break a nigga's pockets or what?"

She grinned, twisting in her seat to face him, her almond eyes sparkling. "Ummm…" she hesitated not knowing how to accept things from Bu. He was just released from prison and trying to start his own business. She knew he had to be strapped for cash while she had a nice amount in her account. "Bu, you know you don't have to buy me stuff, right?"

"You know you trippin' right now, right?" He mimicked her light and airy voice with irritation. "I might not be the richest but, baby trust and believe I ain't never the type of nigga to trick on a girl. You ain't just a girl though… you make me wanna give you the world— lay that muthafucka at your feet. Let me spoil you with every dime I have if that's what the fuck I want to do."

He wasn't asking either. Bu got out the car heading around to her side. His dark eyes seemed to be piercing her skin. To cool her body, she licked her lips and accepted his hand once he opened her door.

"What's up, Noodle," Fink greeted with her, with Ben coming up behind him. They slapped hands with Bu while she looked on with a confused expression. "You know you ain't going nowhere without us."

She snapped her neck towards Bu, jumping into his arms. "You are so special," she hummed in his ear, squeezing him tightly.

He hugged her back. "That's all you, baby."

. . .

Instead of putting her back on her feet, Bu carried her down the walkway, all eyes on them. Ben and Fink stayed close enough to block a threat but far enough to give them personal space.

The November air in Madison Heights carried a crispness that made everything feel more alive. The flowers had shifted to burnt oranges and deep yellows, a soft breeze tugging at their petals. The salty scent of the nearby ocean mingled with the coolness of fall. The shopping district stretched out before them like a postcard - palm trees swaying between buildings, pops of greenery tucked along the sidewalks. People strolled leisurely, laughing and chatting with arms full of shopping bags, while cars moved at a slow, respectful pace.

She looked at him, her gaze traveling over his gold-framed glasses that added a lowkey vibe to his larger-than-life presence. He winked at her, the corner of his mouth tilting up into that signature, slow-burn smile that made her stomach flip.

"You're trouble," she said softly, her lips curving into a grin she couldn't hold back.

"You ain't seen nothing yet," he shot back, leading her into the first store.

A sales associate greeted them as soon as they crossed the threshold. "Welcome to Chanel. Are you looking for anything special?"

Noodle looked at Bu, searching his eyes. What the hell were they doing here? She didn't need a bag. On most days she didn't even carry a purse 'cause she was always with someone that could hold her valuables, like her I.D. and a credit card. That and most places accepted phone taps as a form of payment.

Bu sat on the expensive looking loveseat, speaking to the saleswoman "Give her a few options. She doesn't wear a lot of bright colors... she's more into muted tones or pastels," he said, giving her outfit choice a once over.

Noodle looked good in her two-piece skirt set. It hugged her curves perfectly. Her taut stomach peeked out with each small movement and her nipples pressed against the fabric. Since she hadn't been working or doing any appearances, she wore her hair in its natural state of ringlets that swept across her shoulders and back. Wispy lashes framed her almond eyes, and her skin looked moisturized. On her feet were a pair of strappy heels he thought about being draped over his shoulders while he fucked her in them.

When he licked his lips, her body shuddered. "Com'ere, baby." Bu patted his thigh.

The saleswoman smiled, recognizing Jay Jay before going to the back to find the perfect bag for the man that wanted to trick on the child star. She was well aware who Jacory was and that made her pockets tingle from the potential of a great commission.

Huffing, Noodle sat on his lap, examining his facial features. "You're beautiful." She swiped her hand across his bushy brows.

"That shit don't sound flattering, baby," he muttered.

"It's the truth," she snickered. "And these..." She squeezed his arms. "Phew, I know the girls been going crazy over these."

"Nah...I was fat before I got locked up."

"That's why they call you Big Bu?"

Bu burst into laughter. "Who the fuck you been talking too?"

"Lunar and Pimp." She shrugged, still eyeing him to etch his beautiful features in her brain. She never wanted to forget the first man that made her feel something.

He hummed. "What else they told you?"

"Your name is Bethune... I can't figure out how your mama looked at you and gave you that name," Noodle cackled. "You don't look like a Bethune."

His mind went to Bee. He missed his mama bad. There wasn't a day or night when he didn't think about her. He smiled, in a daze, thinking about his mama saying, 'y'all came out my coochie - I can name you what I want'.

"Pimp over there tellin' my business, he tell you his hoe ass name is Princeton?" Bu laughed when Noodle giggled, bending over to clutch her stomach.

"It's still better than Bethune," she hollered. "But I can work with Bethune," she teased, her finger back on his face and in his brows. "I would kill for pretty, thick eyebrows like this."

"Your shit perfect though, baby."

"So, I pulled a few pieces…" The saleswoman came back with an arm with different bags dangling from it.

"Get whatever you want, baby." Bu nodded for her to try them all on.

———

"I love the beach." That syrupy, sweet voice pulled Bu's eyes to her. "I want to be a beach," she added, lost somewhere in the ocean as she watched the moon reflect off the calm waves.

"The tattoo?" Bu inquired, hoping she'd explain that one piece of *fuck you* she gave to KidVerse. He could spot a rebellious act from a mile away. He'd scolded Pimp many times for doing shit like that.

He wanted to show the hood, niggas were gay, so he kissed a boy, not caring about his friends seeing them. That one act of being who he was, landed Bu in prison for four years. Not directly, but Bu knew karma came to collect in many different ways.

Her loose tresses swung when she nodded her head. "It's an ode to my sister and Qamar."

"You love that nigga, huh?" Bu smirked, playfully because there was a time he wanted to be just like Qamar. So much so, he didn't trip when Bee signed him up for the little league soccer team.

They were laid out on a blanket he'd scooped from a vendor when they made their way to the sand. Madison Heights was calm but raging with people from all walks of life. He could tell why some worked in the city but rested their heads here. Being able to live a double life was high on the list of the rich and famous—or those that wanted to be famous and rich.

"I do... I love him because he loves my sister."

"But he loves you too, right?"

She snickered, taking a sip from her cup. "Mhmmm."

Silence wrapped around them as they sipped on some wine the beach vendor they bought it from said would sneak up on them and give them the feels. It was infused with marijuana and black owned or some shit. So far, Bu still preferred to smoke it over drinking it.

Their day had been filled with so much fun. He let Noodle tear down the shopping district, even grabbing a few things for himself.

Fink and Ben kept their distance the whole time, only needing to intervene when kids rushed Jay Jay for autographs and pictures.

Now, they were tucked on the beach under the stars like he knew where her heart lay. Noodle's love for the beach and the stars went beyond the tattoo on her back. It was her happy place...he knew it because he felt it anytime she talked about her life on Lynn Beach or when the air blew the ocean's scent past her nose. It was the reason she loved coconutty scents.

"I love the sound of the ocean... feels like I was born in it. Maybe I was, "cause on the surface it looks calm and welcoming but below it's dangerous, chaotic, deadly," she gulped. "You think you can splash in it, swim in it... like on those cutesy movies but as soon as you get in, you realize your feet don't touch the bottom. Then you start to panic just before you realize you're drowning, but the people on the surface think you're having a good time playing with the cute fish. When all along, you're just drowning, struggling to see your feet."

Bu's strong hand gripped the back of her neck, yanking her to him. "Hey," he spoke softly while staring into her eyes. "That's why you gotta yell for help. Why you out there just splashing around, hoping they see you drowning when all you gotta do is yell *help*?"

Noodle smashed her lips into his, pushing her tongue into his mouth because she needed to feel him... to know he was real. "How are you so beautiful? That's what your mama should've named you instead of Bethune."

They laughed with their lips still connected, their teeth lightly grazing each other because pulling away to laugh felt like too much distance.

His eyes grew serious. "If you ever need me, just ask for help, baby."

"I will," she lied, knowing she'd never ask for help. Something inside of her wanted to figure it all out by herself.

"Real shit, Jacory... I'm here even when you think I ain't."

She straddled his lap, her eyes screaming fuck me as she humped on him.

Bu gripped her face again. "You gotta get on some birth control, baby."

12

It was another late night. Bu had let her sleep in, knowing he was going to drag her into the studio against her will. Noodle hated the studio. It didn't feel real to her, and she wanted to be anywhere but there.

Lunar and Pimp had tagged along which meant there were also some extra bodies of girls she could've done without. One in particular had been laughing at any and everything Bu said, and he wasn't that damn funny.

Jealousy coated her skin because a whole week of having Bu all to herself had her seeing the world differently. Different in the way of, reacting to hoes trying to get next to him. Before she would've smiled and sat quietly. Now, she was ready to show his hoe-mirer how Lynn Beach gave it up.

"You keep rolling your eyes they gon' get stuck like that," Pimp bumped her shoulder with a laugh as he inhaled the blunt, he was smoking.

There was a heavy rotation of weed and bottles floating around, making the already dark room darker. It didn't matter though because she could see that hoe pushing up on her Bu.

Noodle kissed her teeth, rolling her eyes again. "I don't even want to be here."

"Why?" he asked, his voice muffled from the plume of smoke he exhaled.

She scanned the room. A beat played on the surround sound speakers, the bass knocking heavily. The engineer bobbed his head as he flicked his wrist across the sound board. Lunar was off in a corner pushing up on some girl that looked drunk in love, while Bu leaned back listening to whatever his hoe-mirer was yapping about.

"You ever felt like you the best at something, but when people dimmed your light enough, you start to second guess it?" she blinked.

Pimp let her question sink in, and surmised he was probably too high to answer. The desperation in her eyes had his brain scrambling to find an answer for her. He liked Noodle. They'd spent a good amount of time around each other. She knew he was gay and never mentioned it or pretended he was one of her little friends. Inhaling deeply, he allowed the smoke to fill his mind, hoping it spurred something prolific. "On some real shit, I can't relate, Noodle. My big brother never let a nigga play on my mind enough to have me out here confused. He protected me when I didn't even know I needed protecting. He ain't never judge me or made me feel less than a man. So, I ain't never gave nobody free range of my mind or soul...might've made some questionable mistakes... ones I got Bu paying for to this day, but I know who I am. I know how dope I am."

Noodle let his words sink in as her heart skipped beats watching Bu watch her. She understood the way Pimp described him because in her heart she knew he was trying to do the same with her. It felt like pity more than anything, but she noticed how he tried to slowly pull her out that ocean she kept taking her crazy ass into.

Pimp's coughing pulled her attention back to him. "You got folks that'll do the same for you, but little Noodle is a glutton for punishment." One side of his lip curled.

Lunar stood in front of her with a cheeky grin on his face. "You ready?" he asked, his eyes darting from her to the booth.

Noodle finally noticed the song from the other night that she bombed on. Now, he wanted her to do the same in a room full of people? "No, Lunar!"

"Jacory, come on," he begged, his hands in the praying position. "You got this shit. You the only one I want on this song." Lunar bared his soul to her, begging she do him this solid and get on the song. He knew he was going to be fire and they'd own all the rights to it since he was an independent artist and Noodle hadn't signed to a label yet.

Pimp egged her on, hyping her up and telling her how she was made for this. Noodle continued to chew on her lip, contemplating her next move. She held her hand out. "Pass me that."

"The weed?" Pimp asked, confused. He didn't know she smoked.

Noodle looked him upside the head. "Yes, boy."

Lunar hollered. It was funny when he heard Noodle cuss in public. Growing up all they did was cuss each other out when the adults weren't in the room. Noodle sometimes got away with it in front of them because she was more of a little sister to the adults than a child.

"Noodle," Bu called her name from across the small room. "Don't play with me... com'ere man."

"You in trouble," Pimp snickered when he saw his brother give her that look.

The girl beside Bu twisted her face.

Noodle rolled her eyes, about to put the blunt to her lips. Just as it touched her pink lips, Bu took quick, long strides towards her, snatching it from her hands. "Here," he bent down, twisting the blunt to his lips where he inhaled, before pressing his lips to hers. She was being defiant. He smirked, gripping her chipmunk cheeks and making her lips pucker while he exhaled the smoke into her mouth before sticking his tongue in to swish around.

Her fingers clung to his shirt and her eyes fluttered, a redness coating them after a few seconds.

"Shit," she heard a female say in a lusty tone.

Bu's dark eyes fussed at her without him having to say anything. He gave her a few more guns like that one, making sure to leave a kiss after each one.

"You ready now?" Lunar cut into their intimate moment, a reminder that they weren't alone.

That was what her time with Bu felt like. Like he pulled her from the raging waters. She looked around the room, sucking in a deep breath. Her head bobbed. "I guess," she muttered, walking towards the booth.

Lunar rubbed his hands together, following behind her to get her set up.

Bu watched their every move, taking her seat after she got up. His hoe-mirer flopped back, hating that she lost his attention. Noodle smirked, feeling like she was victorious without having to try too hard.

Lunar's vocals blasted, with the hum of the R&B style beat. Everyone's head bobbed instinctively. Noodle must've listened to his verse ten times before she started to even hum a harmony.

Lunar had come out the booth to give her some space. Leaning against the wall he held his breath hoping she could push through. This album had to be his best yet. It was on his heart to make something so timeless, he'd never go broke off it.

Somedays he felt his back was against the wall. The world had a perception of him, and he felt he had something to prove. Noodle did too, so the way he saw it, it was only right they make it to the top together. It was a family thing, and he wanted to make both his daddies proud. So, he needed her voice to work.

"She's stuck in her head," Bu observed.

Noodle spent thirty minutes trying to find the right words, hit the right note. Her voice sounded good because it was just that effortless for her, yet the words and the cadence didn't come off smooth.

Hoe-mirer, cackled one time too many. Bu, jumped up, his dark eyes raging. "Aye, everybody get the fuck out!"

It was like a record scratched. Everyone's head turned towards him.

"Did I muthafuckin' stutter? Get the fuck out... even you, nigga," he barked at the engineer.

Noodle watched everyone file out, wondering what was going on. She could see his mouth moving but couldn't make out what he was saying. She felt naked and foolish that she was having such a hard time finding her groove. It was in her but she just couldn't push the shit out.

Bu cocked his head at Pimp and Lunar. "Y'all niggas gotta go too."

"Man, what?" Lunar laughed but grabbed his bottle to leave.

Pimp gave Noodle one last glance, winking, making her blush. Pimp was so handsome to her.

Slowly, Bu turned towards her, just staring at her through the glass. Removing his hat, he flipped it to the back. His slow gait towards her was sexy with just the right balance of hood in it. Everything he did seemed to turn her on, it was as natural as breathing.

"Hey," she whispered when he pulled the door open to get to her.

"Why you always in your head, baby?" Bu asked, closing the door behind him.

They were in a top of the line studio and you could start and stop tracks from inside the booth too so they didn't really need anyone else there

Noodle shrank. "I'm trying."

"I know, baby... here let me help you." Bu stood behind her, massaging her shoulders to loosen her up. He witnessed her true star power at The Music Factory, but he didn't recognize the girl standing before him. This girl had walked her crazy ass back into the water once he'd already thrown her a lifesaver.

His large hands ran up and down her bare arms. "You better

than every bitch out right now. You can do this song with your eyes closed. Just let it flow, baby."

"Play it again," she huffed, praying she could get something right. Her fingers grazed the headphones like she was setting a dangerous temptation in motion.

Bu's eyes narrowed, trying to decipher her unreadable expression. He was good at reading people, but Noodle was an enigma sometimes. When she began layering delicate runs over the intro of the track, her voice almost humming in perfect sync with the music, he couldn't help but be pulled in closer. His instinct flared, and without a second thought, he slid closer to her, his presence warm and deliberate.

As they listened to the playback, the air thickened with the tension between them. The music was almost too seductive, too intimate to be merely background noise. Bu's gaze dropped to the curve of her neck, his lips pressing into a half-smile as he leaned in. He hovered just behind her, tall enough to make her feel his presence without completely overshadowing her.

Lunar's verse was first.

'Your love's the kind I wanna feel when I sleep.
    Astronauts in orbit, we got that connection,
    Floatin' through the night, feelin' every reflection.
    Touchin' down, the space between us gets tight,
    You and me, baby, we gon' burn up all night'

Bu bobbed his head to Lunar's verse, feeling the little vibe it gave mixed with that coconut scent Noodle carried around her— hoping to take the beach everywhere with her.

Then, without warning, he exhaled a soft breath right against the shell of her ear, his tongue tracing a quick, teasing swipe across his lips. The sudden contact sent a shiver down her spine, the sensation sharp and electric. The unexpected jolt of heat made her body convulse.

She froze, her breath hitching. "What are you—?" The words were almost lost in the music.

But Bu didn't linger there. No, he was a tease and challenged her at every turn to take what she wanted, both figuratively and literally. Her body shook when his smooth baritone started spitting sexy shit in her ear, not giving a fuck about the mic picking up his voice. "Open your legs, baby."

Noodle listened, doing whatever he said. Her body on fire. She leaned into the microphone to freestyle a hook that melted her insides. Suddenly his finger, found that moisture seated in her panties. Her pussy creamed more as she sung the words that came to mind with him stringing her like an instrument.

"Chasin' galaxies, feelin' your gravity,
   Every touch, every kiss - its sweet melody.
   Lost in the stars, we're just you and me,
   Chasin' galaxies, you're my ecstasy.
   (Oh, oh, oh) Chasin' galaxies, feelin' so free.
   In your arms, that's where I wanna be.
   Lost in your love, in your fantasy,
   Chasin' galaxies, you're my ecstasy."

Bu yanked her by the shoulder, spinning her to face him, his eyes pleading with her not to stop him. The song created a stir in his belly that caused his dick to throb. He was a man who had bedded plenty women back in the day, but none of them accelerated his heart or created a deep lust that almost choked him like Noodle did, not even the ones he could've seen taking home to Bee.

Noodle blinked a few times before her breath was taken away by Bu's kiss.

He was a really good kisser— perfect if you asked Noodle, and her declaration wasn't because he was her first. No, she'd kissed boys before, but no one made her feel what his lips and tongue did. None of them took her to the places he did with just one look.

Without her permission, a moan slipped between their kiss as she tangled her hands into his shirt.

Bu wasn't letting up. His hand dipped deeper into the fabric of her pants and then her panties, in search of something he'd been desperate to feel for a while now. One finger turned into two. The natural heat from her body greeted him just before his fingers splashed into her the wetness of her bare pussy.

"Ugh," Noodle moaned, making sure to spread her legs more, so he could really get inside. "Shiit." Bu sank his teeth into her shoulder. She lifted one leg slightly, balancing on her tippy toes to encourage him more.

"Good girl," he praised, entering another finger into her greedy pussy.

Noodle's folds were tight, warm, wet, and like a fuckin' vacuum. "Oh, Bu," she panted her eyes rolling into the back of her head.

"Show me how this greedy ass pussy is gonna suck this big ass dick up."

Noodle's head fell back. Her teeth dug into those plump lips Bu seemed to love to kiss. But like the good girl he'd just proclaimed her to be, she popped her pussy on his now three fingers slowly.

"Just like that," his voice hissed and his hand lifted to her back for stability. "Tell me how good you feel."

"So good."

"Un uh. I need more, than that, baby." His teeth raked across her ear. "This just an appetizer… if you can't praise the cook off this, I might have to stop feeding you."

His words…his tone. All of it had Noodle floating… chasing something. "It feels like I'm chasing galaxies," she blurted out, gaining her a wide smile and beautiful rhythmic tapping of her insides.

Bu couldn't take the anticipation anymore. He pulled her

leggings all the way down, freeing his dick afterwards. His hand ran down her spine gently making her bend over.

"What if somebody comes in here?" Noodle looked at him with fear in her eyes, but she was still hoping he filled her up.

"They ain't coming in here, baby. Just let me get one out you… It'll be fast." He slapped his dick on her pussy lips. "Spread it open for me."

Noodle did as she was told, gaining her praise. "That's it, baby."

Her body convulsed when Bu bottomed out. "Ugh," she panted, one hand resting on the bottom of her stomach. That was where he was. In her damn stomach.

"This pussy so good, baby! Fuck!" Bu's head fell back. "Can I get it like I want it?"

Biting on her lip, she nodded.

"I can't hear you, baby. Your voice too pretty for me not to hear it."

"Yes!"

"I can?" he asked again to make sure, knowing she was still new to it all.

"Bu, yes! Baby, you can—" Noodle moaned. "You can get it like you want it." She was so delirious that her thoughts were just that, thoughts and somehow getting them out became a choppy mess.

A low animalistic growl filled the booth, followed by her yelping when he pulled his dick out. She glared at him, but Bu was on a mission. He hiked her up, wrapping her legs around his chiseled waist. When his dick was lined up perfectly, Bu fucked Noodle all over that booth. In his arms, she just bounced like she was on a pogo stick.

"Baby!" she yelled, tucking her face in the crook of his neck. "Baby, I—"

"Shhh," he shushed her. "You did so good today. I gotta reward you, baby."

Bu's kisses danced across her face, each one a whisper of

affection that warmed her flesh. His mouth lingered on her forehead, her chipmunk cheeks, and the tip of her nose, making sure she knew that although he was beating her pussy out the frame, he cared for her. The gentleness of his kisses were a contrast to his wild and deep strokes that shook her core.

Bu wanted her to understand his feelings through his actions because words never seemed to be enough for a woman as special as Noodle.

Through it all, he also made sure to thank her for giving him her body. He praised her for being a good girl and taking all the dick he had to give her. Noodle could only moan and hold on for dear life because he drained her of every ounce of liquid her aching pussy could produce.

13

"You're glowing," Aku assessed as they sat next to each other in the nail salon.

It had been weeks since they'd been able to spend time together and that was a hard pill for both of them to swallow. Yes, Aku was a socialite and always on the go but she always made time for Noodle whether it was a chill movie night or going to a lounge to let their hair down. They had never gone so long without spending quality time together.

Today, they were making up for lost time at Tranquil spa. After they'd stumbled into the place, lured by the lavender scented air, the two of them quickly dubbed it a fave.

Noodle blushed. "You doing too much," she snickered.

"Oh no baby, you been out here doing too much… all booed up, pun intended." Aku wagged her tongue, teasing Noodle more. She was happy for her girl. The way Noodle was eager to get out the house today to bask in the sun and be around people, was a testament to how much had changed over a short period of time.

Aku glanced over at Noodle's nails, her brows lifting in excitement. "You getting long red nails? Oh let me find out my bestie boo is a gangbanger now."

Noodle cackled. "Aku, please... I'm just trying something new."

"And it just gotta be red, huh?"

It was no secret that Noodle typically got short neutral colored nails and only wore muted tones. Now, red seemed to have snaked its way into her color palette and Aku knew why.

"You look happy, though."

"I feel happy," Noodle smiled, her stomach fluttering from thoughts of Bu.

Aku's face lit up too. "And you're coming to the club and I didn't even have to bribe you with a movie night after."

Noodle rolled her eyes. "I gotta mingle and show my face more. You know I'm thinking about signing to Lunar's label since ain't nobody else trying to take any meetings with me. I wonder why..." she mumbled the last line, knowing KidVerse was trying to blackball her. They were so salty about her cutting ties with them and seemed to have started a smear campaign in the background.

In public, they had yet to comment on whether Noodle was dropped or if she quit and that left the internet speculating every day on what had occurred. Then images of her and Bu had the world in a frenzy, trying to figure out who the fine thug in glasses was.

Aku pulled her hand from the LED lamp, turning her body towards Noodle. "Girl, fuck them. They know what it is and I find it funny how you're going to sign to Lunar's label."

"What you mean?" Noodle asked, confused. "He's asked me before," she shrugged like it was no big deal. "You know he has this idea of us doing what the family did and building it up as a family thing."

Aku twisted her lips. "And Bu is fifty percent owner."

"What?"

"You didn't know?" Aku asked. "Oh, I forgot you had years of not being in the mix...but girl yes." She looked around, leaning in closer so her words were only heard by Noodle.

"When he got locked up, they say he had some crazy amount of money that he gave to Pimp to hold. Well, Pimp cleaned the money by funneling it through Lunar's label. Like Lunar comes from money so no one thought too much about it. Except, I hear my daddy gave Pimp the idea. Anyway, after four years, he has at least a milli in his account."

Noodle let everything Aku just dropped in her lap sink in. So many moments she'd shared with him since she'd met him replayed in her mind. All along she thought he was finding his way when everything Bu showed her, showed he was very much well off. He blew a bag on her at The Shopping District, purchased his truck brand new with cash. Resting her head on her hand, her face twisted, her eyes shut as she thought over every moment she'd shared with Bu. He was so humble and allowed who he was to be at the forefront of how he showed up for her. So, even if she felt slighted by not knowing, the parts of him that her heart knew, knew Bu was just a black man capable of kingly things.

"Yea," Aku nodded, chuckling to herself. "You were just enjoying yourself not thinking about what he did or didn't have. That's why you deserve all the things. Your heart is good and you see people past the amount in their bank account."

Noodle's heart galloped in her chest listening to Aku express why she was a good person. It was one of the little things she missed hearing from her people. Aku made sure to give it to her in abundance. As children, they learned to lean on one another a lot until Noodle found herself in Cali most of the time. It never drove a wedge between them though. French made sure to have his girls together at least one weekend out of the month. Had it not been for him, their bond might've wavered a long time ago.

"I wonder why that nigga didn't say anything," Noodle poked out her bottom lip, thinking about all the *not so subtle* signs.

Aku laid her hand on Noodle's lap. "Did you ask him?"

"How would I know to ask, 'hey do you own Lunar's label?'"

"Girl you know what I mean." Aku stood from her seat with her card out to pay. "Did you ask him about his money situation?"

"No, 'cause I didn't want to make it seem like it mattered."

"If it didn't matter then... it shouldn't matter now." Aku slid her card across the counter with a flick of her wrist, settling the tab for both of them for their pedicures, and then the acrylic nails with hand massages wrapped up their three-hour salon visit.

Noodle nodded, letting the conversation go for now.

They stepped out onto the sidewalk, with Fink and Ben trailing behind. Without Bu around, Noodle noticed they didn't give her as much space. Instead, they stayed at her twelve, subtly keeping an eye out for both her and Aku.

Arms linked, the two walked without a care in the world. The weight of everything else disappeared for the moment, and if Noodle could live in that peace forever, she would. She'd always been a girl's girl. It started when she realized how much Siasia needed someone to lean on. Her love for Black women had only grown from there.

"You still on the prowl for your *forever thing*?" Noodle asked, breaking the silence.

Aku sighed dramatically. "I don't know... I think I'm just gonna let it find me."

"Let it find you?" Noodle smirked, her head jutting backwards. "Like it's out here on these streets waiting for you? Not my Aku being an optimist..."

Aku bumped her lightly with her shoulder. "What, you don't think I deserve an urban romance moment? Maybe I'll drop my phone in the middle of traffic, and some fine ass man will rescue it. Or maybe I'll meet my soulmate after he kidnaps me."

"Kidnap?" Noodle tossed her a side eye, raising an eyebrow.

Aku shrugged. "Hoe, it's possible... look at me."

Their laughter spilled out, drawing glances from others. As

they rounded the corner, Noodle caught a glimpse of a street vendor selling bracelets.

"Let's stop," she said, pulling Aku toward the stand. "I wanna get something."

"For you or Bu?" Aku teased.

Noodle waved her off. "For me... sometimes a girl just needs a little sparkle, you know?"

Aku grinned. "Now you're speaking my language."

As Noodle picked through the display, Aku leaned against the counter, squinting at a group of people crossing the street. One of them looked vaguely familiar, but she shook it off. She turned back to Noodle, who was holding up two bracelets - one gold, one silver.

"Which one?" Noodle asked.

"Get both. You're worth it."

Just as Noodle decided to add a matching one for Bu, that familiar face Aku had spotted, eased over.

"Jay Jay," his light voice called out.

Noodle's face bunched up before turning to see what adult her stage name was coming from. When someone called her KidVerse name, they were usually kids, but even with his voice not being deep, she could tell he wasn't a child.

"I knew your face looked familiar," Aku nodded, examining him and how much he'd grown up.

Luther shoved his hands deep into his cargo pockets, shoulders hunching slightly. "Yeah... I look a little different, but it's me."

Noodle squinted, her head tilting as if angling her gaze might help her place him. Then it clicked. "Oh, hey!" she said, her face lighting up as recognition hit her.

He wasn't a kid anymore. The last time she'd seen him, Luther was all elbows and knees, with a voice that cracked halfway through every sentence. He'd been a season regular on her show. The shy boy with the big heart who everyone loved. She could still remember his face the day his storyline ended.

The final episode of season three, when his birth mother showed up at the ranch to take him home. It had been a tearjerker, both on-screen and off.

But now? Now, he was standing in front of her - taller, broader, his voice steady and a little deeper.

She blinked, half expecting the scrawny kid she remembered to reappear.

"You really grew up, huh?" she said, crossing her arms as a smile tugged at her lips.

His eyes lit up at her remembering him. "You did too, Jay Jay." His eyes roved over her body. Even dressed in a baby doll tee, jeans, and flat sandals, Noodle looked really good.

Aku cleared her throat.

"Oh, hey..." Luther snapped his finger a few times, jogging his memory of her name.

"Aku," she reminded.

He smirked. "That's right, Aku... Jay Jay's beautiful cousin."

"Mhmmm," she pursed her lips.

"Well..." Noodle looked from Aku to Luther. "It was nice seeing you."

"I heard you're no longer with KidVerse. Me neither. I have a manager that's good at her job. You in the market for one?"

Noodle nodded. "Ummm, I might be trying to do something."

"Let me get your number and I'll make the introduction." He handed Noodle his phone, watching her type in her number. "I'll be in touch," he licked his lips.

"Okay... and it's Jacory— my name."

His eyes brightened, picking up what she had put down. "My bad, Ms. Jacory."

He walked away, so Noodle and Aku turned their attention back to the street vendor with the pretty bracelets.

———

"How many bedrooms again?" Bu asked, looking up from his phone. His schedule was hectic, but he really needed to get a more permanent solution to his living arrangements.

Sleeping in Noodle's bed every night was comfortable, but he could feel how delicate the space was. She was new to relationships, and to sex, so the last thing he wanted was to crowd her or push things too fast.

Besides, there was a weight in his chest telling him it was time to leave The Jig behind for good. Something quieter, something that felt like peace, was calling out to him...some shit Bee seemed to be whispering to him in his sleep. Madison Heights had that vibe - close to the water, slower paced. *Close to Noodle.* He could see himself starting over here.

"Five," Pimp answered for the realtor, his tone flat.

The realtor looked up sharply, annoyed that he'd asked the same question she'd already answered before they stepped foot inside. She didn't say anything, though. He wasn't the first distracted buyer she'd dealt with.

Bu finally looked up from his phone, clutching it in his hand by his side before glancing around the open concept living room. The sunlight poured in through floor-to-ceiling windows, hitting the polished wood floors just right. He had to admit, the shit felt good.

Going from a cell, to a small home in his hood...to this? This was the type of shit he had only dreamed of. "This nice," he said, more to himself than anyone else.

"You could do something with this," Pimp added, opening a cabinet in the kitchen and peeking inside. It was clean with no remnants of squished fast food ketchup packets. He gave an impressed nod, moving onto the next one, just being nosey. "Me and Lunar can have a time in here."

"Who said y'all niggas was crashing here?"

Pimp laughed. "You ain't gotta say it... we gon' be wherever you at. You see we ain't found another hotel. If you couped up in Noodle's house, we there too."

No matter how hard Bu wanted to suppress his smile, he couldn't. He loved both of them and knew if he was getting a new spot, he had to have room for them too. "I'll think about it."

"Yea, you do that," Pimp jested.

Bu noticed Pimp's vibe was more relaxed today. It wasn't often they got time like this, just the two of them. Lunar had a way of pulling most of Pimp's focus and understandably so, but Bu appreciated moments like this when it was just them. He wanted to talk, to ask his brother how he was navigating every-thing... life, work, relationships, but he didn't know where to start.

Pimp handled business with Lunar but held his personal dealings close to his chest. Bu understood why. Having a straight best friend, Pimp didn't want to bring any bad press or nega-tivity to Lunar. Pimp was protective of those around him like that. He understood how the world viewed people like him.

Black people hadn't fully grasped the concept of a straight man being tight with a gay or bisexual, and Pimp wasn't about to let anyone throw shade at someone he cared about.

"You good?" Pimp asked, closing a cabinet and leaning back against the counter, staring at his brother because the realtor was waiting to see what the next move was going to be.

Bu smiled faintly, shaking off the weight in his chest. "Yeah, my bad... okay, where do I sign?"

The realtor perked up, her hands clasped together like she'd just won a prize. "You want this one?" she asked, her brows arching as if to make absolutely sure. This was house number five today, and she'd sent him at least twenty listings over the past week. If this was it, she was more than relieved.

"Yeah, I'm sure." Bu's voice dropped, his southern drawl curling over the words like honey. He couldn't help the way his eyes lingered on the kitchen counter, his mind wandering for a brief second. *Noodle.* She was the only one he wanted to break the house in with, and the thought of her spread out on the counter was enough to make him cough and refocus... enough to have him to buy his first house in a city he'd only been in for a couple of weeks.

"Both names?" she asked, glancing between him and Pimp.

"Oh, nah, just mine." Bu's attention was already back on his phone, his fingers scrolling fast.

Pimp laughed, the sound cutting through the room. "Noodle got you in your phone like that?"

"Man..." Bu's face lit up, a grin spreading before he could stop it. "She just be texting about nothing."

"And you be texting back about nothing," Pimp shot back, or raising his brow. He wasn't mad at it, though. Noodle and Bu seemed to need each other in a way that worked, balancing each other out in all the right ways.

Bu didn't even bother responding. His focus was split between his text thread with Noodle and the messages from the business attorney he'd reached out to earlier in the week. Starting his business in Madison Heights felt like the right move, but it came with its own set of challenges. But, this house, this life he was slowly building felt like the foundation he needed.

"You ain't even here right now," Pimp said, snapping his fingers in front of Bu's face.

Bu laughed, finally tucking his phone into his pocket. "I'm here. Let's make this shit happen."

The realtor nodded quickly, pulling out the paperwork. "I'll walk you through the process. If you're ready to make an offer, we'll need to lock it in today. Properties in this area don't stay on the market long."

"I'm ready," Bu said, his tone steady. He could feel Pimp watching him, probably proud that he was taking a step forward instead of staying stuck in the past.

As the realtor went over the details, Pimp leaned in closer. "You sure you're ready for this? This ain't just about having a spot to crash. This is a whole house."

Bu met his brother's eyes, his expression serious. "I'm ready, Pimp... for real. I need this."

Pimp studied him for a moment, then gave a small nod. "Cool, but you ain't making no big decision like this based off some lust filled feelings, is you?"

"You know that ain't even me," Bu glared, trying to see what his little brother was getting at.

"I'm just asking." Pimp threw his hands up in mock surrender.

The hesitancy was valid but Bu couldn't bring himself to admit that because the truth was, his motives were fueled by feelings. It wasn't lust but maybe it was too soon to claim it as love. Plus, Noodle had drawn her line in the sand on the four letter word. Regardless, Bu knew he couldn't move his life in the direction he wanted to, if he remained tied down to Sapphire City.

Finding help and getting things rolling here had already proven to be a challenge, and by no means did he think doing it in Cali made getting it done any easier. He wasn't sure what drove his heart to make the moves he was currently making— all he knew was, it felt like the path was being laid out for him and he'd never been one to turn away when felt like divine intervention.

Something about all this felt like Bee pushing him by signing him up for soccer or dragging him to church. Bu could feel his mama smiling over him. That was all the motivation he needed.

14

Noodle bobbed her head to the music, sipping from the hot tea she had the club owner have made for her. She was beyond nervous and the bubbles in her stomach did nothing to rest her racing heart. Over the rim of her warm styrofoam cup, her eyes darted around the section. Everyone seemed to be having a good time, while she talked herself out of running out the building.

Their section was filled with some of the same people from the studio the other night. Bu's hoe-mirer tried to stay close to him but like the other night, he wasn't paying her much attention. She rolled her eyes, hating to see girls in his face. She understood their infatuation with him. It was probably the same thing that had her running through the woods with him.

The two of them hadn't spent much time together over the last few days. Lunar had her in the studio a few more times since the last time and Bu was doing whatever it was, he did. They did spend nights together though.

Lunar had their song on the radio and got them a few club appearances to push the record. Everything was moving so fast her head was spinning. She hadn't even heard the song a full three times before they had it mixed and mastered, after she put a few more runs on it. Noodle was proud of it but damn, could she sit in it for a while?

"Get out your head, baby," Bu whispered in her ear from behind, creating another round of crazy butterflies in her belly.

"Am I that easy to read?" Noodle smirked, pushing the cup back up to her lips.

His rough hands rolled down her arms leaving a trail of goosebumps. "For me, hell yea... see I took a masterclass in all things Noodle. Once I aced that, I signed up to study the book of Jacory."

"They ain't the same people?"

He laughed. "Hell nah."

"What you get in that class?"

"A muthafuckin' A, baby," Bu laughed, with a duh look on his face.

Pursing her lips, Noodle fought against her smile. "I'm nervous as hell."

"My baby cussing, must mean big business... com'ere." It wasn't a question. He pulled her into his arms, her chin resting on his chest. Staring down into her eyes, he felt like he could get lost in them forever. It was the only place he wanted to be lost and never found. "I'm gon' be in the front row, focus on me baby. They gon' love you regardless. You belong on stage."

"And where you belong?" Noodle licked her lips, her pussy thumping so hard, thoughts of taking him in the bathroom filled her mind.

Bu leaned down to kiss her lips. "Between your legs."

She shivered.

"Ummm... let her breathe," Aku cut into their intimate moment. The two of them got so caught up sometimes, the real world disappeared.

"Don't hate, girl," Noodle laughed, still looking in Bu's dark eyes, wondering what was going through his beautiful mind.

Bu smiled, pulling his rolled joint from behind his ear.

Without removing himself from her arms, he sparked it up, letting the weed fill his lungs.

Noodle's needy eyes perked up and her lips made an O. She felt his chuckle through his chest as he flipped the joint to blow smoke into her mouth. She inhaled it then blew it back out in his face.

"Ugh," Aku faked sick. "Y'all are too cute for me, hunny."

"She hatin' again, baby," Bu laughed as he hit his weed again.

It didn't take long for Noodle's eyes to lower and her body to sway to the music. The DJ was spinning good songs that had the club rocking. Noodle turned around, bending over to one of Devin Ports new songs about his little *yea yea* holding his attention with her body.

She started poppin' her ass on Bu, making a silly lopsided smirk dance across his face. Finishing his joint, he sat it on the cocktail table beside them, gripping her hips. Smoothly, he rocked into her, matching her rhythm with his slow wine.

Her bone straight hair swung freely because Noodle hadn't figured out that straight hair wasn't more polished or professional like they made her believe. Still, she was fine either way.

His eyes found the tattoo on her back. He ran his hand down it, letting her know he was all in. The red backless top accentuated her frame perfectly. The hip hugging jeans dipped more when she touched her toes. His dick jumped at the sight of her red thongs. A satisfied smile rested in his eyes thinking about his baby all of a sudden loving the color red. Bu loved and hated how pliable she was. It was cool when the person molding her had good intentions but history had proven, most people she encountered didn't have her best interest in mind.

When Noodle made her ass cheeks bounce, he pulled her back into his chest. "I'm dying to fuck you." Bu's voice was smoother and the hint of weed in his pores made her feel high. His hands were on her, leaving a trail of heat as they roamed her body not caring about being in the club.

Her tongue swiped across her lips at the feel of his dick

pressed into her lower back. Thinking about him folding her up like a lawn chair, she reached behind her to grab it through his jeans. She needed to see how bad he wanted to fuck her and by how hard he was, she knew Bu was ready.

Lunar made his way over to them. "You 'bout ready, Noodle?" He was feeling good and didn't pay attention to the lust in their eyes. He was ready to hit the stage.

Bu groaned when she removed her hand. "I—"

The DJ blasted air horn sounds through the speakers to get the club more hype, drawing their attention to what was going on. The way he played them over and over, each blare louder than the last, rattled Noodle's chest, stealing her breath away.

"Devin Port is in the building!" He announced, making Aku's ears perk up.

Lunar cheesed, happy his big homie could make it. Rubbing his hands together, he waited for Devin to make it to their section. As soon as he walked in, Lunar met him halfway slapping hands with him. "Glad your old ass could make it."

"You know I wasn't gonna miss it, my boy." Devin pulled him into a brotherly hug. His eyes went to Aku, making her blush.

Lunar pulled back, looking over at Bu. "Let me introduce you to my big bro."

Devin nodded at Bu, but went to Aku instead. Pulling her into a tight hug, he whispered in her ear. "What's up, mahmah?"

"Oh, you speaking today?" Aku asked with her arms around his waist. She was tall but Devin was taller, even with her being in heels.

"Damn, you smell good, mahmah," his low tenor made her ear vibrate.

"You too," Aku said, pulling back from him, and smoothing down her sleek bob, to distract herself from how flustered his fine ass was making her feel.

Noodle wiggled her brows at Aku.

Devin turned towards Bu with admiration in his eyes. "The

man, the myth, the muthafuckin' legend," he slapped hands with Bu. "I heard nothing but good shit about you, bro."

"Likewise." They dapped each other up, ending their handshake with their fingers twisting into b's.

"I see Madison Heights treating you good," Devin commented on Noodle being tucked under Bu's arm. "Little Noodle... I need to get with your management, I'm looking to do a song or something with you since you back."

Noodle blushed. "I'm getting my feet wet."

"Well, let me know when you're ready and I got you on a feature or something." He looked around the section. "Where Pimp crazy ass at?"

Bu sniffled, seeing his brother off to the side standing next to Bobby Jr and a few girls. Devin followed his line of sight with a head nod. "But let me chop it up with you while they get ready to perform," he laid his hand on Bu's shoulder.

Bu kissed Noodle on the side of her lips, wishing her luck.

As the men walked away, Aku fell into Noodle's side. "We gon' be gang sisters."

"Aku, please," Noodle cackled, still watching Bu's sexy ass walk away. The way he walked, you could tell he was carrying big dick. She shuddered thinking about finally putting it in her mouth.

———

More horns blared from the speakers.

"Time for the main muthafuckin' event!" The DJ yelled, grabbing everyone's attention to the small stage in the center of the club. "The way Chasing Galaxies has been on repeat, it was only right we got them in the building! We know Nar... the hottest new comer in the game right now."

Lunar pinched the top right shoulder of his shirt between his thumb and index fingers, making his shirt wiggle and the girls scream.

"And you might know little Jay Jay…except she ain't Jay Jay no more. Our girl is grown… matter fact say fuck KidVerse!"

"Fuck KidVerse!" the crowd yelled back.

Noodle cringed, but Lunar rubbed her arm, letting her know it was okay. Everything was going to be fine.

"Introducing… for the first time as a solo R&B artist, Jacory!" The DJ did her introduction justice. The crowd was hyped to see her and Lunar.

Smooth like butter, the R&B trap beat poured through the speakers as Lunar's voice slid in, painting pictures with his words. His verses were a double-edged blade, spinning lustful dreams while hinting at something far more carnal. An unapologetic ode to chasing orgasms.

The bassline hit her chest, vibrating through her ribs, and Noodle felt a flush creep up her skin. Her breath caught, teetering between excitement and fear, as if the stage lights had sharpened into a thousand tiny suns aimed directly at her.

Just as her head went under the water, her fearful gaze darted to the crowd, desperate for an anchor. That's when she saw him. Bu, was posted up in the front row just like he promised. He didn't cheer or call out, but his subtle nod said everything - *You've got this, baby.*

Noodle's pulse steadied. She swallowed her fear, letting it dissolve into the music. And then, like a spark hitting dry kindling, she ignited.

Bu's face split like a proud daddy. His baby was up there looking like the professional she was. Even with fear coursing through her, she sung and commanded the stage effortlessly.

Noodle and Lunar owned that stage, moving in sync as if the music had been written for their connection alone. The chemistry between them was magnetic, a force so raw and undeniable it was bound to set off a flood of think pieces. There'd be rumors, no doubt and whispers of secret love, of passion simmering beneath every glance and touch. And maybe once, when they were younger and life was a little messier, those rumors might've been true. Back then, crushes had bloomed between late-night studio sessions and laughter so pure it felt other-worldly.

But Noodle preferred it this way now. Lunar as her friend who blurred the edges of family. That was the real magic of their bond, forged when she walked into their lives at ten years old, scrappy and determined. No romance could touch the kind of love they'd built— rooted in trust, unshakable, and just as eternal as any galaxy Lunar could dream up. Because he chased galaxies too, except his would be the finding of his roots. Lunar's chase was of feeling grounded in who he was and who he came from. Noodle knew it. They'd talked about it as children.

Just as she rolled her body, she almost tripped over her line when she saw her sister Siasia walk in with the rest of the family behind her. She snapped her neck to Lunar who only shrugged while rapping adlibs.

The crowd was vibing and Bu sung her parts word for word, even her adlibs. She felt so good as the song ended. Her back perspired from nerves and the lights shining down on her.

Lunar wrapped his arms around her. "Show all the love to Jacory and it's forever what?" he pointed the mic to the crowd.

"Fuck KidVerse!" they yelled.

"You did so good," he whispered in her ear, his wet forehead pressed against the side of her face.

"Thank you," she said pressing a kiss into his cheek. "Like, for real… for everything."

"We family, Noodle."

"Oh, I'm your cousin?"

Lunar hollered. "Hell no!"

She cracked up in his arms seeing the cameras flash out the corner of her eyes. They were flicking it up and she had to accept it. Once her and Lunar left the stage, she rushed to Bu who was leaning against the wall with one leg kicked back at the knee. Seeing his face, she slowed to gather herself. In the blink of an eye, she envisioned this being her real life. Performing in front of thousands of people and getting off stage to be comforted by her man. The vision felt so real, she could touch it, but she was afraid. Fifty, fifty didn't feel safe— the odds didn't seem to be in her favor.

"Get out your head, baby," Bu's deep, southern voice pulled her back to him. He opened his arms, showing her she was safe with him. "I'm so proud of you."

Noodle looked up into his eyes. "I'm proud of me too."

"As you should be. You are a fuckin' star. You do this music shit with your eyes closed. You're up next."

"And you are beautiful," she muttered.

"Watch out, baby," Bu's head fell back with laughter.

She heard heels clanking against the floor pulling her eyes to its direction. "We came all this way and my sister runs to everyone but me," Siasia said, cocking her head to the side with a slight smirk on her face.

Siasia was shocked to see her sister look so grownup. The way Noodle clung to Bu reminded her of herself with Qamar. Ahhh, to be young and in love again.

Noodle laughed before looking up at Bu as if to ask him could she leave his side. Bu, ever so charming and all about her, nodded.

Siasia kissed her teeth, resting her hand on her curvy hips. Siasia's brown skin looked healthy, and she was still very much young. At only thirty-one, she was thriving in both her professional career as well as her personal life. The life Qamar built was rooted in all things love. His stars revolved around Siasia's planet. It worked so beautifully because Siasia loved everything that came with him. The two extra kids and the loving family he was born from.

Noodle hugged her. "Sisi!"

"Don't Sisi me when you ain't care to see me... all you worried about is Bu's fine ass," she whispered, the last part making them fall out in laughter. Pulling Noodle back, she looked at her sister. Memories flashed in her mind of Stacy bringing his new baby home. Noodle was wrapped up in a blanket, with her pale skin and boney as hell. Siasia dubbed her with the moniker— and Noodle was born.

"So, what you think?" Noodle picked at her fingers.

"I think you the shit!" Siasia yelled. "My baby ain't a baby no more." She swiped a tear from her face. "And I am so proud of you. You did it, Noodle."

Noodle fell back into her big sister's arms. Siasia had been more of a mother than anything. "I love you, Sisi."

"And him," Siasia muttered in her ear, her eyes connecting with Bu, who stood back watching them. "Them glasses... girl!" she fanned herself.

Noodle pinched her. "Stop for real."

"Girl, I got a man, but I can appreciate another fine black man."

Noodle just shook her head, her thoughts still buzzing from Siasia's claim of her being in love with Bu.

Did she?

If love felt like a warm hug wrapped around her or the heady rush of spinning too fast on her favorite ride, then maybe she was drowning in it. Head over heels, no question. But as the idea swirled, that nagging fifty, fifty rule crept back into her mind. Half the time, love was everything they said it was— light and magical. But the other half? It was terrifying.

This was the part no one ever warned you about. The part where love swelled so big and full inside of you that it became suffocating. Like holding your breath for too long. It consumed you, chewed you up until you thought you might burst from the sheer intensity, and then came the panic.

This was the moment when fight or flight kicked in. The crossroads where people ran for their lives, scared to death of loving someone so much they'd shatter if they lost them. Noodle could feel it now, the quiet urge to flee, to take off before the fall. It wasn't the love itself that scared her, it was the risk. *What if she loved him and lost everything?*

She didn't get time to explore that with Siasia, before she was pulled back into the mele of the club. Her whole family greeted her with hugs, praise, and kisses. They were proud and her face ached from all the smiling she'd done. Of course, Bu gave her space until she found herself nestled into him while everyone around them turned up in celebration.

She smiled at Luna and Javen partying it up. They hardly ever popped out. The two of them preferred a more intimate setting where they could cut the hell up in private. She felt loved, seeing all of them pause from their busy lives to support her and Lunar.

15

Her body buzzed, and not from the hangover of excitement from her performance. The crowd was nice, but it was seeing him reciting every lyric— word for word like he was her biggest fan. It was different because he was usually so laid-back- calm, cool and collected, but tonight Noodle could see Bu's heart beat outside of his chest.

That and the mix of the weed he let her indulge in only with him. And truthfully, it was the only way she wanted to enjoy the earth's green.

Her ear lay against his body. She could hear the beating of his heart. "Is this weird?"

"Is what weird, baby?" Bu kept his voice low, but the deep-ness was felt by the way it vibrated through his body.

"Being chauffeured."

"Nah… ain't no different from the times I ain't have no car and had to bum a ride with my boys."

Her ears perked up. Any little details she could get about the Bu before prison was always a treat. "Your friends? You never talk about them."

"Ain't nothing to talk about. Most of them still locked up or dead and any of them that still walk this earth, are dead to me."

Bu never gave much emotion when he spoke but something about him made you hang onto every word he said.

"Oh," she snapped her mouth closed, looking up through the moon roof at the twinkling stars.

Bu let his body sink deeper into the backseat as his eyes followed Noodle's upward gaze.

"I used to dream about being a star," she said softly.

"You *are* a star."

She snorted, shaking her head. "I mean a *real* star... like the ones in the sky."

"Why?" Bu asked, his mind wandering. He pictured her as a star, far away, unreachable. Then he imagined a version of himself that had never met her. Then his thoughts shifted to Bee. She felt like a star too, always pulling at him, her gravity undeniable. What was it about stars that made them stick in your mind and tug at your heart like that?

Noodle tilted her head, as if searching for something up there. "I don't know. Just feels like I've been chasing something out there, trying to figure out where I fit in."

"Chasing, drowning, you do everything but live, baby."

Her words struck a chord deep inside him. How was it, that a girl who had the world in her hands, could be so desperate to figure out who she was. He ain't never had shit in his hands but drugs and guns and he knew exactly who he was.

Bu's mind drifted back to Bee. She had spent so much of her life grounding him and Pimp, making sure they understood their worth. Their fathers had left an absence so loud it could've swallowed them whole, but Bee filled the gaps. She taught them about their roots, about the other half of their family tree. She was never bitter or petty about anything she went through. Bee could've torn their dads apart with her words, but instead she handed them a narrative steeped in dignity. It made Bu think about the weight of identity and how it shaped who you were and who you *thought* you were supposed to be.

"You never talk about your mama." He felt her eyes on him now, no longer looking at the stars.

"I talk about Cynthia... Stacy too," she said, brushing him off.

"Yeah, the woman who raised you and your real dad," he pressed. "But never the woman you *look like*."

Noodle's smile was faint, almost mocking. "How you know I look like her?"

"I know," he said, his voice softer now. "Tell me about her."

Noodle's shoulders stiffened, her exhale shaky, as if she were holding back something heavy. "Ain't much to tell," she muttered, but her tone betrayed her.

"You don't know her?" Bu asked. His hand found her hair, fingers threading gently through it, tracing her scalp. It was a gesture meant to anchor her, to tell her it was okay to float into the deeper waters of herself, or the sky— whichever surface she preferred today.

Noodle hesitated, her lips parting and closing again. She was fighting it...fighting herself. Finally, she let the words spill, her voice tight, laced with unshed tears. "She sold me," she revealed. "Not really, but literally. After my mama and daddy died, the police brought me back to Jackie. Then Qamar came along, waving deep pockets. She didn't even blink. She let me go for six figures."

Bu frowned, tilting his head. "Is that the real story, or the story you remember?" He didn't mean to defend Jackie, but something didn't sit right. There was a crack in the story— a missing piece. "You say Qamar paid her for you like you didn't want to go back to your sister. Am I missing something?"

Noodle swiped at her eyes, frustration burning in her chest. "Siasia was all I knew, but maybe Jackie could've given me something... some kind of meaning to my life." Her shoulders sagged, the weight of her words dragging her down. "I don't know, Bu. I'm just... chasing something."

Bu's eyes softened, but his voice was steady. "Sounds like you're running from something."

She laughed bitterly, swallowing hard. "Life... love... freedom... maybe galaxies," she whispered. The tears she'd been holding back slid free, and she let them fall unchecked. "I think we're all chasing or running from something. What's the difference anyway?"

Bu sat with her words, his hand still resting against her head, grounding her. Maybe there *wasn't* a difference. Maybe the line between chasing and running was as blurred as the stars in the sky.

"Seems like you're looking for something already inside of you."

Noodle pulled her head from his shoulder and her eyes from the stars. Those almond eyes seared into him. "What about you? Are you chasing or running?"

He looked over at his Noodle - a ball of clay, ready to be whatever the artist decided. "I'm just moving my feet, praying it aligns me with whatever God has in store for me."

"God?" She bunched up her face.

He snorted a laugh. "You don't believe in God?"

"I mean... yea."

Fink snorted from the front seat making Noodle roll her eyes.

"You just didn't think I did? Damn, that's cold, baby," Bu lay his hand on his chest, his gold watch catching her eye. "I grew up in church, Bee made sure of it. When I started running the streets I pulled away, but locked up, I ain't have shit else to do, so I started reading and understanding the word."

She looked at him in admiration. How did he get finer and finer, the more she pulled back the layers of him. Noodle was so caught up in Bu's red world, she didn't notice the drive to her condo being extra-long. She also didn't notice the smell of salt growing stronger.

"Jackie been asking me to come to church with her," she confessed.

"I think you should, baby."

"I just can't forgive her like that...like my heart is so conflicted. Besides, I don't want to hurt Siasia neither." Her hands rested on her head. "I don't know what I want."

"You can't heal if you keep pretending it doesn't hurt." Bu sat up, gripping her hand in his. "Be real with Jackie, I bet she's ready for you to give it to her raw 'cause she knows going through is the only way to make it to the other side." He kissed her hands, acknowledging her new red nails. "We've been chasing galaxies, but maybe we were meant to find our own."

———

Noodle's eyes hung low from exhaustion and feeling about him getting his own space hurt Bu had thrown her off by bringing her to his new house as if she didn't enjoy his brown sugar scent in her room, filling her bathroom, or just in the air when she woke up midafternoon. The beach house was nice. Still her bruised heart wouldn't let her acknowledge it.

It was empty, with only the night sky shining in through the massive wall to wall glass doors that led to the infinity pool and beach. If she was in the market for a bigger house, this would be her dream.

"It's cute," she said snidely, making her way to the kitchen.

He'd been following behind her, catching each subtle facial expression that told him, his baby wasn't feeling him getting his own place. He understood why she wouldn't understand without him explaining. "You really acting like that?" His hands wrapped around her body, spinning her around to face him.

"Nooooo I'm just a little thrown off by all of this," she whined. "You think you slick... how long you had this spot?"

"I just got the keys today. The seller was very motivated to sell, so it only took three weeks to close on it," Bu nuzzled his chin into her neck. "I ain't got nothing but a bed and some throw on clothes in here."

"So, you leaving me?" Noodle asked, staring off through the nice-sized window that sat above the sink.

Swaying her to the island, Bu placed soft kisses on her neck. "I'm just giving you your space back. I can still come over by you or you can come over here, baby. This is new for you, and I want you to fully prepare for what we're getting into. Like, ain't no skipping steps over here."

She wrapped her hands over his arms, which held her tight, keeping her close to him. "Then why you just now telling me?"

"Don't make this more than what it is," Bu groaned. "Get out your head and see me as being a gentleman, not taking advantage of this being your first time dating."

"We dating?"

"Man," Bu, pulled back from her, his hands resting on top of his head. "Come on, Noodle... like you gotta grow up one day. Yes, we're dating."

"Why you mad 'cause I'm asking questions?" She flailed her arms in the air. "You just said this is new... How am I supposed to know if what we're doing is dating?"

She was right. Bu was just getting frustrated with how green she could be sometimes. It wasn't good for her 'cause the music industry and Hollywood were cutthroat and dream stealers were able to smell that shit on girls like her.

Bu yanked Noodle back to him. "Sorry," he crooned, making his eyes sad. "I gotta be gentle with you."

"Not all the time," she whispered, her voice dipping low. "Sometimes you can be rough with me."

"Oh, this how you feeling?" Bu's voice rose when Noodle's hands ran against his dick print in his jeans. "You went from not knowing if we're dating, to wanting me to fuck you?"

"Un uh," she shook her head. "I want you to teach me how to suck your dick."

His front teeth sunk deep into his bottom lip as Noodle eased to her knees. He cringed, thinking about how uncomfortable that might be. The sound of his zipper had him quickly tossing that thought. Pulling his phone from his pocket, he played some music low to fill the empty space.

Noodle looked up at him with those almond eyes and that upturned nose. "Are you going to teach me?"

"Baby, you know I'll teach you anything... go on and pull that muthafucka out."

Noodle loved when he talked to her like that. Usually, he was gentle and soft with her, but on the rare occasions his gritty language snaked its way into her ears - she melted.

"Okay?" She gripped his dick once she had it free.

Her red nails wrapped around it perfectly.

"You got them nails for me?" he asked, his voice low but loud enough for her to hear.

"Yes! Now tell me what to do... please," she whined, her mouth watering and ready to taste his salty skin.

"You ever sucked a lollipop?"

"Yes..."

"Don't suck my dick like that... get nasty with this mutha-fucka... sloppy, baby." Bu sat his glasses on the island he was leaning back on.

Noodle stared at the pubic hairs staring back at her. He was clean shaven but left some hair, probably because being bald didn't feel manly to him. She took a deep breath before slowly wrapping her mouth around his dick sheathed in brown skin. His mushroom head was slightly lighter than the rest of him.

"Wait," he stopped her before stepping out of his clothes. He wanted no barriers between her and him. She didn't budge. She watched his every move, taking in how thick and muscular his thighs were. There was also a bible scrip-ture on this thigh, in a sexy font that she hadn't paid much attention to before now. Running her fingertips over it, she watched bumps prickle his skin as a low hum came from his mouth.

Bu allowed her time to ogle him with her eyes before his dick jumped to get her attention.

"Okay," she hummed. "Not a lollipop," she coached herself, wrapping her warm mouth around his fleshy dick.

"No teeth," he said through gritted teeth as her teeth grazed him. "Shit!"

Noodle wasn't a pro yet so she used her two hands to work the parts of him she couldn't get in her mouth. Her mouth juiced, coating him in her saliva.

"Just... like... that." His voice came out tattered while his toes curled. "Good girl...keep sucking this dick just like that... tell me who taught you this?"

"You," she garbled.

"I can't hear you, baby... tell me who taught you how to suck dick so good?"

Her pussy leaked and her knees ached, but Noodle wanted him to keep talking her through her dick sucking lesson. "You." She wasn't audile but Bu felt her reply.

"That's right, and who's the only nigga who gets to feel those pretty ass lips wrapped around his dick?" His rough hands found their way into her hair, scraping her scalp while feeding her his dick.

Noodle pulled back enough to answer him before she was back to that slow rhythm she'd gotten comfortable with. The sound of her slurping him bounced off the bare walls.

Bu hissed when her teeth scraped him ever so slightly, but he didn't mind. The act of her being on her knees made it feel like the best head he'd ever received. His hips thrust forward, and he could feel her spit dripping down his thighs. Blood rushed from his toes to the head of his dick. Instead of finishing in her mouth, he removed himself from her.

Noodle's lips popped and her eyes begged him to put it back in. But the way his dark eyes scorched her skin, she was on her feet ready for the next round.

"Take those clothes off, baby. Let me see you," Bu stepped away from the counter to wipe himself off, giving her a little space to get naked.

Noodle didn't hesitate to quickly remove every piece of clothing she had on, dropping them on the floor. Instinctively she covered her hard nipples.

He lovingly pushed her arms down. "Don't do that. I wanna see you."

The A/C chilled her skin but not enough to put out the flame he always seemed to ignite inside of her. "Did I do good?" that syrupy, sweet voice asked with her pretty face all wet and disheveled, mascara was smeared across her face.

"The best," Bu said, hiking her up on the counter. "I chose this house just so I could spread your fine ass across this island and eat."

"Wait!" Noodle sat up on her elbows, eager to ask him something. "Do you like giving or receiving?"

What she really wanted to know was did she do a *really* good job.

"I like giving… I like seeing the look on your face when my head is between your legs and my tongue is so deep inside of you, we feel like one." He kissed her toes, making them wiggle. "But I *love* seeing you on your knees with your small hands wrapped around my dick."

Satisfied with his answer, Noodle lay back down and spread her legs with a big smile on her face that was washed away just as quickly from his peppered kisses.

His calloused hands roamed up her moisturized legs. Bu didn't explore her naked body for too long before his head was buried between her legs. His tongue work was lethal and her taste was addicting. He wrote his name in every language. She felt English and Spanish, she died when he wrote it in Arabic and French and was resuscitated when Jacory spelled in German came next. He shared all the languages he lazily learned when he had nothing to do but stare at 4 walls.

But he still wasn't satisfied with that, Bu needed to feel her wrapped around his dick.

Noodle's breath was yanked from her soul when he slid inside her. "Hmmm." Her eyes rolled to the back of her head.

His warm hand pressed against her face. "Open your eyes for me... watch me while I'm feeding you my dick and my heart, baby. Open your eyes and enjoy me loving on your body, so you know how this shit supposed to feel. Open your eyes and watch me spell love all over you. When I get done with you, you'll walk lighter." He kissed her. "... breathe better" Another kiss. "... love easier... that's my purpose on this earth... *You.*" Bu circled his tongue between her puffy lips while his hips swirled inside of her.

Noodle cried like a baby as he worked her over and over.

"I love you," he confessed, with the music still crooning in the background and her legs still wrapped around him, accepting his long deep strokes. "You ain't gotta say it back but I wanted you to know that."

"Why?" Noodle asked, as her body rocked backward and forward.

"I'm obsessed with loving you because it feels like God's energy... like it's what he wants me to do and I never disobey God."

Noodle shed more tears, releasing more fear.

Noodle felt like she could die that day and be transported to God feeling full and whole.

Instead of saying anything back, she pulled his mouth to hers, kissing him deeply and staring into his eyes as her body shook from the most powerful orgasm she ever had.

16

Noodle limped into her condo. Her body was on fire from the figure eight Bu had her in all night long. Now, she was tired and wanted to crawl in her bed to catch up on some sleep. She'd been on go over the last few days and if she didn't rest, she was going to crash out.

"I never thought I'd see the day," Solar teased from the couch, one leg crossed over the other, her foot flopping lazily in the air.

Noodle let her head fall back, her shoulders sagging under the weight of exhaustion. "I should've called first," she said under her breath.

"Where you been?" French asked, emerging from the kitchen with a cup of something in his hand. She knew it couldn't be coffee since she nor Aku drank it.

Her tired eyes swept the open-concept living area, scanning the room like she was counting witnesses. The walk of shame hit differently when the audience was in your own house. She glanced down at herself - Bu's underwear knotted at her hips, one of his oversized shirts swallowing her whole, his socks and slides on her feet. It didn't help her case.

"Where's Aku?" she asked through a yawn, already bracing for judgment.

French gave her a hard look over the rim of his cup. "Shit, you tell me. I'm just over here trying to figure out if this is how y'all are out here living now?"

"Huh?" Noodle blinked, genuinely confused. She and Aku were twenty-one years old, grown women who made their own money and barely leaned on their people for anything. Sure, Aku still got a monthly allowance from her parents, and Siasia and Qamar slid Noodle money whenever they felt like it, but they didn't *ask* for that.

French got closer, the look in his eyes something between concern and disappointment. "Don't *huh* me. I'm asking, is this how y'all living it up?"

"I mean..." Noodle licked her lips, searching his face for what he was really getting at.

"French, sit down," Solar fussed, waving him off. "Them girls are grown."

"They still my babies," he muttered, his glare softening but not disappearing. His voice dropped lower. "Who you was with? That nigga Bu?"

Noodle stiffened. His brown eyes looked tired, like he was carrying some unspoken weight, like the answer might break his heart.

"Stop being a hater," Qamar finally cut in, sparing her from the confession she wasn't ready to make about being tossed around Bu's new kitchen like a ragdoll. "Com'ere, Noodle," he said, opening his arms wide.

"I'm sleepy," she mumbled through another yawn, stumbling into him without hesitation.

Qamar rubbed her back, his voice soft against the shell of her ear. "Your sister and Luna are in your room. Just wanted to give you a heads-up."

Noodle gulped but nodded, grateful for the warning. Her eyes sagged more but she toed off the slides before padding down the hall and into her room. She inhaled deeply as she pushed the door open. Two sets of eyes glared at her.

Siasia and Luna were propped up in her bed like they belonged. Siasia looked down at her phone. "Good... afternoon."

Noodle snickered at the sight before her. "Where is Javen?" she asked Luna, trudging over to the bathroom.

Luna's lips popped. "You're worrying about the wrong things... where's Bu?" She smirked teasingly.

Siasia watched her sister from the back as Noodle entered the bathroom not worrying about closing the door. "Limping and shit," she commented, making Luna roll around on the bed, die laughing. "Well I know you ain't no virgin no more."

"How'd you know in the first place?" Noodle asked while she peed, then wiped herself and washed her hands.

"I know 'cause I was a virgin before too," Luna held her head up proudly.

Siasia cut her eyes at her. "Like everyone wasn't a virgin before... Luna, please," she swatted her away. "I know you Noodle, so of course I can smell when you done gave that coochie up."

Noodle crawled into her bed not caring about either of them being there. She needed to rest her eyes at least.

"You smell just like him," Luna commented, sticking her nose close to her.

Siasia tugged at the durag on Noodle's head. "This his too?"

"Mhmmm... I woke up to my hair tied down. I didn't fall asleep like that."

Siasia cocked her body back, her eyes saying, 'excuse me'. "I hope you on birth control."

Noodle pursed her lips. "I am... he told me to get on it."

"Oh, Bu is a keeper," Luna swooned at the way he seemed to be taking care of Noodle instead of exploiting her being new to sex and situationships.

Noodle smiled big thinking about the way Bu took care of

her. He was always so sweet, making sure to teach her the things she needed to know along the way. He rooted for her, encouraged her, and pushed her to do things she tended to shy away from. He advised her even when it might've hurt his chest. Like telling her to have dinner with Luther and his manager. Bu told her if she really wanted to take her career to the next level she would need a good manager and after they did their own research on Luther's manager he nudged her forward.

Even after Noodle told him she thought Luther liked her, Bu still told her to take the meeting. He even told her what to say when she texted him this morning.

Siasia smoothed her hand over Noodle's durag-wrapped head. "That makes me feel better about you growing up... I know you don't tell me a lot, but I'm okay knowing you have someone like Bu in here to see the snakes in the grass."

"That's true. You know Noodle likes to do it by herself. Seems like Mr. Bu ain't letting her do it without him, though." Luna added her two cents.

Noodle's smile fell thinking of all the things she kept to herself. Things that would shatter her sisters' hearts had they known what the industry did to her. If they knew the one secret she held back, knowing nothing good would come from sharing it. Now, she had to add Bu to the list of people who absolutely couldn't find out.

"Can I get some sleep now?" Noodle tugged the covers over her body. "Oh, Luna you know someone named Bridgette?"

"Bridgette who? What she do?" Luna tapped on her chin in thought.

"She's a manager."

"Oh, yea, I've heard of her. From what I hear she's pretty good but if you're ready for a manager, I know someone perfect for you," Luna suggested.

Noodle shook her head. "Let me see what she's talking about first... I'll let you know after." She pulled the covers to her eyes.

Siasia and Luna made eye contact, shrugging at the typical Noodle— wanting to conquer the world on her own.

"Luna?" Noodle called out, again.

"Yes?"

"Was Javen your first and only?" Noodle asked, her eyes closed, ready to fall asleep.

Luna shook her head even though Noodle couldn't see her. "Not my first and only sex partner or love."

That had Noodle's eyes popping open as she twisted to look at Luna who was positioned behind her. "Wait... what?!"

Luna laughed. "I'm surprised Candi ain't told you that."

"Not too much on my girl now," Siasia joked. She and Candi's relationship was rock solid. That was the big sister she always wanted. Luna too but Candi held a special place in her heart, probably because she wasn't attached to Qamar in the ways Luna and Solar were.

"Jay?" Noodle's voice held a whisper. "Oooh." Her mouth made an o as if it was all coming back to her.

"Mhmmm," Luna nodded, thinking about her brief time with Jayshun Black. Javen held her heart even then but she'd be a liar if she didn't admit Jay gave her something special too. "Jay had a piece of my heart, but Javen owned my soul. That man slithered through my body like blood, so even when my Jay laid claim to my heart, he couldn't fuck with that soul tie I had with Javen Cooper." There were stars in her eyes. "Love is complicated like that, Noodle."

"Love is scary like that," she mumbled, getting comfortable again.

———

Bu read the headline of the image making its way around the internet. It was an image of him and Noodle at the club after her performance. He'd been photographed with her before only then, they only caught blurry glimpses of him. This time his face was front and center, clear as day. His stomach twisted as he scanned the comments. People could be so brutal, cutting deep with words they'd never dare say to him in person. For him, it didn't sting. He'd learned to brush off the noise. But Noodle? He knew her... knew she was probably sitting somewhere with her phone in her hand, reading every cruel thing people had to say about her... about him... about *them*.

Most of the heat fell on him, but it was the comments about Noodle that made his blood boil. They picked apart her character like scavengers, calling her desperate and painting her in a light so far from the truth it made his chest ache. She didn't deserve that. She never had. But the world loved a story they could tear apart, and right now, *they* were the story.

She cared too much about what people thought... always had.

It wasn't just about keeping her image clean. It was like she needed the world to see her a certain way, and every critique felt personal. Bu exhaled sharply, tossing his phone onto the passenger seat. He didn't have time to get wrapped up in this right now.

He had a meeting to get to.

Bu pulled up to Devin's house, taking in the five acres of lush greenery and perfectly manicured landscaping. The hills stretched endlessly behind the house, the kind of backdrop that made you stop and stare. Devin, stood waiting for him on the stone patio.

Bu shuffled out the car with Noodle on his mind but he needed to seal this deal with Devin. It was what they'd chopped it up about in the club. They were cut from the same cloth so Devin was ready to lend a hand to any man that wanted better for themselves, and that red flag they both wore like a badge of honor didn't hurt.

"What's good, my boy?" Devin greeted him, extending a hand as Bu stepped onto the patio.

"Not much," Bu replied, shaking it firmly, finishing it off with their fingers twisted in bs. He took a moment to glance around. "This shit is nice." He whistled.

Devin grinned. "Yeah, it's decent. But it needs some work. That's why I called you."

They sat down at a table overlooking the property, the breeze carrying the scent of weed and blooming flowers. Devin laid out his vision— he wanted to take the landscaping up a notch, turning his already impressive yard into something award-worthy. Some shit that'll make his neighbors heads turn. They were a cool bunch but his rugged features did gain him some not so nice greetings in passing.

"I need somebody who knows what they're doing," Devin said, leaning back in his chair. "Not just someone who cuts grass, you feel me? I want this place to look like it belongs in a magazine."

"You're talking about a lot of work," Bu said, glancing out at the acreage. "But I can handle it. I'll need about a week to get everything rolling... you know, since my company is new. Gotta find a crew too."

Bu was a man unashamed. He was also going to let anyone know up front that this was all new to him. If someone didn't want to take a chance on him, he was cool with that but at least he knew he'd laid it all out for them to make a good decision.

Devin nodded. "That works for me. I'm not in a rush, just want it done right."

The business talk was quick and straightforward. Bu respected that about Devin— he didn't waste time. But as the conversation shifted, Devin brought up what Bu knew was inevitable.

"So, man, you seen the internet today, right?" Devin asked, resting his elbows on the table. "You and Noodle are all over it."

Bu's jaw tightened, but he nodded. "Yeah, I seen it."

Devin studied him for a moment, his expression thoughtful. "You think she's strong enough to cut through the noise? All this attention, the negativity— it's loud, man... real loud. Then

KidVerse ain't making it no better with that slick shit they pulled."

KidVerse finally issued a statement about Jacory being let go because her image didn't align with what they stood for. They boasted shit about them being a family and kid-friendly oriented company. Bu knew that was bullshit. They were a fuckin' billion dollar company eating off the backs of children.

Bu leaned back, running a hand over his jaw. He knew the answer, but saying it out loud felt heavy. "No," he admitted finally. "She's not built for this shit. Noodle's too pliable. She cares too much about what people think. All that noise? It's gonna eat her alive."

Devin frowned, his gaze dropping to the table. "That's tough. She seems like she's got something special, though."

"She does," Bu said, his voice low. "But it don't matter how special you are if you let the world get in your head. I've tried to tell her, but..." He shrugged, his words trailing off.

Devin sighed, shaking his head. "That's the game, though. You gotta have thick skin or it'll chew you up and spit you out."

Bu nodded, his eyes drifting out toward the hills. "Yeah. That's what I'm worried about... my baby too soft for them to do her like this."

The two sat in silence for a moment, the weight of the conversation settling between them. Bu knew he couldn't protect Noodle from everything, but that didn't stop him from wanting to try.

———

Noodle tapped the hem of her skirt, her finger trembling as she fought to steady her nerves. Her eyes darted around the restaurant, certain that every pair of eyes was fixed on her, watching, waiting for her to fall apart. Each glance felt heavier than the last, pressing against her chest, tightening her throat. She wanted to throw up the shots she had the waitress bring her while she waited.

The Ambi was a nice mid-scale restaurant that any and everyone found themselves crammed into because it was small. Girls crammed themselves into the bar waiting for an unsuspecting bachelor or married man looking for a sugar baby. It was her second time being there. The first was an outing with Aku while she was prowling for the love of her life who never showed up.

She stared at the door, begging Luther to walk through it. He was ten minutes late. Her pulse quickened with every second that passed, her patience wearing thin. The phone on the table buzzed again, rattling against the wood like it was mocking her. But she didn't reach for it. She couldn't. It felt radioactive, like it would burn her skin if she touched it.

Her stomach churned. The timing of all this was cruel. For once, the world was on her side, buzzing with praise about her performance, calling her more incredible than they'd ever imagined. She should've been riding that high, basking in the glow of validation she'd worked so hard for.

But instead, it felt like the rug had been ripped out from under her... again.

KidVerse's statement had hit like a wrecking ball, unraveling all the good she'd built in a single blow. The narrative shifted before her eyes. Praise turned into speculation. Celebration to scandal. She wanted to clap back, fire off the words already forming in her mind, but she couldn't risk it. She wasn't naïve enough to think they wouldn't use it against her. She was already teetering on the edge of being blackballed. One wrong move, and she'd fall.

They were trying to figure Bu out. So far, they'd come up empty handed but she knew it was only a matter of time before they had his whole rap sheet on display for the world to judge him. The red flag that hung from his pocket had already been zoomed in on and America's sweetheart was now a fraud with a thing for bad boys. They didn't know Bu was actually more than that.

Her chest ached as she swallowed her frustration, pressing her lips together to keep from screaming.

The door finally opened, and Luther strolled in, unbothered, like he wasn't fifteen minutes late. He scanned the room, spotted her, and sauntered over... his pace infuriatingly slow.

Noodle's jaw clenched, but she didn't say anything...not yet.

"Sorry... got held up," Luther said casually as he slid into the seat across from her, not even bothering to offer an explanation. He flagged down a waiter for water, completely ignoring the tension radiating off her.

His nice dress shirt and slacks looked stupid. Even his caramel skin made her sick to her stomach.

"You're late," she said, her voice tight.

"And Bridgette's later," he shot back, leaning back in his chair like he had all the time in the world.

Noodle's foot tapped beneath the table, the motion too small to release the storm building inside her. "Did you talk to her?" she asked, forcing her voice to stay calm.

"Yeaaa," he said, dragging out the word. "She's on her way." His annoyingly, soft voice squeaked out.

Noodle let out a slow breath, her frustration simmering beneath the surface. "You could've texted me."

His gaze flicked to her buzzing phone, a smirk tugging at the corner of his mouth. "Looks like you've been busy anyway."

She didn't take the bait, didn't even look down at the device. She knew what was waiting for her there. Messages she didn't want to read and notifications she didn't want to see.

The door opened again, and this time it was Bridgette, rushing in with a harried expression, her bag slung over one shoulder. "Sorry, sorry," she said, sliding into the seat next to Luther. "Traffic was hell."

Noodle didn't respond. Her eyes flicked to Bridgette, then back to Luther. The air between them was thick.

Bridgette sighed, brushing her hair out of her face. "Alright, let's get to it."

Noodle sat up straighter, her pulse pounding. She wasn't sure what she was walking into, but she knew she had to keep it together... for now.

Noodle had ordered more shots, indulging alone. The two of them enjoyed glasses of wine showing her how different from Luther she really was.

Yes, she'd been taught business etiquette... she'd been primed on how to look happy and unbothered, yet she was everything but that. Deep down inside she was just a girl from the trailer parks of Lynn Beach born to a daddy who couldn't keep his hands to himself and a mother who sold her to Qamar for five digits.

Luther looked like he'd gone off to private school and had a two-parent household that was warm and overbearing. He didn't have to watch his big sister cry from doing God knows what for the rent money. Nah, Noodle didn't fit in with them. It was even clearer when Bridgette looked her in her face and told her, she needed to rethink whatever it was she had with Bu. He was a hoodlum that would only bring her down.

"I'll be in touch," Noodle said, standing from her chair. Even that was uncomfortable.

Luther stood too. "Let me walk you out," he offered while she shook her head. Her eyes red from the numerous shots she took to the head without eating anything.

"I have my security," she nudged her head to the table beside them where Fink and Ben had been sitting and listening.

Luther's eyes widened. "Oh..." he stuffed his hands in his pockets. He was so lame to her. "Well, give me a call when you get home."

Bridgette just sat there like she knew she wasn't going to hear from Noodle ever again.

Noodle only nodded at him, with a slightly sympathetic smile on her face. Ben and Fink wasted no time flanking her sides. They walked out the restaurant militant-like, their heads on the swivel as paparazzi swarmed her. They ushered her into the back of the truck. Her head slammed against the back of the headrest exhausted. For the first time, she picked up her phone, bypassing everything but his name. Clicking on it, she listened to it ring.

"Baby," Bu answered.

"Can you come over?"

"On my way."

They stayed on the phone a few seconds just listening to each other breathe before Noodle hung it up.

"I don't like her," Fink broke the silence in the car. "Bridgette," he specified.

Noodle huffed her eyes going to the moon roof. "Me neither."

17

"Aye, where you at?" Bu asked the person on the other end with the phone sitting on his shoulder, on speaker.

There was shuffling on the other end before Pimp's voice broke through. "Why, nigga?"

"Because I'm asking you where you at? Lunar in the studio but you ain't, so where you at, Princeton?"

Noodle snickered, slapping her hand over her mouth. She didn't want Pimp to know she was close enough to be in their business.

Pimp smacked his lips. "I'm grown and I don't have to be up under Lunar all the time."

"You right... but where you at?" Bu asked again, the annoyance evident in his voice. He seemed a little riled up since he showed up at her door with food. She didn't ask him what his problem was because she had her legs spread wide before she could think.

"You let that nigga rile you up but you bring that pussy to me?"

A tingling sensation washed over her as she thought about Bu's face between her legs, and his deep southern drawl in her ear making her feel so good. Now she lay in her bed naked with her head on his chest and one leg draped over him.

Bu didn't ask about her meeting. It was like he knew he wasn't going to like what she had to say. But Noodle would be lying if she didn't admit Bridgette's suggestion was ringing loud in her ear. It was a matter of how bad she wanted a music career.

"I'm with Bobby," Pimp muttered.

Bu kissed his teeth. "Yea, we gon' have to have a fuckin' talk, Princeton."

"You calling me the name my mama gave me don't scare me, Bethune," Pimp's words were low and slick.

Bu sat up, her head rolling off him. "I ain't never been the type of nigga to use words to scare another nigga... I'm all action. *You* know that better than anyone."

"Yea, whatever... let me go." Pimp ended the call without another word.

Noodle wanted to mind her business but she also wanted to peel back another layer of him. So instead of letting the after-glow of sex fill their space, she pushed the barrier. "You always so hard on him... why?"

Bu rolled his neck, probably working out all the kinks from the weird positions Noodle put him in when she tried to run from his tongue lashing. "What happened at your meeting?"

"Oh no, Bethune! You don't get to answer my question with a question. You go first then me." Noodle sat up, her perky little breasts bouncing, catching his eyes.

Bu licked his lips.

"Nope!" Her lips popped playfully, but she made no move to cover herself.

With Bu, she didn't need to. There was no shame, no hiding. She could be raw. Physically, emotionally - in every sense of the word. He'd unraveled her layers one by one, peeling back the guarded parts of her that even she didn't fully understand. With him, she was free. Free to be every messy, complicated, beautiful version of herself.

And to think Bridgette wanted her to let him go.

How? How could she even begin to untangle herself from the man who had embedded himself so deeply into her bloodstream? It wasn't just love... it was something primal... something she couldn't fight even if she wanted to.

This was that fifty-fifty love that scared the shit out of her. The kind that balanced you on a razor's edge between joy and destruction. The love Luna had talked about the other night. She'd laughed it off then, but now? Now she understood. She was so caught up in Bu that even the thought of life without him felt suffocating, like someone was pressing a pillow to her face, stealing her air.

It wasn't just physical even though the way he looked at her made her body hum. It was his presence... his essence. His soul had tangled itself with hers in a way that felt eternal, unshakable. It was magnetic, something she couldn't explain but felt in every breath, every beat of her heart.

No matter who else came along, no one could touch her like this. No one could own her the way Bu did, not just in her body but in the marrow of her being. He *knew* her... saw her... claimed her with his actions because they had yet to place a label on whatever it was they were doing and because of that, she was his. Entirely... irrevocably his.

Pushing his hand down over his weary eyes, Bu swallowed the fear of telling her the one thing that might make her run for the hills. Because even though his Noodle wasn't as green as she wanted to believe she was, she still had yet to experience the life he'd experienced.

"I killed for him," he sighed roughly, forcing the words out.

Noodle's mouth dropped, her eyes stretching wide because she knew she didn't hear what she just heard. Well, she heard it clearly but wasn't expecting him to reveal that. Like what was he even talking about? She knew Bu had gone down for gun possession... the whole world probably knew by now.

He continued, his head somewhere in the past. "That gun possession should've been murder because that's what I really did. Pimp had always been cool with who he was... didn't care if other people knew either. Then he liked a certain type of boy—"

"The down low kind?" Noodle whispered, staring off into the past with him. Her body heated thinking about it.

Bu nodded. "I told him that shit wasn't cool but he didn't listen. Bee always said people thought I was the problem child when it was really Pimp." A ghost of a smile peeked through his frustration as memories of his mama crossed his mind. "So, he kissed the boy when others were around. Of course, that bitch ass nigga wasn't with anyone knowing, even though he'd kissed Pimp a dozen times before... I know because I seen it myself. He was just a pussy ass little boy that liked to kiss my brother behind closed doors." Bu's face furrowed, pulling at Noodle more. She landed on top of him, anchoring him like he'd done so many times for her. She wrapped her arms around him, her tiny fingers digging into the waves on his head, coaxing his truth out of him. "You already know what a group of seventeen year old black boys did to him... even the nigga that had pledge his heart to him."

"So, you took care of it?"

He nodded, scared to look in her face. "Even after I promised him I wouldn't."

"The promise you broke?"

"Yea... but I ain't know it was going to go down like that. I was just going to beat his ass but seventeen year old boys from The Jig carried guns. He ain't know I was cut from the same cloth." He closed his eyes trying to hide from her judgement.

She kissed his eyelids in acceptance of his truth.

"So, karma came back around two years later. When I got pulled over riding dirty with an unregistered gun," he snorted out a laugh. "I had to take that chance because ol' boy's family had a price on my head."

"Maybe it wasn't karma though because it could've been worse, baby... maybe it was God slowing you down because you was moving too fast."

"Bee died while I was in there... I ain't get to see my mama in her last days. She was mad at me and I couldn't make it right when she was here, so I'm trying to do right now that she's gone."

"...and you are." She gripped his face. "I know Bee proud of you, baby... I'm proud of you. You have ownership in a record label and you still so humble."

He smirked because he didn't know she knew that.

Her head bobbed. "Yea I know." She smiled

His hands finally touched her. His fingers dug into her sides as his dick stirred, flicking against her pussy that was just as greedy. Noodle lifted her needy body up sinking down on him. His lips parted, a moan escaping.

Her head fell back when her ass hit his balls. "Bridgette told me if I want to take my career to the next level, I can't be with you," she crooned, her voice shaking from the slow stroke he gave her from the bottom.

His head fell back, his eyes closed. "Oh yea?"

"What you think about that?" she asked, still riding him nice and slow.

"I think if you have to ask then you know the answer. No one should be bigger than your dreams." His fingers dug deeper into her skin.

The pain was pleasurable. She gritted the back of her teeth, already close to the edge. "Don't talk me into circles, Bu."

"You deserve to be happy and if letting me go drives you to your destination, who am I to stop you? I ain't even good enough for you... our worlds don't mix, they collide like two trains on the wrong track." His pace picked up, fucking her from the bottom.

"And you deserve everything. The sun, the moon, the stars... the ground we walk on. Bu, you deserve all of it. I think you deserve more than anyone else I know." Her eyes glossed over, staring into his marred face. "God you are beautiful... your sons will make women weak in the knees."

Bu only stared at her, his pace stopping. The anger that had been sitting on his chest started to vanish. Years of pent of rage, gone just like that... because of a girl. It explained the unique thumping of his heart, but it didn't explain the war inside his head.

"I wish life hadn't ruined me so just maybe, I could love you, but if it's one thing I loathe is what love turns people into."

"What if I love you first?"

Her thumb smoothed across his brow. "I loved you the first day I saw you. When you came over to me, I saw a forever thing... I saw all the shit Aku talked about... the shit my sister lived... the pain I saw in Cynthia's eyes and Jackie's because she wanted Stacy to love her too."

"What else you see?"

"That no matter what anyone says, even my own mind..." she licked her lips, rocking her hips forward searching for the good feeling only he could give her. "...no matter how scared I am of loving you... I welcome it. I want to love you so good, baby. Just... just be patient with me because not even the war in my mind gon' make me come up off you. And Bridgette stringy hair ass can go to hell. I want to chase galaxies with you."

He kissed her so hard, her teeth scraped his lip. "And I'll love you until the galaxy dies," he declared, slow stroking her, melodically playing the perfect song to soothe her worrisome heart.

18

Noodle bobbed her head to the slow, hypnotic rhythm pulsing through the studio, the beat wrapping itself around her like a warm blanket. Pimp had the track on a low hum, just enough to let her thoughts simmer but not overwhelm them. She was deep in her zone, legs tucked under her, her pen moving across the page like it had a life of its own.

Her new notebook was already filling up. Half-finished verses spilling into fragmented choruses and random ideas scattered across the pages. To anyone else, it probably looked like a mess of scribbles and scratched-out lines. But to her, it was something else entirely. Each word, each line, was like layering flavors in a pot of hot gumbo on a cold winter night. Every piece building toward something richer, something fuller.

She bit her bottom lip, tapping her pen against the paper as she worked out a tricky rhyme. The croon of the track pushed her forward, pulling pieces of inspiration from deep in her chest. Flashes of Bu filled her brain, making her hand move even faster.

This was her magic, the place where nothing else mattered. No headlines, no judgement, no noise from the outside world... just her, the beat, and the art spilling out of her and Pimp. "What you thinking for this?" he asked, bumping her shoulder to pull her from her word-induced daydream.

"This melody feels sad."

Pimp nodded. "Okay, so what you got for it? You been sad before, let's put some words on it and make it feel like something people can relate to."

Noodle had officially signed to Lunar's label and she was trying to record as many songs as she could in hopes of having an ep to put out soon. It was imperative she capitalize on the buzz of her song with Lunar. He was already on his way to the top so riding his coattails could be beneficial.

"You scared of love? What that feel like?" Pimp tossed out a few questions to get her mind buzzing and her heart thumping.

Noodle tapped her pen on the paper, allowing his questions to linger between them. "Scared of love?" she repeated, letting the words roll around in her head. Her mind went to Bu, to every time she thought she had it figured out and every time she realized she didn't. But all those times weren't her times. Her brain looped the love of the women around her. Cynthia, Siasia, Jackie, Luna, Solar, and even Tiny... the love stories of every woman she'd encountered flashed through her mind because that was all she had to go off of.

"What it feels like?" she echoed softly to herself.

"Yea," Pimp pushed, getting up and walking to the board. He adjusted the levels on the board like he had more experience than he really did. "Like, when it's good... when it's bad... when it's gone." He glanced at her, his usually playful face now serious, like he knew exactly which buttons to press.

Maybe he did because Pimp had been around. He'd seen her being a shell of herself, seen her ignoring the eyes of men that vied for her attention. Then he saw her come alive when his brother walked into her life. So, just maybe he did understand that love had been the bane of her existence and was the rawest thing she could talk about and hopefully sing about.

Noodle exhaled sharply, leaning back in her chair as her

thoughts spiraled. "It feels... dangerous," she murmured, her hand on her beating chest.

"Dangerous how?" Pimp asked, his voice low and coaxing.

"Like you're walking on a tightrope over a fire pit... but the fall might be worth it. And when it's gone..." Her voice trailed off, the lump in her throat catching her words. She tapped the pen against her notebook rhythmically, trying to shake the emotions creeping in.

"When it's gone, what?"

"The fall might kill you but it'll be the greatest fall you ever experienced."

"Write that," Pimp said, his voice gentler now. He knew exactly how that fall felt. He was currently on a downward spiral praying Bobby caught him when it was all said and done. But this session wasn't about him, so he kept his feelings to himself.

Noodle's pen hit the page, her hand moving faster than her brain as she scribbled her thoughts down. The melody still played in the background, soft and haunting, and her words started to spill onto the paper.

"Walking on fire... but the fall feels right. Love's a gamble... until it burns you alive," she muttered— half-singing, half-writing.

"That's it!" Pimp said, his eyes lighting up. "You hear that? That's a hook right there. Simple but deep."

She smirked, shaking her head. "You think everything's a hook, Pimp."

It was true because everything she'd said during their last session, he'd felt was a good hook. He wasn't very objective and that made Noodle feel insecure about what she wrote. She needed criticism.

"That's because it is when you say it. Don't overthink it... just let it flow."

He stood, stepping over to the booth in the corner of the studio. "Run it back. I'mma loop this part," he said, nodding to the beat. "Get in there and lay it down rough... see how it sounds."

Noodle hesitated, staring at the notebook for a beat longer. Her chest tightened from the weight of everything, she was trying to prove, pressing down on her. Producers still weren't calling her back, and she'd signed to Lunar's label hoping it would open doors. But so far, it felt like she was still knocking, her knuckles bruised from trying.

"Get out of you head, baby," Pimp teased, trying to sound like his brother.

She narrowed her eyes at him, standing and grabbing her notebook. "You not funny," she rolled her eyes, wishing Bu was there with her, but he had his first landscaping job and couldn't make it.

Pimp only laughed. He tapped on a few knobs and buttons, returning the beat for her to start.

Sliding into the booth, Noodle adjusted the headphones on her head and closed her eyes. The beat swirled around her, pulling her back into her thoughts. This was her chance to prove she was better than KidVerse... to prove that she was something, someone, worth betting on.

The words came, shaky at first, but then stronger. As she sang about the dangers of love and the fire it left behind, she could literally feel it— the art spilling out of her, raw and real.

When she opened her eyes, Pimp stood staring through the glass in awe. She could've sworn she saw a tear roll down his face but it was gone just as fast as it came. With two thumbs up, he coached her on what to do next.

The studio felt so right. It didn't seem to scare her anymore. She was ready to fully embrace her purpose, Noodle could finally say she was ready. With each word she sang, doubt rolled out of her mind and heart. It was her time and no one was going to take that from her.

When she stepped out, she saw Pimp with the phone to his ear. His face was balled up and serious as he listened to whoever

was on the other end. Finally he spoke. "Nah, I'm in the studio…
I got another session with someone after this. Let me see if I can
push it back… alright," he said before hanging up.

"Everything good?" Noodle asked, inching closer to him.

"Bu said the one man he hired didn't show up and Devin's
yard too big to do alone or he gon' be there all night," he huffed.
"I gotta a session with this new rap girl but… let me see if I can
cancel her shit."

"No!" Noodle stopped him. She knew she had to be out of
her mind for what she was about to say. "I'll go."

Pimp hollered, grabbing his stomach from the laughter.

She cocked her head to the side, annoyed. "I'm for real… I'll
go help him. I mean it's just mowing the lawn. It can't be that
hard."

"Yea, I need to cancel just so I can see you out there sweating
and crying."

"Pimp, please." Noodle mushed his face. She pulled out her
phone to dial Fink who was outside in the car with Ben.

"Yea, Noodle?" Fink answered.

"Ummm," she chewed her lip. "Do you know where I can
buy a riding lawnmower for like now?"

Fink snickered. "I mean, with money you can get anything
when you want it. What's up?"

Noodle looked over to Pimp who still had a goofy look on his
face and tears in his eyes. "You got the address?"

"Yea…" he said before rattling it off for Noodle to give to
Fink.

She ended the call when Fink told her he would call up a few
businesses to have it delivered before she got there.

"You do whatever you do to this song then go to your session
and let me go be superwoman to my superman." She winked
before strutting out the studio.

———

Bu swiped a hand across his damp forehead, flicking away beads of sweat before they could roll into his eyes. His glasses slipped again, threatening to slide right off his slick nose. With an annoyed grunt, he pushed them back up, only for them to fall again within seconds. It wasn't even *hot* not technically. But the January sun was relentless, beaming down on him, making it feel like summer was around the corner.

Devin was out of town and left him clear details and access to his home. Now Bu stood in the middle of five acres of lush grass and way too many hills. It made Bu feel both inspired and overwhelmed. The space was massive and the pressure to execute felt heavier than the sun beating down on him.

The truth was, he needed this shit to work.

Starting Bumble Bee Landscaping hadn't been the hard part. The initial capital had been easy. Almost laughably so, considering how much his drug money had grown during his time away. But finding reliable people was proving to be the real hurdle.

Back in Sapphire City, it had been one thing, but even here in Madison Heights, good help was harder to come by than he'd expected.

Some might've wondered why he even wanted this. Like why bother with a landscaping business when he already had a stake in Lunar's label? He could've stayed in the music game, riding the wave of Lunar's meteoric rise, helping get more talent because he had a good ear for music, but that wasn't him. It never had been. Lunar's world was too messy, and Bu had always preferred structure, order, something he could build with his own hands.

Bumble Bee Landscaping had been his dream long before he'd known how deep his pockets really were. Back when the only thing he had were ideas and enough hustle to back them up. Even as a kid, he'd loved the simplicity of working outside, the satisfaction of seeing something grow under his care. It was about more than cutting grass and planting flowers. it was about transforming spaces, making them something people could be proud of.

In prison, he had no issue with signing up to tend to the little greenery they had. It was an escape, even when Bee put that soccer ball in his hands to keep his mind off the streets.

Now, standing on Devin's property, Bu felt good even knowing he would be out there until well into the night without help. He didn't mind though. This was the crawling phase no one wanted to talk about. It was the part of the story the entrepreneurs no longer talked about when they sold you expensive tickets to their seminar that was a bunch of nothing. The crawling phase was where God showed you who he was…when he showed you why he was the alpha and omega, 'cause if your faith in him waivered slightly, you could fold. Instead, you had to face each day by placing one foot in front of the other with Him at the forefront of your mind and heart, he would see you through.

Bee had instilled that in him and Bu felt she was still helping God guide him. She loved her boys too much to be too hands off. He laughed to himself thinking about her.

Bu adjusted his gloves, wiped his forehead one last time, and set his sights on the task ahead. This wasn't just about landscaping. This was about proving to himself that he could thrive on his own terms.

Just as he settled into shaping the hedges, he heard another mower in the distance. Devin's house had neighbors but they weren't that close with the way the roads curved and dipped. The acres each home sat on made it difficult for you to run over quickly to borrow a cup of sugar.

He squinted, seeing the ride on lawn mower coming up the hill with a black SUV trailing behind it. Bu tilted his head slightly when the mower seemed to be swerving. Thankfully, Devin's home was the last on the street and there was no traffic coming that way.

Sand colored boney arms wailed in the distance. "Bethune!"

Bu's face split at the sight before him. "This girl crazy," he laughed to himself, but his heart did that hopscotch thing it did whenever he thought about her.

"Come help me get off," Noodle yelled when she got as close as she could without driving it on the grass.

Bu doubled over, clutching his stomach as laughter rolled out of him. Ben leaned out the truck window, his phone held steady, recording every second of the scene before him. Fink also had tears in his eyes, holding onto the steering wheel cracking the hell up. Noodle, sat perched on the shiny new lawnmower, gripping the steering wheel like she was in a street race. Her face was a mixture of confusion, concentration, and determination as the machine started creeping up the hill in jerky starts and stop.

"Noodle, you gonna flip it over!" Ben hollered, wiping tears from his eyes.

Noodle shot him a bird. "Mind your business!" she yelled back, focused on trying not to run into anything.

After a quick Google search by Fink and some hollered instructions, Noodle finally figured out how to put the mower in drive. It lurched forward with a loud sputter, and she had let out a laugh, hyped that she got it started. Now that she'd made it to Bu, she really felt accomplished.

Bu shook his head, still laughing as he jogged over to her. By the time she made it to the top, he was already reaching for her. He plucked her off the mower like she weighed nothing, pulling her into his arms.

Sweat dampened his shirt, sticking to her clothes, but she didn't care.

"What you doing here?" he asked, his voice low in her ear, his breath warm against her cheek.

"I came to help, duh," she replied, batting her lashes at him dramatically, knowing he was a sucker for it.

Bu smirked. "You don't even know how to drive, baby."

"Okay, and?" she shot back, feigning offense. "You don't need a license to drive a lawnmower."

"But it don't hurt to know how to drive," he teased, his voice laced with amusement.

Noodle tilted her chin up, challenging him with a playful glint in her eye. "Then teach me, cause I ain't leaving until you done. How is this gonna work if you the only one making dreams come true?"

Her words hit him like a brick, cutting through the humor and landing somewhere deep in his chest. He swallowed hard, his smirk fading as he looked at her. She always had a way of reminding him why he was wrapped around her finger.

Instead of responding, he turned his attention back to the mower, his voice softer now. "Where you get that from, anyway?"

"I bought it," she said matter-of-factly, her heart-shaped face twisting into an expression of pride. Her lips pursed just slightly as she held her head high.

Bu blinked at her, stunned for a moment, before shaking his head in disbelief. "So, you trickin' too now?" he asked, a grin tugging at the corners of his mouth.

"Anything for my Bu," she sang, throwing her arms around his neck.

He kissed her cheek, then her nose, pulling her closer. "You something else, you know that?"

"And you love it," she said, dreamily.

"I love you, baby," he doubled down, loving the way he sounded saying it… the way it made him feel… the way loving her made him feel. He loved it all… *he loved her.*

Bu couldn't argue with that.

He set her back down, laughing as she tried to swipe at the sweat on her clothes.

"Eww," Noodle teased, knowing damn well she didn't mind his sweat on her.

"Alright then, let's see if you're serious. Come on, partner, let's make these dreams come true."

19

"You done lost your mind, baby," Bu said as they sat out on her balcony. His place still wasn't fully furnished, so they still spent a lot of their time at her condo. That and Lunar and Pimp were at his crashing while Aku was always in and out at hers.

His finger swiped across the newest tattoo on her thigh. Proverbs 4:23— 'Above all else, guard your heart, for everything you do flows from it.' In red ink it looked like it belonged and popped against her tanned skin from being in the sun all day with him three days ago.

His heart swelled, he couldn't believe she had gotten a tattoo to match the one on his thigh. His baby was just coming out of her shell more and more showing who she really was— a boughetto girl from the trailer park in Lynn Beach once afraid of love.

A child star stepping into her womanhood under the scope of the world.

His eyes went to the sleeve tattoo she started the same day. Noodle thought she would be able to get the whole thing finished but the pain and the intricate details of it said otherwise.

"You got me out here loving red, ready to throw up bs...

show me how you do that lil handshake thingy." Noodle forced her body between him and the railing.

He tucked her curly tresses behind her ear. "Nah, baby. Leave all that to me. When they see you, they see me so they know what type of time we on."

"How they see you?"

"Real niggas can look at a girl and tell she belongs to someone. It's in their pores, their smile, their eyes... I see all that when I look at you. That lets me know I did right by you."

"You do great by me." Noodle whispered, loving the feel of being wrapped up in his arms. "I feel like I'm swimming when I'm with you."

Bu placed a gentle kiss on her forehead. "You make my dick jump when you talk like that... my heart hopscotch."

"Oh, that's a line... let me find out you a songwriter."

"I'll be whatever you need me to be."

"Mine?" her voice dipped.

"All yours, baby."

A comfortable silence filled them as the wind brushed across their skin. Southern Cali was expected to get some rain. No one believed it, but the wind felt good even if the clouds didn't open up.

The sun had set but the neighborhood was still alive. People walked their dogs and friends cackled on their way to wherever they were going.

Her syrupy voice cut through the silence. "I wonder what that's like..." she stared at the people below her.

"What what's like?" Bu asked, his beard tickling her neck.

"Walking to the neighborhood restaurant to catch a drink and eat some food," she spoke dreamily.

Her life wasn't spontaneous. She had to plan out everything and always had to have security with her. She loved Fink and Ben but she wished she could go places without having them stalking behind her.

Bu huffed. "What you want me to do with that baby?"

"Nothing… I'm just talking," she sighed.

Bu spun her around to face him. Her back dipped on the cool railing making those pesky butterflies do crazy things in her belly again. "If you tell me some shit you ain't get to do…some shit you never got to feel, it becomes my mission in life to give you that."

She gulped. "But sometimes, I'm just talking."

"But I'm always listening." His dark eyes twinkled from the glare of his glasses. That red hat creating a stir between her legs. "Get dressed, let's hit the town, baby." His face was dangerously close to hers, she could smell the weed on his breath.

"O— okay," she stammered, breaking out of his embrace to do what he told her to do. Her body fell back into him when he yanked her arm.

His soft lips pressed into hers, making her wanna say fuck that night on the town. "I needed that… now go." He released her making sure to tap her ass on her way in. "Don't take all day either," he called out behind her.

———

The wind was still wild, blowing Noodle's hair and pressing her dress against her body, as she walked the sidewalk in pure bliss. Each rain scented gust carried a sense of freedom she'd dreamed about as a little girl in the trailer park, staring out her bedroom window at a world she longed to reach.

Bu held her hand firmly, his presence steady against the chaos of the wind. He kept her on the inside of the sidewalk, shielding her from the street like it was second nature. Fink and Ben trailed behind them, just far enough to make her feel like a regular girl and not someone who needed protection. It was how they typically operated since Bu always kept something cold and steel on his waist.

The city moved around them, but all Noodle could focus on was the moment. They were on their way to a local eatery she'd been dying to try, and her excitement bubbled over keeping a smile on her face.

"You think we should get a dog?" she asked, stopping to crouch as a fluffy white dog sniffed her leg before rubbing its head against her. She cooed softly before scratching behind its ears.

Bu nodded without hesitation. "If you want a dog, we'll get a dog."

"But do *you* want a dog?" She straightened, brushing the windblown strands of hair from her face and tilting her head to look at him. "You give me what I want, but what do you want, Bu?"

He glanced over at her, his dark eyes steady, taking in just how pretty she was. "I'm just happy to be here, baby. I'm supposed to be serving a life sentence or in a grave."

Her throat tightened, and she swallowed hard, her voice going low. "Teach me how to love you the way you want to be loved. This can't be all about me. Your heart beats just like mine, baby." She deepened her voice, trying to mimic the way he said *baby* to her all the time, hoping it worked the same magic on him that it did her.

A smirk played on his lips, one side curling up like he couldn't help himself. "The fact you even acknowledged my need for love is enough. You loving me enough... probably more than I deserve."

"But I wanna love you more," she pressed, stepping closer to him. "I want you to feel the way you make me feel." Her voice dipped as she began to sing, crooning Sabrina Claudio's *Teach Me* under her breath. "I wanna know if you feel this too... if you don't, I can't be in love with you."

She stretched her arms out as if she were on stage, spinning on her toes with a natural confidence that felt straight out of a sultry black love movie. Her voice floated in the air, smooth and soulful, drawing the attention of everyone around them.

Heads turned, and when people realized who she was, their

expressions shifted, and their eyes widened like they had stumbled upon a secret concert in the middle of the street.

Bu watched her twirl and sing, his hand still in hers, his smirk softening. There was no doubt in his mind that Noodle was truly one of a kind, special like...like Sunday mornings... like winning big in a dice game. She was undoubtedly the prize because he'd won big.

When she stopped, catching her breath and grinning, he tugged her close, his voice low and steady as he said, "You keep loving me like this, I'm never letting you go."

Her smile widened, and for a moment, they were alone drifting into nothing. And it wasn't scary because nowhere with him was better than anywhere with anybody else. The sea or the sky, Noodle didn't mind because Bu made everything feel safe, like he had her no matter what.

They continued their walk, holding hands only stopping if she was recognized. Bu was observant and noticed she had been noticed by more people who respected her space. Some people could tell she was trying to have a private moment and only smiled while others didn't understand that celebrities were humans too.

When they made it to the restaurant, Bu ordered a glass of whisky while Noodle tossed back a few shots. He didn't mind because she would sober up on the walk back to the house. That and he'd never be able to tell her no anyway, so he let her enjoy her night, ordering everything on the menu.

"I gotta make a stop in Sapphire City soon. Gotta check on the house and shit," Bu revealed, after swallowing a handful of truffle fries.

Noodle sucked the juice from her lime. "Are you coming to Javen's retirement party in Emerald City?"

"I wasn't invited... I don't really know them like that. They were older than me and had moved up in life before I could fully understand. I know Qamar because he came back more than them in the beginning and Bee wanted me to kick a ball just like him," Bu laughed, thinking about the many run ins he had with Qamar where he'd always toss him a couple dollars.

"You coming with me," she shrugged because it wasn't a big deal.

Javen and Luna could be intimidating because of the highs they had reached, but Luna was the sweetest girl's girl she ever met and Javen had always been so laid back only showing emotions with his wife, kids, and extended family.

Bu only nodded, his expression steady, but deep down he knew if she wanted him to do something, he was doing it without a second thought. There wasn't any room for hesitation when it came to her. It was all the shit Bee had warned him about, all those late-night conversations about love, loyalty, and finding the one who shifts your whole world without trying.

In those moments, Bee was just a woman deprived of love. It wasn't noticeable back then but now, Bu was able to see his mama's heart for what it was.

'One day you're gonna meet a woman who moves your soul, not just your body. And when that happens, you better be ready to handle her the right way.' Bee's southern voice rang in his ears.

At the time, Bu hadn't thought much of it. Back then, his world didn't leave much room for daydreams about love. But now, with Noodle, he understood exactly what Bee meant. She was that girl for him. The one who made his heart do a little tootsie roll in his chest every time she looked at him, and loving her didn't take effort. It wasn't complicated or forced. It came as naturally as breathing, like she'd been designed just for him.

If every day could be like this, simple and easy, then life would finally feel like it was worth all the hard times he'd been through. But Bu knew better than to believe it would stay this way. God didn't work like that. God didn't hand you blessings without also testing your strength. He'd make sure to drag you through the fire, letting the flames lick at your skin until you bore the battle scars that would forever remind you where you been.

And the scars weren't just for memory's sake. They were lessons etched into your soul. The real lesson wasn't just remembering that God brought you through. It was understanding *what* He brought you through. Because in the midst of all the chaos, when the walls feel like they're closing in and it seems like everything is out of your control, it's easy to lose sight of Him. It's easy to forget that you've already been here, already fought through, already come out stronger on the other side.

Bu's eyes found hers. Noodle smiled back like she'd been as much in his head as she been in his heart.

God didn't just give him a second chance at life. He gave him *her*, and Bu wasn't about to waste it because the lesson wasn't just about survival, it was about thriving in spite of it all.

Bu paid the tab and they made their way out the restaurant. Noodle's eyes were glossed over and every time she hiccupped, the scent of liquor breezed out. Even her fingers danced while Bu tried to hold her hand.

Fink shook his head laughing. The difference in Noodle before and after Bu were night and day. He loved to see the love that washed over her in everything she did now. The studio was easier for her now. He knew her life seemed more colorful than ever before.

As they all fell into small talk and laughing at Noodle who kept trying to do silly little dances, everyone's phone started going off.

Ben pulled his phone out first, stopping in his tracks when he saw what was blowing up his notifications. He stopped walking, his posture stiffening as he stared at his screen. His phone began ringing almost immediately.

Noodle's phone buzzed again, pulling her attention. She glanced down, still smiling faintly, but her face froze the second her eyes landed on the screen.

Bu looked over to Ben with questioning eyes. When Ben shook his head, Bu tried to grab her phone from her hand but he was too late.

"Wh—wait…" she stammered, tilting her head like the angle might change what she was seeing. She tapped the screen, scrolling, her fingers shaking. "This can't… this ain't right. No, no, no…" Her voice wavered, and she backed up a step as if distance could shield her from the flood of images and words.

"Noodle, gimme the phone," Bu said, stepping forward when he saw the panic rising in her eyes.

"Wh— what is this?" Her voice broke as she clutched the phone tighter. Her chest rose and fell with short, shallow breaths. "This can't be real. Tell me this ain't real!" she yelled.

"Baby." He reached for her, but she pulled away, her feet stumbling backward until she hit the edge of the sidewalk.

Her knees buckled as the full weight of the situation hit her. She fell, landing hard on the cold concrete, her phone slipping from her hands to the ground. She stared ahead, her eyes wide, but she couldn't see anything but the replay of the video on her phone. Her breathing turned into panicked gasps.

"Why would they do this?!" she cried, her voice rising, cracking under the strain. Her hands flew to her face, trembling as she tried to cover the tears streaming down her reddening cheeks.

Bu crouched down in front of her, his broad frame shielding her from prying eyes. "Noodle, look at me. Baby, look at me." His rough hands found her face.

She didn't respond, her cries growing louder as her body shook.

Gently wrapping his hands around her wrists, he pulled them away from her face. "Breathe… you gotta breathe, baby."

Her eyes flicked to his, filled wild and glossy with tears, her lips trembling. uncontrollably. "They're lying," she choked out, her voice barely above a whisper. "They're lying, Bu. I didn't do what they're saying. I swear—

"I know you didn't," he said firmly, cutting her off. "I know, baby." His dark eyes grew cold, with murderous thoughts.

As if reality just hit her, Noodle's face broke even more. "I wanna go... take me somewhere... I just wanna get outta here."

Listening to her pain, sliced Bu deep. She was unraveling and rightfully so. His trigger finger itched, but what KidVerse did couldn't be handled in the way he knew how to handle things. This was bigger than him and that reality didn't make him feel any better. This was what his heart hadn't prepared him for. How could he protect and seek revenge for his baby— the girl that held his heart in her hands when the enemy didn't run the streets or carry a flag?

20

Noodle sat on the edge of the couch, her hand trembling while her phone vibrated as she stared at the trending hashtag, #JacoryExposed. Her heart pounded like it was trying to escape her chest and she could barely breathe. The tears had yet to stop.

How could she stop crying when the one thing she vowed to take to the grave stared her back in the face. The nasty, vile video didn't just stare her in the face, it laughed at her while pointing, adding more cuts to her already raw flesh.

"They really hate me... but why?" she whispered, scrolling through the hateful comments.

Bu snatched the phone from her hands, tossing it onto the table. They were on their way to her condo when they saw the swarm of cameras waiting. Thinking quickly, he ducked off to the side of a building and ordered a rideshare. Now they were tucked away at his beach house. "Stop reading that shit!" He slid his hand down his face. "They don't know shit."

She sighed, running a hand through her curls. Her face was crimson and had the situation not been so bad, Bu would've commented on how cute her nose was. "It ain't about what they know. It's what they think they know. That video..." her voice cracked, and she stood, pacing the living room. "It makes me look like I was... like I wanted it."

Bu leaned forward, resting his elbows on his knees. "Talk to me, baby. What happened because I know what I see, but I also know what I know."

Noodle stopped pacing, her arms crossed tightly over her chest like she was holding herself together. "I was eighteen, feeling closer to be grown... thinking I could handle anything." She stared into the distance. "That party... I shouldn't've been there. It was all industry people— older men with big titles. I didn't know anybody but wanted to be seen." She hesitated, glancing at him.

Bu's gaze was steady, his tone calm but firm. "Keep going."

She nodded, taking a deep breath. "That man, Jordan... he was a casting director at KidVerse. Big name, had all these girls around him. He kept calling me 'baby girl' all night, talkin' slick 'bout how he could help me out. I wasn't thinking anything of it until he cornered me in the back room."

Bu's jaw tightened and his leg bounced. That itch in his index finger started up again, but he stayed silent and let her finish.

"He tried to kiss me, Bu," she said, her voice shaking. "The video doesn't show it, but I pushed him off me. I cussed him out and left. I never spoke to him again, but now they're out here actin' like I... like I was down for it." Her eyes filled with tears she refused to let fall anymore.

She didn't understand how a company that was pivotal in her journey of growing up could do something so low. And for what? Were they that upset about Noodle's fame picking back up?

It seemed every time she was pictured out living her life, they came up with something to tear her down. It didn't make sense to her. Maybe it wasn't for her to understand, but it hurt like hell. Now, her family was blowing up her phone ready to ride at dawn and burn the whole world down for her. It was all too much, when all Noodle wanted to do was make good music and be happy.

"I'm drowning," she tugged at the collar of her dress. It wasn't tight before but now, she couldn't breathe. " I—I can't breathe!" Noodle panicked.

Bu stood, closing the distance between them in two strides. "Look at me, baby... you gotta calm down. Fink!" he yelled.

Rushing into the living room that now housed one leather couch, Fink directed Ben to get her a cup of water. Noodle was hyperventilating. He'd seen her do it before when work and life got too overwhelming for her.

"Here," Ben pushed the shot glass up to her lip.

"Really?!" Bu looked him upside his head.

"Man, this all that's in there," Ben defended himself, feeding Noodle little sips of water.

Fink rubbed her back. "Take deep breaths, Noodle... you gotta calm down."

After a few minutes of deep inhales and slow exhales, Noodle's eyes crawled over to Bu, who hadn't taken his eyes off her yet. She could feel his blood boiling and hated that this might've been a trigger for him. It wasn't the same, but she knew his mind started working like it did when Pimp had his incident. "Com'ere, baby." She patted the spot beside her.

Reluctantly, Bu hiked his jeans up, before stalking over to the couch.

Noodle crawled into his lap, her soft body melting into his from the heat that radiated off him. "I don't know what's going through this beautiful mind of yours... I mean I think I do because for some strange reason, I feel like I'm in there with you... maybe I am." She relaxed her shoulders. "I know I am," she clarified, "because I am. I know what you wanna do but we ain't doing that. We're doing this the right way."

"Hmph," Bu grunted.

She removed his hat, sitting it on her head. Watching the range of emotions play on his face, she remembered just how bad that video was, coupled with the statement. Tears rolled down her face again. Noodle buried her face in his neck and cried hard.

"That ain't on you," he said firmly. "You hear me? That's on *him*. And them muthafuckas at KidVerse? They gonna regret tryna play with your name." Bu tapped her chin, turning her face towards him. "Remember, I said when people see you, they gon' see me? They gotta see me, baby."

Her phone trilled on the table. Looking over at it, Jackie's name flashed across the screen. "Pass me my phone." She held her hand out where Fink placed it. "Ma," she sniffled.

———

Bu had never been to Lynn Beach. After catching a redeye, they touched down at the airport a little after four in the morning. Noodle slept most of the flight, clinging to his side as she sniffled in her dreams. He hated not being able to fix it all. He had a mind to say fuck what she was talking about and handle the situation the only way he knew how.

The rideshare pulled up to a nice home with rose bushes nestled in the front yard. The weather was cool but not cold and in the driveway sat a Benz. Bu looked over at Noodle who only grinned.

"You didn't think I took care of Jackie?"

"Oh, she's back to Jackie now?" Bu laughed. "You something else."

Noodle waited for the driver to open the door before she got out. Still in her dress, she stretched her arms out, rolling her neck. She had an eventful day and he could see the weariness in her eyes.

They walked up the sidewalk to the front porch where the light flickered. Noodle didn't even get a chance to knock before the door was snatched open.

Jackie pulled Noodle into her arms and Noodle broke down.

"Oh, Jacory," Jackie squeezed her tightly, looking like the older version of his Noodle.

Bu stood back, allowing them to cry in each other's arms. His heart swelled, thinking about running into Bee's arms. He wished he was able to fall into her when he walked out the prison gates. His eyes misted, knowing no matter how much Noodle wanted to pretend she didn't care, it was clear she needed a mama... needed her mama.

"Oh Jackie, this is my boyfriend, Bu," Noodle finally gathered herself enough to make the introduction. Saying boyfriend felt weird because he was more than that. Bu was her soulmate. The protector of her heart. He knew what she needed before she could open her mouth to even ask.

Bu removed his hat, extending his hand. "Nice to meet you."

"I'm a hugger, Bu." Jackie wrapped her arms around him.

Like Noodle, he melted into her. He didn't know how much he needed a motherly hug until he felt her. Jackie felt like Noodle.

"Come on, let's get in the house, it's already late." Jackie led them inside.

It was clean, but what did Bu expect? Maybe he didn't expect anything, because Noodle barely talked about her mother. It smelled like coconut. Again, he should've expected that too. The house was mid-sized with a mix of traditional and modern furniture. There were pictures of Noodle plastered above the fireplace in what looked like the *don't sit in here* room. He chuckled under his breath, thinking about Bee wanting a house like this. His mama talked about hitting the lottery to be able to afford it. Now, he could've bought her one— would've bought his mama everything her heart desired hoping to make up for her struggle.

"Y'all hungry? Thirsty?" Jackie asked, running her hands down her pajama pants. She was nervous.

Her own child made her nervous.

"Just tired," Noodle ran her fingers through her hair. She was just as nervous.

She bought Jackie the house three years ago and this was only her second time being there. So much had changed. It was a brand new home when she gave her mama the keys. There was no furniture and Jackie declined every attempt she made to pay to have it furnished. Noodle also had to fight her about the brand new car in the driveway. For Noodle, it didn't matter if their relationship was strained, she was going to take care of the woman that birthed her. Even if she loved a man so much she handed her only baby off to him to raise with the next woman.

"Well, I got the guest room ready for you. I even sat a little nightgown in there for you. Let me know if you need anything. Good night, baby."

"Good night."

"Night," Bu smiled.

———

Bu sat on the edge of the bed with his head in his hands. The situation with KidVerse had a knot in his chest that tightened with every passing hour. The video they posted wasn't just a violation of Noodle's privacy. It was an attack. A calculated move to humiliate her. His instinct was to handle Jordan the way he'd handled problems his whole life. But he promised Noodle he wouldn't go that route, and the last time he broke a promise it cost him everything.

His phone rung beside him. Glancing down, he saw it was the attorney finally returning his call. He knew he was on a different time zone but as one of the best attorneys in Cali, Bu expected him to be available all times of the day. Bu had to damn near cuss the answering service out when they tried to brush him off. Yet, like all things, money talked.

With a heavy sigh, he answered the phone, pressing it to his ear.

"Mr. Bennett," the voice on the other end said, brisk but professional.

"Yea?" Bu's eyes darted over to Noodle when she stirred in her sleep. He wondered what she was dreaming about and if he was there to protect her from it.

"Mr. Bennett?"

Bu pinched his eyes tight. "I'm here."

"Oh, okay. Well, this is Strickland, and I was woken up out of my sleep about an issue you felt needed to be started right away." Bu could hear the sleep in Strickland's voice, making him wonder had the nigga even brushed his teeth before he called. It didn't really matter, since Bu couldn't smell it over the phone. His mind was just all over the place overthinking and underthinking shit.

Bu rubbed his eye. "Yea."

Strickland sighed, probably annoyed with the short answers. From what he could tell, Bu wasn't having a dire emergency like he'd told the answering service. "I reviewed the details you gave my answering service, about the case against KidVerse."

"Yea, so what you thinking?" Bu didn't have time for small talk. He needed to know if he was going to have to continue his search for a good lawyer.

"I'm thinking I can help, but this is going to be expensive, Mr. Bennett."

Bu's face soured. "Throw a number at me."

"It's not going to be easy, going up against a corporation of that size."

Bu clenched his jaw, his patience thinning. "I didn't call you for easy. I called you to win…what's the number?"

Strickland hesitated. "Understood. But to even begin, we'll need a retainer. For something of this magnitude, given the resources KidVerse has at their disposal, the retainer will be $250,000."

"Quarter of a mil?" Bu inhaled sharply.

"Yes, Mr. Bennett. Cases like this require extensive research, multiple filings, and the ability to counter a team of high-powered corporate attorneys. We're talking about a company with billions in revenue and a strong legal team. If we don't prepare thoroughly, they'll bury us before we even get to court."

Bu let the number roll over in his mind, his chest tightening. "Fine," he conceded, his voice rough. "You'll have it. Just make sure you do what you said... win."

"Of course," Strickland replied. "I'll send over the paperwork to get started."

Bu ended the call, tossing the phone onto the bed like it burned his hand. He had the money, so it wasn't about that. But it felt like throwing cash at a problem that couldn't be resolved, at least not in the way he wanted to solve it. A quarter of a million dollars wouldn't ease the ache in his chest or erase the memory of how broken Noodle looked since that video dropped. However, taking them for all they were worth and humiliating them on a public platform would make him feel better. Waving his red flag would be even better.

He looked over at Noodle one last time. She looked tormented but still beautiful. The tip of her nose was still red from crying all night. His eyes scanned down her body, observing her one leg kicked from under the cover, Bu smiled at the red ink on her thigh. His baby had been through so much, but you couldn't tell by looking at her.

With his mind churning, Bu headed to the kitchen. His body moved on autopilot. Pulling open the cabinet, he scanned the shelves for something that would numb the heaviness inside him and he was really hungry. The food from the eatery in Madison Heights was long gone.

As he reached for a bottle, Jackie's voice came from behind him. "Looking for something strong, huh?"

Bu looked at her, his dark eyes blank. Jackie leaned against the doorframe, her arms crossed, watching him with a knowing look.

"Rough morning?" she asked, stepping into the kitchen.

His head darted towards the window off to the side of the eat-in dining room. The sun had started to wake up the sky.

"Something like that," Bu muttered, sitting the bottle down without opening it.

Jackie came closer, her eyes soft with concern. "You wanna talk about it?"

Bu hesitated. He wasn't the type to open up, especially not to someone he barely knew. But Jackie was Noodle's mother, and there was a quiet strength in her presence that reminded him of his own mama— a story worthy of listening to because black women told the best stories tangled with life lessons.

"I been calling around all morning trying to find a lawyer to take this case," he revealed. "Found one, but it's gonna cost a quarter of a million just to get started. Money's not the problem, though." He paused, his voice thickening.

Her lips pursed, knowingly. "Red hat... you ain't used to fixing things this way, huh?"

Jackie had lived a life before. She knew men like Bu and there was no judgement in her words. She understood because justice for black people was hardly ever acquired in a courtroom. How, when the system had never been set up for us to win?

Bu's lip curled, his eyes amused. "I don't know what you talkin' 'bout."

Jackie cackled. "Oh okay, Mr. Bu."

Pulling out a chair, she gestured for him to sit down. Bu didn't hesitate, as he took the seat across from her.

"She's the best parts of this fucked up world, you know," he rasped after a long pause. "Your daughter... she's got this light in her, but she don't see it." Bu stopped talking, raking his hand over his tired face. "She's terrified of life...and love, like it's always trying to take her down. And it's not her fault— it's the hand she was dealt. But she's stronger than she thinks... stronger than anyone I've ever met."

Jackie's eyes softened, her hands folded on the table. "She doesn't think she's strong?"

Bu shook his head. "She thinks she's just surviving. But she's been through hell, and she's still standing... that's strength." He looked down, his voice growing quieter. "She thinks I saved her, but the truth is, she saved me too. I ran into her on accident, but I fell in love with her on purpose."

Jackie swallowed hard, her eyes glistening. "She's lucky to have you," she said softly.

Bu shook his head. "Nah. I'm the lucky one."

Jackie reached up, dabbing at her eyes with the corner of her sleeve. "I wish I'd been lucky enough to find a love like that," she said, her voice trembling.

Bu leaned back in his chair, his gaze drifting to the window. "My mama used to say love ain't about finding someone perfect. It's about finding someone who makes you better, someone who makes you want to be better… I don't think that only applies to a spouse." He looked back at Jackie. "I think it can come from our children too."

"Your mama sounds like she was a wise woman." Jackie smiled faintly, her tears spilling over.

"She was," Bu agreed. "I wish she was here. She always knew what to say, how to keep me grounded. I feel like I'm flying blind half the time, trying to figure out how to be good enough for Noodle."

Jackie reached across the table, resting her hand over his. "You already are," she said firmly. "You love her. That's more than enough."

Bu looked at her, the heaviness in his chest easing a little. He squeezed her hand before standing. "Thanks, Jackie, I needed that."

Jackie smiled, watching him as he left the kitchen. She dabbed at her face wiping the tears that never seemed to end when it came to Jacory. Talking to Bu gave her the courage she would need to finally break the ice with her one and only baby. Jacory was all she had and she wanted to cherish their time together, hoping to create lasting memories. But first, Jackie had to rip the band aid off.

21

Noodle spent the next week wrapped in a bubble, shielding herself from the chaos that had upended her life. In Jackie's house, she found a kind of uneasy solace. The college coastal town was quiet and far removed from the flashes of cameras and relentless questions. For the first time in what felt like forever, she had silenced the world by turning off her phone. No calls... no texts... no updates.

Bu, had become her shield, anchoring her to the shit that mattered. He managed the details she couldn't face— food, necessities, even the calls from Siasia. Fink and Ben, once they'd arrived a day after her had stepped in too, keeping her family in the loop enough to reassure them that she was safe, without revealing where she was. Noodle appreciated it, but guilt gnawed at her because Siasia didn't deserve the silence, not after all she'd done for her.

The guilt didn't outweigh her exhaustion, though. Noodle had buried herself under the covers, forming a cocoon where she could breathe without expectation. *Her happy den.* The dim light filtering through the curtains didn't reach her, and the city outside was a muffled hum beneath her thoughts

Bu had left early that morning to stock up on shit they needed because they left Madison Heights in a hurry, with nothing but the clothes on their backs. He kissed her on the forehead before he left, murmuring something reassuring, but she barely registered his words because she felt him. She was always in his head like that.

He mentioned flying to Sapphire City later in the week to handle business, but even that felt distant. The only thing Noodle knew for certain was that she wasn't ready to face the world.

A soft knock came at the door. She froze, holding her breath like that would make it go away.

It was Jackie. Noodle could feel her mama's presence even before she heard the tentative voice. "Jacory, baby? You awake?"

The words hung in the air. Jackie waited a moment, and when Noodle didn't answer, the door creaked open.

"Jacory," Jackie tried again, this time stepping into the room.

Noodle's pale face peered out from under the covers. Jackie stood there awkwardly, her hands twisting the hem of her sweater. She looked out of place, unsure, as if one wrong move might make her daughter disappear.

"I—I know you probably don't want to talk," Jackie stammered, her voice shaking slightly. "But I was hoping we could."

It was hard to get one on one time in with her because Noodle clung to Bu like he would disappear if she didn't. It was cute but Jackie couldn't relate to such affection. Even after Stacy's passing, Jackie had yet to really date anyone. Instead, she thrust herself into church getting right with the Lord, hoping her daughter would make her way to her.

Noodle exhaled, letting the blanket fall to her shoulders. She propped herself up on one elbow, staring at her mother.

Jackie looked older than Noodle remembered, maybe it was the lines around her eyes or the way her shoulders sagged under the invisible weight. It struck Noodle how strange it was, that she could recognize these things in a woman she barely knew.

"What is there to talk about?" Noodle tsked, her voice flat.

Jackie flinched, but she didn't retreat. Instead, she moved closer, pulling out the small chair by the desk and took a seat. Her hands clasped in her lap, her eyes searching Noodle's face. "I just want to know how you're feeling," she said softly, "with everything that's happened."

Noodle studied her mama. Jackie had the same color skin, same curly hair and eyes. The upturned nose Noodle loved to look at— Jackie had that too. She was the spitting image of the woman who stood before her, which made being given up harder to understand. Her eyes went to the door, hoping Bu would come back to be the buffer between them. She needed him there to get through the terrible conversation she'd been avoiding for eleven years.

Noodle shrugged, pulling the blanket tighter around herself. "I don't know. Tired, I guess."

Jackie nodded slowly, her gaze dropping to her hands. For a moment, neither of them spoke. The only sound was the distant voices of whatever show Jackie had been watching.

"I'm sorry," Jackie said suddenly. It came out like air from a popped balloon. *Loud... Fast... Unexpected.*

Noodle blinked. "For what?"

"For not being there," Jackie said, her voice breaking. She looked up, her eyes glistening. "For not being the mom you needed, for... for everything I missed— I know I can't make it right, but I'm willing to try."

Noodle swallowed hard, her chest tightening. "Why now?" she asked, her voice sharper than she intended. "Why do you care now? You had years to care, Jackie. Years!"

Jackie flinched again, but she didn't look away. "I've always cared, Jacory," she pleaded. "I just... I didn't know how to be a mom. I was stupid, and I let my own problems get in the way. I let my fear get in the way."

Noodle laughed bitterly. "Fear? That's your excuse?"

"It's not an excuse," Jackie said firmly. "It's the truth. I was scared. I didn't know how to raise a kid, and I thought... I thought you'd be better off without me."

Noodle sat up fully, her blanket falling to her lap. "You thought I'd be better off without my mom?" she said, her voice rising. "Did you think I would be better off when the woman who was just as fucked up as you died? Did you think maybe, just maybe - I needed a mama then?"

Noodle sat up, her wet eyes - angry. Her body heat rising from emotions overflowing and her heart breaking at having to relieve things she'd rather move on from. "Do you know how many nights I cried myself to sleep because I wanted you?"

Tears spilled down Jackie's cheeks, but she didn't interrupt. She let Noodle's words crash over her, her own pain etched deeply into her face.

"You wasn't ready?" she scoffed. "You gave me up for love then turned around and gave me up again for money... but *you* were stupid... not ready? Thought I'd be better off with a man that put his hands on women?" Noodle mocked, her voice shaking. "Now, when my life is falling apart, you decide to care? You don't get to do that, Jackie. You don't get to waltz in here and pretend you my mama."

"Stacy never hit you though," Jackie defended, pissing Noodle off even more.

"As if that matters!" Her hands went up in the air. "I was ruined because love scared the hell outta me! I'm still scared, but my heart is telling me I at least have a fifty percent chance of a man not beating me to death. Stacy beat Cynthia so bad...and his death didn't just leave Siasia without a mama, but it left me stranded too. But you loved him so much that you gave him that much power over me because it wasn't about you." Noodle's voice broke. "I've been silently drowning and I didn't ask for help. I didn't complain. I thought I could fix it by myself, but I couldn't and I didn't." She tucked her face into her knees crying hysterically. "You ain't the only one at fault but I do blame you the most."

Jackie took a shaky breath. "I know I don't deserve another chance, Jacory. I understand that. But I'm here now, and I'm not going anywhere. I want to be there for you, if you'll let me."

Noodle stared at her, her emotions warring inside. Part of her wanted to scream at Jackie, to push her away and slam the door on this conversation. But another part - a quieter, more vulnerable part— wanted to believe her.

"I really thought a life with Siasia was better for you... better than a life with me," Jackie added, looking down at the floor, her hands back twiddling her sweater.

"You seem to think everywhere but with you is better... maybe Siasia was the best place but she's still not my mama. I want her to be my big sister and taking care of me shouldn't've been her responsibility. She was just a child too! I'd taken away so much of her youth already. It's why I never went to her when I should've or when I could have used her help. I still *need* my mama... I need you."

Jackie nodded, tears streaming down her face. "You're right," she said. "It should've been me, and I'll never forgive myself for leaving you. I wish I could but we can't erase the past. But I'm here now, Jacory. I'm ready to do whatever it takes to make all this up to you."

The room was silent for a long moment. Noodle stared at her mama, searching her face for any sign of insincerity, but all she saw was pain and love... all she saw was the future version of herself... all she finally saw was Jackie had been drowning too! Noodle groaned her eyes brimming with tears, totally drained from the past few days.

"I don't know if this'll be easy, but I mean it when I say I need my mama," Noodle said in a low hushed tone allowing her constant tears to fall freely.

Jackie nodded again. "And I need you, too."

Another silence stretched between them, but this time it felt different, softer.

"Bu said I can't heal if I keep pretending it don't hurt. So, I'm letting you know, it hurt… I'm hurt," Noodle said quietly.

Jackie's lips trembled into a small smile. "He sounds like a good man."

"He's the best man," Noodle's eyes swelled with love and pride thinking about Bu and how her life had been all wrong until he showed up. Bee had done her big one when she raised him.

Jackie hesitated, reaching out, her hand hovering in the air between them. "Can I— can I hug you?" she asked.

Noodle hesitated too, her heart pounding. Slowly, she nodded.

Jackie leaned forward, wrapping her arms around her daughter. Noodle stiffened at first, the gesture unfamiliar and overwhelming. But as Jackie held her, something inside her broke. She let out a shaky breath and leaned into the embrace, her tears soaking into Jackie's sweater.

They stayed like that for a long time, holding onto each other as if they were afraid to let go.

Eventually, Jackie pulled back, her eyes red and puffy. "Thank you."

Noodle nodded, wiping her own tears away. She didn't trust herself to speak.

Jackie stood, smoothing her sweater. "Come on," she said, a small smile tugging at her lips.

"Come on where?" Noodle asked, confused.

"To the kitchen," Jackie smiled. "Bu's a good man, but he's not your babysitter, and if you want to keep a man like him, you need to learn how to cook."

Noodle blinked, caught off guard by the sudden shift in tone. "Are you serious right now?"

"Dead serious." Jackie's smile widened. "Now get up. We've got work to do."

Noodle stared at her for a moment, then let out a reluctant laugh. "You're ridiculous," she said, throwing off the covers.

Jackie grinned. "Maybe, but you're still getting in that kitchen. This is what mama's do. They teach their little girls how to cook."

They walked to the kitchen together, the tension between them a little lighter but not gone. It wasn't perfect, and it wasn't everything Noodle had hoped for, but it was a start.

As Jackie pulled out ingredients and started explaining the basics of cooking, Noodle found herself smiling despite everything.

The little girl drawn to the water knowing she couldn't swim, stood on the coast only dipping her feet in. The little girl smiled because now she was sure that if her stubborn heart ever pushed her to wade into the water, someone would be there to pull her safely back to shore.

———

"I don't think I'm really ready, Luna," Noodle huffed, yanking her foot back from Bu's lap.

Luna fussed on the other end. "Jacory, come on...who I'm gon' get if you not comin'?"

"Qamar," Noodle snickered knowing Qamar could sing but he was no singer. "Do it yourself, Luna."

"Wow... so original," Luna rolled her eyes.

They were on facetime and after almost two weeks, Noodle was back to answering her phone. The minute she turned it back on, she was bombarded with calls, voicemails, and texts from her family. The social media notifications weren't important so she ignored them.

Bu pulled her foot back into his lap, daring her to snatch it away again. His hands kneading the balls of her feet, soothing any aches she may have had from them being out at the beach all day. Then they came home to a full spread that Noodle had insisted on making before she left. The food was really good. It had been a while since Bu had enjoyed a homecooked meal.

Noodle moaned out loud as she relaxed, his foot massages were sooo good.

"Ummm are you?" Luna cocked her head sideways as if she'd be able to see more. "Where Bu?" Luna asked, curiously.

"No Luna! I'm not having sex and he's right here rubbing my feet."

"That's still so intimate." Luna's face was still balled up. "Have you talked to Siasia?"

"No." Bu interjected. "I told her to talk to her sister but she over here being scared."

She cut her eyes at him. "When did we become Chatty Pattys?"

Luna kissed her teeth. "He's telling you the right thing. Siasia was worried about you. Fink had to convince her not to plaster your face all over the news. I never seen her so... broken." Luna didn't want to make Noodle sad but she needed to understand how worried her sister had been— how worried they all still were.

Noodle had yet to explain the video to them. French was ready to paint the whole Cali red behind her and of course Qamar was going to be right beside him doing life in prison. It was selfish to Luna that Noodle thought it was okay to pop back up with no real explanations, like nothing happened.

Sagging her shoulders, Noodle nodded in understanding. "You think she gon' be mad at me about wanting to build a relationship with Jackie?"

Bu's brows dipped. She was back to Jackie when all day it was mama this and mama that. He shook his head at her need to make everybody else comfortable while dismissing her own true feelings.

Noodle didn't make eye contact with him, reading his mind.

Luna huffed, "If anybody knows about strained mother relationships, it's me. I love Stephanie. Solar still ain't feeling her but that doesn't affect how I show up as a daughter to Stephanie and a sister to Solar. I love 'em both and you're gonna have to put your big girl panties on and handle your shit like an adult. My mama once told me, give me back my purse... you've been holding a grown woman's load when you should've just been a child living your life. So, Noodle, give them back their loads and show up in the world the way you want to show up... forget everything else."

"Okay," she whispered.

"Why don't you try putting your feelings into your music? That's what helped Siasia. It's the reason God gave you this gift. Use it wisely because you never know how your experiences could help the next little girl from Lynn Beach or The Jig, and before I forget, I'm sending you my friend Dejanay's number. I was supposed to give you before but with everything going on– I forgot. She's a beast when it comes to music management. Call her, she'll get you together."

22

"Oh my God!" Noodle buried her face into the bed, while Bu delivered mean back shots.

Sweat trickled down her back tattoo. He licked it up, making her body spasm as she tingled all over.

"It's mine, right?"

"Yes!"

"Tell me, it's mine...let me hear that pretty voice the world loves so much." His hand came down on her ass hard.

"It's yours...they don't hear me like this, baby." Noodle huffed, throwing her ass back to the best of her ability.

Bu's fingers scraped her scalp, before gripping her hair. His strokes slowed but even going slow, his dick was powerful. "I love you so much. You feel all this love I got for you?"

Frantically, she nodded her head yes.

"I want to hear you, baby... let me hear you."

"Bu I feel your love all over me. I— I love you so much," Noodle screamed, tucking her lips into her mouth knowing the thin walls had their business all in the streets. She put her hand up, he was sooo deep... too deep.

"You betta move that fuckin' hand... you said it's mine,

right?" Bu dug deeper into her. "Huh?" His hand sounded off again.

His rough hand, grabbed her neck, pulling her to him with his dick still deep inside of her. "Kiss me, baby."

Something about his rough loving turned her on. Noodle was desperate to do anything he asked. Greedily, she twisted her neck, sliding her tongue in his mouth, her pussy pulsing around him. "Baby?" Her soft eyes yearned for him.

"That's my baby... give me all you got."

Bu had been waiting to feel Noodle on his dick again. Two weeks in Lynn Beach was too long but he wasn't a disrespectful man, so he practiced restraint in Jackie's house. Now that they were at his house in Sapphire City, it was the first thing he did. Bu wasted no time getting her naked and putting his face between her legs.

"Hmmm," Noodle panted, enjoying the slow strokes he delivered, easing all her juices out of her. Bu was a passionate man both in bed and every day in every way.

"Hmmm," Noodle panted, melting under his slow and deliberate strokes, savoring the way he drew every drop of pleasure from her. Bu was a passionate man in every way. His touch always tender yet consuming being a true reflection of the passion he poured into every part of her.

"You ready for me?" His deep voice tickled her ear. "Turn around so I can watch you taking this dick before I fill you the fuck up."

Noodle did exactly what she was told, giving him her body any way he wanted it.

Tears leaked from her eyes when he flipped her around and fucked her missionary style, whispering how much he loved her, declaring how the universe had conspired with Bee to give him the best thing on earth— her.

"You my home, my safe place, literally my favorite fuckin' person, baby. You my universe and my world only exists in you."

———

Noodle didn't wanna leave him. She knew she had a two hour drive to Emerald City, but leaving felt like peeling herself away from the one thing that made her life feel steady in a crazy, unsteady world.

The Sun dipped lower, casting a honey glazed gleam over the neighborhood, making it too picture perfect for her to go. Or maybe it was the fine man she'd just been under that made the neighborhood movie worthy.

Javen's retirement party wasn't until Saturday, but she decided she would show up early, even if she wasn't ready to peel herself from Bu.

Javen had given Emerald City all of him so it was only right they send him off properly and she had to be there to show him love too. But in true family fashion, they were saving the best for their private party. Luna booked her to perform at the stadium party through her new manager, Dejanay. So far, Noodle felt good about her. She seemed cool and down to earth. She also had sad eyes when they Face-Timed but Noodle wasn't worried about that— hell, she could relate. Pain was something they all carried, some heavier than others.

Bu leaned against the SUV, a cloud of smoke curling from his lips. His eyes sat low but stayed locked on her like she was the last person on earth.

"You sure you can't come before Saturday?" Noodle asked, pulling him closer to her as if he could get into her skin. Feeling his warm body against hers almost had her saying fuck Emerald City.

Blowing the smoke from his mouth, his eyes hung low as his lips tugged up lazily. "You can't wait three days to see me?"

"Nooo," she whined. Her voice soft, with a slightly teasing tone.

"What you gon' do when you traveling around the world?"

He sucked in another plume of local weed. He missed that Cali weed and hated he wasn't able to bring any back with him.

The sun hit her face perfectly, making her glow more than she naturally did. "You coming with me, duh," Noodle said seriously.

A smirk slid across his face as she gripped his lips, signaling for him to blow her a shotgun. Bu didn't hesitate, spreading her lips with his tongue and pushing the smoke into her mouth with deliberate precision. The moment felt like everything was in slow motion. Intimate, hypnotic— a quiet rebellion against the chaos awaiting them beyond their bubble.

Their lips lingered – smoke curling between them, as if it were the only thread connecting them to this moment.

Fink pulled them out of it by rolling the window down, just as Ms. Linda stepped out on her porch.

"Bethune... I been looking for you boy." She stood with her hands on her hips.

Noodle snickered. "You in trouble."

"Shit, cause of you." Bu kissed the tip of her nose. "You gotta go, baby. Fink and Ben ready."

"But—" She stomped her feet.

"Here I come, Ms. Linda." Bu pulled the back door open, prompting Noodle to get in. She was still pouting.

"Get out your head... you need to talk to your sister anyway."

"I know," she said, sliding into the backseat. "Just see if you can get there before Saturday."

"Alright," Bu yelled over his shoulder, as he had already started making his way to Ms. Linda's house. "Drive safe, let me know when you get there."

"Uh un... let me see your little girlfriend, Bethune." Ms. Linda waved Noodle over, curiosity in her eyes.

She wasn't ready to leave her man anyway, so she hopped out of the truck, making her way to the porch. The scene was like a picture perfect snapshot of the life she was slowly starting to believe she deserved.

Bu had just stepped onto Linda's porch when a small black Honda creeped down the street. It was like everything moved in slow motion. The windows were dark, and as they rolled down slowly, Bu saw his heart being ripped from his chest.

"Fink!" Bu hollered, startling Noodle.

Fink and Ben hopped out the car militantly.

Bu removed his gun from his waistband just in time when suddenly shots rang out everywhere. Bu shot back, knocking Noodle onto the ground. "Stay down!" he barked, his voice raw but urgent.

But Bu didn't stay down. He was back on his feet in a flash. He seethed, thinking about something happening to his baby. So mad and only seeing red, he walked the car down, his arm fully extended like he'd been handling firearms his whole life. Well, he had been around them his whole life, but Noodle didn't know that. She saw glimpses of who he used to be, but never the full version of him… never *this side of him*. Bu kept firing shot after shot, reloading just as quickly, while Fink and Ben let loose too.

The car swerved wildly, bullets ripping through the black paint. The tires screeched as the car spun out of control, crashing into a light pole at the end of the street. The whole street went black.

Bu took long strides rushing to the wrecked car, his eyes alert for any movement. He needed to see their faces, needed them to see the last face they'd ever see. His mind was a blur of red. He didn't hear Ms. Linda screaming his name, he didn't feel Noodle in his mind begging him to come back to her. Bee had disappeared too. All he could see was having to bury his heart when he'd just gotten it back. Bee had been the treasurer of his heart - she had been the one to pray for his soul until he looked into Noodle's eyes and gave all of him to her hoping she'd find something she could take with her on her journey. She wasn't supposed to stay but in some way, he realized he needed her just as bad she needed him. So no, God wasn't with him when he clutched his gun in his hand, reaching for the door to end it all.

He reached for the car door, but before he could pull it open, Ben ran up behind him, wrapping him in a bear hug and hauling him back. "Let it go, Bu! Let it go!" Ben's voice was strained, his grip firm as he dragged him away from the wreckage.

Noodle scrambled to her feet, her heart pounding as she ran to Bu, tears streaming down her face. "Bu!" she cried, her voice breaking as she grabbed his face, her hands trembling as she searched him for injuries.

Bu stared at her, his eyes wide and vacant, the adrenaline coursing through him like a drug. His glasses were gone, but he still looked like the man who'd pulled her from the depths when she thought she'd never breathe again.

"Baby," she whispered, her voice trembling as she cupped his face.

"Look at me. Baby, please look at me."

Bu blinked, his gaze finally focusing on her. He reached up, his hand covering hers as reality crashed over him. He'd been here before… standing in the wreckage of his past, trying to make sense of the chaos. He thought karma had already taken its due from him, but this moment felt like a brutal reminder that his debts weren't paid in full.

Noodle pulled him close, holding him as tightly as she could, her tears soaking his t-shirt. "I thought— I thought—"

"I'm okay," Bu murmured, his voice thick with emotion. He buried his face in her hair, soaking in her coconut smell, his arms wrapping around her like she was the only thing keeping him upright.

Sirens wailed in the distance.

"Bethune, give that here, baby," Ms. Linda appeared beside him. Her frail old hands clutched the gun.

"Nah, Ms. Linda… I—"

"Hand it here like I said," Linda's voice dipped, her eyes glaring at him daring him to tell her no again. Just as she had the gun and was back on her porch, the police had everyone surrounded.

"On the ground!" they yelled.

Fink and Ben did as they were told but yelled to identify themselves as peace officers.

Noodle lay beside Bu just crying non-stop. He hated himself for thinking he could have a little piece of heaven after sneaking out of hell.

23

THE FLUORESCENT LIGHTS in the visiting room buzzed, but not as loud as Noodle's heart while she sat across from Bu. His orange jumpsuit felt like an insult, like the system was mocking everything good about him. She'd spent the whole drive rehearsing what to say, but now her mouth was dry, her words caught somewhere between her chest and her throat.

Bu leaned forward, resting his chained hands on the table. "Don't cry for me," he said softly, as if he hadn't just walked through fire for her.

"Why?" Noodle didn't say hey… she didn't have sympathy or anger or disappointment in her eyes like Bee had when she sat across from him for the first time. Noodle just asked one question. It had to make sense to her. "Why, Bethune?"

Without effort a lazy grin curled his lips. "I just want to make you happy… at least I didn't ki—"

She shook her head, her eyes scolding him. "I've watched enough crime shows to know you shouldn't say shit."

So he didn't. They just sat across from each other breathing.

Noodle was so mad, she could feel her body heating up every time she thought about those men that tried to take her Bu from her. They tried to rip her anchor away when she'd just found him. After the police showed up, they were notified that one man in the car was pronounced dead on the scene while the other one would probably never walk again. The injured one they rolled away started yelling how Bu had took his son from him, so Noodle put the pieces together and realized he must've been the down low boy's father. That made it sadder because Bu didn't even mean to kill his son. And had he been a better father — an accepting father, maybe his son would still be alive and living in his truth.

It took the police hours to make sense of the mess. Ben and Fink were cleared for self-defense but told to stay close, since the cops believed one of them had been the one to actually fire the kill shot on the deceased.

But when they got to Bu, as soon as they pulled his name up, their demeanors changed. All they saw was a convicted felon in a shootout. They had yet to determine if he even fired any shots since Ms. Linda had already hide his gun. Noodle was a mess that day, begging and pleading with them to not take him, but her sweet and syrupy voice that broke Bu to his knees, didn't work on them. They weren't trying to hear anything once Bu was identified. His name came up flagging gang affiliation and that he'd just been released almost a year ago.

They didn't want to hear that Ms. Linda had the whole thing on tape. It didn't make a difference when Ms. Linda came out the house with her own 9mm gun claiming, she had handed it to Bu when they checked his hands for gunshot residue.

So now, Noodle had to wait until Monday to see her man behind bars.

Javen's retirement party came and went like a blur. She performed as best she could, but immediately left to get back to Sapphire City just in case they released Bu.

"They don't give us a bunch of time for visits baby... don't waste it saying nothing."

Noodle kissed her teeth and rolled her eyes.

How was the world trying to take him away from her?

"How was the party? I saw the parade on TV..." Bu tried to make small talk, hating the sadness in her eyes. It was a reminder to him of what his actions helped wipe away. He lowered his head, hoping his tears wouldn't fall because he was just as fucked up about possibly being gone from her as she was.

Noodle didn't want to talk about the retirement party or the stupid parade. She wanted to talk about the quarter of a million dollars he spent to fight KidVerse that he never told her about. She wanted to talk about all the places they would go when he came home. She didn't care about anything else.

Those dark eyes looking into hers, that she'd never let the world trick her out of loving, were her only concern. The way she could feel his heart through hers was both criminal and whimsical.

At the same time, they touched their chests.

Bu cleared his throat. "I'm good, baby... this ain't nothing new."

"But it is... it's new because I won't survive without you... I keep getting in the water... keep getting tricked by how familiar it looks and I know it's not safe but the way it calls to me," she swallowed her tears. "No one will hear me yelling for help... nobody but you."

He smiled again with those glasses pushing against his face. "They can't hear you because you ain't really yelling... you gotta let people know you need help, baby."

"How did you hear me, Bu?"

He looked down, his hand pushing against his head before running down the chains on his wrist clinking together. "My heart gotta know morse code or some shit because even when you don't say shit, I hear the thumping of your heart telling me to come get you."

"Do you want kids?" She needed to know because her uterus hurt just thinking about carrying his babies. How could she not when he said sweet things to her like that?

As she waited for him to respond, her eyes moved around

the room. There was a swarming energy of sadness and fake happiness. No matter how much people laughed with their loved ones, the joy didn't sound authentic. She swallowed her own sadness down.

"You pregnant?" Bu stopped, tapping his hand on the table long enough to stare into her face.

Noodle shook her head. "No... my boyfriend is responsible."

"Oh, he be wrapping up?"

"Hell no," she giggled, looking around to make sure no one was listening. "He sent me to the doctor to get on birth control."

Bu nodded, his smile growing serious. "Why you asking about kids then, baby? Never let a nigga make you a baby mama before he makes you a wife. If you think I ain't gon' plant my seeds in you and watch 'em grow, you outta yo mind. But I'll give you my last name first."

"So, how long you thinking?" she fluttered those lashes that made him weak in the knees.

His head fell back, laughing. "What my boy Leon say, carry me home, marry me now and I promise you everything."

"You are my everything." She blushed. "You know I'm in your head, right?"

"What you talkin' 'bout baby?" Bu sat up... even in orange he was fine...even in his state issued glasses. They didn't let him keep his designer ones that she loved to see him in.

Noodle leaned forward. "You think I'm going to run... think I should let you float in the water by yourself, but I'm not. We're locked in and I ain't going nowhere... no running, just chasing love. I'm following you because I'll follow you into the water, the sky, and to hell."

"Wrap it up!" The COs yelled.

———

Walking out of the jail, Noodle held her head up as cameras

flashed from all directions. It didn't take long before the paparazzi had the story on Jay Jay's bad boy getting caught in a shootout. The internet hadn't calmed down from her alleged sex scandal a few weeks ago and now she was back in the press for all the wrong reasons. She was so fed up of this.

"How is he?" Fink asked, once they were safely in the car behind the black tint.

"As good as anybody in jail, I guess. You know he's not going to break down and cry to me. So, I guess he's okay." She flopped back into the seat, her eyes going to the moonroof.

It didn't matter where she went. Fink would always rent a SUV with a moonroof. She appreciated the little things. It showed how they were more than just her hired security. They had transformed into family.

"Noodle, Bu ain't the kind of man to hide his feelings from you. If he wanted to breakdown and cry to you, trust he would. If he says he's good, it's probably because he is," Fink tried to explain to her, hoping it would help soothe her worrisome mind.

"Yea, okay," she sighed. "Has Elle called while I was in there?"

Elle had been hired to handle the case with Bu. She was a beast and better suited to handle what he was going through. The family had her on retainer so she showed up whenever she could.

"No," Ben sighed, looking out the window. "The whole thing is messed up, if you ask me.'

"If you ask anybody," Fink added. "Don't worry though Noodle, he'll be home soon."

"Yea, that's what they say," she muttered, slumping down in the seat as they rode through the city to her hotel. Bu's house and truck had been shot up so she couldn't stay there. Even Ms. Linda's home had bullet holes in it. It was all a huge mess.

———

The car pulled up to the curb in front of the hotel. Noodle stared out the window, her eyes dull as they traced the neon glow of the city reflecting off the rain-slick streets. The ride back from the jail had been quiet and heavy. Seeing Bu in cuffs and that orange jumpsuit, separated from her by a cold metal table, was like feeling her heart break all over again.

His absence was a weight she carried everywhere, pressing down on her chest, making it hard to breathe, even after she'd just seen him.

Fink stepped out first, coming around to open the back door. Noodle didn't move right away. She wasn't ready to face the world outside the safety of the car. When Fink opened the door, her breath caught.

Siasia stood there, just as pretty as she'd always been. She was dressed casually, her arms crossed, but the softness in her eyes betrayed the tension in her posture.

Noodle froze, unsure of what to say. They didn't really talk at Javen's retirement party, She performed, exchanged a few pleasantries, and then slipped out before the night was over. There was too much to unpack then, and maybe she hadn't been ready.

But here Siasia was, standing in front of her like an unspoken question.

"Noodle," Siasia said gently, her voice laced with concern.

The name had been given to her by Siasia. To her, she had always been Noodle. She never called her Jacory or Jay Jay.

Noodle swallowed hard, her throat tight. "What are you doing here?"

"I came to see you," Siasia simply replied. "You left the party so fast. At first I thought you was just so worried about Bu, but then it hit me that you were avoiding me."

Noodle slid out of the car, her shoulders hunched as if carrying a burden too heavy for one person. Fink nodded to both women before giving them space, heading toward the hotel lobby.

"I'm not avoiding you," Noodle said quietly, not quite meeting Siasia's gaze.

"Then what was it?" Siasia stepped closer.

Noodle leaned against the wet car, folding her arms across her chest. "I just... didn't know how to talk to you. There's been so much going on, and I didn't want to ruin things for you. You've got Qamar, and you're happy. I didn't want to bring my mess into your life."

Siasia's expression softened, shaking her head. "Noodle, you're my sister. You can't ruin nothing by talking to me. It's what I'm here for."

Noodle finally looked up, her eyes glassy with unshed tears. It was time for her to tell her truth, time for her to ask for help. "I love you, Sisi... I love you so much for everything you've done for me. You didn't have to step up the way you did, but you did, and I'll never stop being grateful for that. But..." She hesitated, searching for the right words. "I want a mom *and* a sister, not either or. I've been trying to build something with Jackie, and it feels good... like something I've been missing my whole life. But it doesn't mean I don't love you or still need you."

Siasia's lips parted, her expression unreadable for a moment. Then she stepped forward and pulled Noodle into a tight hug. "I will never leave you," she whispered. "And I get it— I do. I just want you to be happy. If Jackie can give you something I can't, I'm not mad about that. You deserve it... Now, I don't know how nice I'll be when she's around but..."

Noodle laughed, knowing how her big sister was.

Her eyes became sad again. She wanted to be happy that her sister was onboard but all she could think about was Bu.

"How is Bu doing?" Siasia asked, knowing her sister was hurting behind that too.

Noodle's tears spilled over, and she clung to Siasia, her voice trembling. "I miss him so much, already, and I don't care how long it takes or what anyone says—I'm staying with him... am I being dumb?"

Siasia pulled back just enough to look Noodle in the eyes, wiping at her own tears. "No, Noodle. You are just a girl in love… I understand because love is both ugly and beautiful… love makes you second guess your morals sometimes too," she chuckled. "But I understand, I see how he loves you and how you love him. Never let anyone take that away from you. Plus, the way I heard he walked them niggas down 'bout you, chile."

Noodle nodded, her chest tightening with relief. "My man don't play about me."

"Y'all want to get in the car?" Ben asked, coming back out since the rain was starting again.

Instead of getting in the car, they walked inside the hotel, making their way to the bar where they found a secluded area.

After a moment, Siasia tilted her head, her expression turning serious. "What happened with KidVerse? That's the shit I need to know more than anything else."

Noodle stiffened slightly, her jaw tightening before she told Siasia everything. The same way she gave it to Bu, she gave it to her sister. Her tears started and stopped throughout the retelling of the story. But once she laid it all out on the table, she felt better. Like some of her pain had been lifted for good this time.

Siasia studied her for a moment, thinking of a way for her sister to spin everything that had happened in her life into something tangible. "What if you put out your own video? Set the record straight, let people hear your side."

"You think that would work?" Noodle blinked, considering the idea.

"I think you've got a voice people want to hear. And it's about time they hear the truth—from you, not from anyone else."

Noodle exhaled slowly, determination lighting up inside her. "Okay, let's do it, but you gotta help me figure out what to say."

Siasia smiled wider, pulling her back into another hug. "Oh baby, I ain't lettin' you do nothing else without me… you done lost your virginity and fell in love." She dabbed at her face thinking about her first baby growing up to be the perfect young woman.

Noodle smiled hard, happy to have both her sister and her mama. All she was missing was Bu. She knew God wouldn't give her a love like this and snatch it back like this. She knew these were the battle scars you stared at once the war was over, thankful for the reminder.

24

The small office in Madison Heights smelled of fresh paint and sawdust, the kind of scent that promised new beginnings. Noodle stood in the center of the space, her arms folded as she surveyed the work in progress, *Bumblebee Landscaping*. She'd painted the name herself, gold letters popping against the deep green of the sign on the back wall behind the desk. It was Bu's dream, and if the world wouldn't give him freedom yet, she'd build something solid for him to come home to. But even as she smiled, pride swelling in her chest, the weight of old wounds pulled at her.

"Man, this shit so nice," Pimp walked in, his eyes already glossing over. "Damn, this is love for real."

"Hell yea," Lunar nodded. "I can't wait to find some shit like this. Noodle was supposed to be mine."

Aku cackled. "Don't let Bu hear you. He shoot 'bout his girl."

Everyone laughed loud and hard. It was funny now that they felt good about him being able to prove his innocence. They tried to offer him a plea deal but he didn't take it. So now they were waiting to present all the evidence to a judge to get the charges dropped.

"Yea, this is nice but you know we have to prep you for your radio interview tomorrow and you have a session with..." Dejanay looked over the calendar in her phone. "That producer you been dying to get up with."

Lunar cocked his head to the side, his eyes questioning Noodle. She had gone rogue. Since KidVerse had so many people scared to work with her in fear of losing their business relationship, she started working with independent artists, producers, and songwriters. Her fans praised her for it because she'd been putting out some fire music while making sure to uplift the little people in the world. Of course, Luna helped her write a lot of music too and kept her in the loop, but she was creating a sound the people had never heard before. Noodle's tone was sultry, hip hop, and soulful. She wasn't the shy America's sweetheart on KidsVerse anymore.

Now she was the girl with tattoos, blinged out jewelry, who had a man that was locked up. When she thought about trying to clean it up, Dejanay told her to lean into who she really was. It made her more relatable because she'd walked on both sides of darkness.

Growing up in a trailer, she was transformed into a princess when her sister fell in love with a rich man. Jacory was the best of both worlds.

And to think she did it all while, building Bu's company up too. *Bumblebee Landscaping* was all over billboards. She had a commercial and everything. They even won the award for Best company for lawns in the L.A. area. Their clientele ranged from celebrities to mom and pop businesses.

"What time is this interview, cause you know Bu calls me every morning, real early?" Noodle flopped down on a folding chair. Before now, she was operating the business from the beach house. But with more employees and equipment, she had to buy a brick and mortar location. She was even in the process of developing their own line of fertilizer and other chemicals for lawns as the business ideas kept flowing once she got started.

"Yea, because I gotta style you," Aku yawned, needing a nap. Outside of styling Noodle, she'd taken on other clients and was constantly on the go. She loved it and felt like she was finally finding her footing.

Dejanay cut her eyes at both of them. "Eight in the morning… don't be late neither! And you," she swung to look at Lunar. "What's up with the album?"

Lunar had been dealing with his own issues of self-identity, making it hard for him to make meaningful music.

His deep dimples sunk as he gave her a boyish grin to mask his inner turmoil. "I can't just put out anything… you know I gotta take my time."

"Bullshit!" Pimp fake sneezed, gaining him a side eye from his best friend.

Lunar shot him a bird, just as the front door dinged.

"Ma!" Noodle ran into Jackie's arms. "When you got here?"

"Just now… you was on the phone complaining about how overworked you felt with the company and trying to make your album, so here I am. I'm going to handle things here while you do your music thing." Jackie squeezed Noodle while mouthing *hey* to everyone else.

"Thank the Lord!" Dejanay lifted her hands in the air. She loved Noodle's drive but it was a lot on her client at one time. Dejanay understood and never tried to make her choose but having someone there Noodle could trust would free her up to really get in the studio and do a few more shows.

Noodle looked around the room, so thankful for the village God gave her. When her nights felt dark and weary, he kept showing up and showing out.

———

The buzzing phone on the counter jolted Noodle from her thoughts. She grabbed it in a hurry, knowing exactly who it was.

The ringtone she'd assigned to him, just the sound of his voice saying *'pick up, baby'*—filled the quiet studio room. Pressing the phone to her ear, she let out a shaky breath.

"Bu?" she said softly, her voice catching slightly.

Bu had a contraband cell phone in jail so there was no pesky operator telling them how long they had or reminding them he was so far away from her. They didn't talk all day though, as they didn't want to overdo it and have him get caught so they talked on a schedule.

"I'm here, baby," his deep, gravelly voice rumbled through the line. "You good?"

Noodle's lips trembled, the weight of him not being out, sitting heavy on her chest. "I'm good enough now that I hear your voice."

"Come on, baby," he cut her off gently. "Don't do that. Don't get in your head about things we can't control."

"You in jail for protecting me…for protecting us, and they're treating you like you're some criminal who can't change— like you didn't just save my life!" she huffed. "The company is so beautiful, you should be here for this. I'm almost done with my album and you ain't here to hear it. The person who inspired it all, ain't here to hear it before the world," she sniffled.

"Noodle," he said firmly, his tone softening. "We knew what this could be. I'm a felon, baby. They was always gonna look at me sideways. But Ms. Linda's cameras show the truth. It's just gonna take time for them to see what we already know. I'm coming home soon."

She didn't respond right away, her throat tightening as she attempted to swallow her tears.

"Tell me about the interview." He tried to change the mood. "You kill it?" Bu asked, his deep voice rumbling through the line.

"I did what I always do," she teased. "Had to let the world know Jacory's here to stay."

"That's what I'm talkin' about, baby," he said, pride evident in his tone. "I can't wait to come home so we can celebrate. I'm tired of hearing your voice through the phone."

She laughed, the sound light and full of joy. "Soon, baby. Just hold on a little longer," she tried to sound like him even though her heart bled every time she talked to him, knowing he wasn't there with her.

Time didn't make it easier and no matter how many songs she wrote about her love for him, she still yearned to be tucked under him. Yearned to hear him critique her music, making sure he pulled the best out of her. Her body shuddered, because she missed her vocal coach.

"Get out your head, baby. Stay in mine…"

"Where we at now?" Noodle tucked her feet under her body, getting comfortable.

"I'm in the water… in *this* galaxy you saved me… *you* pulled me out the water."

Epilogue

THE ARENA WAS ON FIRE, and Noodle's heart had yet to settle. The roar of the crowd outside sent tremors through the walls, vibrating under her feet like a heartbeat she wasn't quite sure she could keep up with. She was excited, yet nervous, because no one ever told her that dreams, when they come true, hit you with a weight you didn't expect.

Her career started rocky, stitched together with scraps, doubt, and survival. But now she stood at the center of her own universe, headlining an arena tour. The girls looked up to her. They accepted every part of her, even the parts the industry labeled as dirty, ghetto, and raw. Her authenticity was a rebellion, and the world loved her for it, and even though it took her twenty-one years to figure out who she really was, she wouldn't change her journey for anything.

The last year had been hard. The kind of hard that leaves scars, but ones she wore with pride. God didn't put anything on her that she couldn't handle, and if anything, He gave her those battles to remind her of just how unbreakable she really was.

Noodle took a deep breath and closed her eyes. She needed to warm up, so she started with a low hum, letting the note roll around in her chest. It vibrated through her like a grounding force.

She stretched her neck from side to side as she raised the pitch, sliding into a soft falsetto. Noodle exhaled effortlessly, then dropped the pitch into a throaty growl, laughing at her own dramatics.

"Hmm... hmm! Hmm... hmm... ha!" she sang, emphasizing each sharp note while throwing her ass in a circle.

Dejanay came zooming into the room with her face in her phone. "You warming up or getting ready to pop that coochie on the pole?" she teased, typing away on one of many phones she carried like her life depended on it.

"Both," Noodle laughed, shaking out her hands hoping to get more of her nerves out of her body. "How did I get here?" The thought poured out when that hadn't been her intention.

Dejanay didn't respond because she'd had one too many conversations with Noodle about self-doubt and self-sabotage.

"You good?" Aku asked, snapping her back to the present. She stood behind her with a bottle of body shimmer in his hands, squeezing a generous amount into her palms. Without waiting for an answer, she smoothed the glittering cream over Noodle's shoulders,, shining her up like the diamond she was.

"Good as I can be," Noodle replied, offering a small smile that didn't quite reach her eyes.

Aku gave her a look, cocking an eyebrow. "Hoe, don't give me that half ass answer. You good-good? Or just faking-it-good?"

She exhaled, tilting her head back to look at the ceiling. "I'm good, Aku...but I'm a little sad too."

Her eyes went sad. "Aww, Noodle...he'll be home soon. He better 'cause baby, I been planning y'all wedding for the last six months," Aku joked.

That made Noodle smile with memories of Bu. The way that man held every piece of her heart in his hands was so powerful. A bigger smile danced across her face when she thought about how scared she used to be of letting anyone love her.

"Are you happy?" Aku asked, reminding Noodle of how close they were... reminding her of their childhood check ins.

It had been a while since she'd been asked that, but Noodle knew even with a little nerves and sadness, she was very happy. "The best kind of happiness... like I feel it even when I'm alone, Aku." Her eyes misted. "My one regret is depriving myself of this for so long...hiding what was really going on with me, allowing my grief to linger, and my hurt to replay on an endless cycle. My biggest regret is thinking I was chasing something when all along I was running from it."

Aku wrapped her arms around Noodle. "You're my favorite person," Aku cried.

"I'm my favorite person, too..." Noodle giggled.

"And not just the happy you Noodle, I've loved every version of you. You are my sister, my secret keeper, and the one person I can't do life without. If I never told you before, I love you."

"I love you too," Noodle pulled Aku back into her. "And whatever you're looking for will find you sooner than you think. What I feel, I wish it on my enemies because that's just how beautiful, whole, and safe I feel."

"Good enough to want your enemies to feel it?" Aku shook her head. "I'll never be that healed and happy."

Noodle pinched her. "Aku, please! Yes you will and I promise when you get this full circle feeling, anger won't even live in you anymore."

"Well tell me something since you know everything now," Aku smirked teasingly before, pulling back from her to continue getting her ready.

Aku had become Noodle's official stylist. When Lunar told them they needed to make it a family thing, he was right. The three of them leaned on each other heavily with promises to always hold one another up. The label was thriving with Lunar looking at signing a few more artists. He said he didn't want too many artists on the roster but wanted to help other black kids—it was what Big Lunar would do.

Noodle's thoughts went to Bu. She'd wished he'd be home by the time she made it to Lynn Beach for her last show. Although his innocence could be proven, the DA had dragged their feet on investigating the shooting. But since he was a convicted felon with a little money, they denied bail every time his attorney requested it.

Aku stepped back to admire her work, her tone softening. "And you know Bu would be here if he could."

She nodded, biting her lip. "I know. I just wish he could see it. Like for real, not just hear about it through his lawyer or see clips online." Noodle huffed allowing her makeup artist to dab away the tears on her face.

"It's almost time Noodle," Dejanay said looking up from her phone for a brief second. Noodle's success was a big deal and she was continuously growing, so she stayed busy.

Noodle nodded, wiggling her shoulders to shake her nerves off.

Aku sighed, running a hand over her signature bob. "The DA is on some bullshit but Bu gonna be home soon. Elle said she's pushing every button she can, calling people, and making noise. You know she's the best."

That made Noodle smile for real this time. "Yea, Elle is a fine ass Pitbull in a skirt."

Aku laughed, patting her shoulder lightly, careful not to smudge the shimmer. "Period! So just focus on your show tonight, and kill that shit. You've got a whole arena out there waiting to lose their minds, and you're the reason why."

Noodle glanced at her reflection in the mirror, taking in the liner that winged her almond eyes, the bold red nails, and glossy lips. Her hair had been straightened, with light curls towards the end. Her outfit of choice was a red two piece pants suit that hugged every curve she'd developed over the past year.

Noodle looked like a star, but there was still a sting of doubt in her chest. "You think I'm ready?" she asked, her voice quieter than before.

"Girl," Aku said, cutting her eyes. "You been ready. You were ready the moment you opened your mouth in that soccer arena all those years ago and told the world to listen. Tonight? You're about to make history."

Noodle blinked, swallowing the lump in her throat. "Okay," she said, steadying herself. "Okay… I'm ready."

Aku grinned, stepping back and giving her a playful shove toward the door. "Been fuckin' ready!"

"Let's go," Dejanay walked through the door first.

As soon as Noodle entered the hall, Fink and Ben were right there always ready to keep her safe.

She could hear the opening artist getting the audience hype. It was so loud, it coated her skin in chill bumps. Hearing the crowd chanting her name would never get old.

"Jacory! Jacory!"

As Noodle turned to head toward the stage she paused, looking over her shoulder. "Aku?"

"Yea?"

"Thanks. For everything. I don't know if I say it enough."

Aku smirked, waving her off. "You don't have to. We're family, remember? Always."

Her heart swelled at that word. *Family.* The kind of family they'd built out of chaos, love, and loyalty. She nodded, turning back toward the stage.

The moment she stepped up, the deafening roar of the crowd hit her like a tidal wave. Her nerves were still there, but so was the fire.

Somewhere out there, Bu was listening. But right now, Noodle belonged to the stage… to the crowd… to the galaxies she was about to chase down and make her own.

———

After an hour and fifteen minutes on stage, Noodle's show was coming to an end. She knew the song everyone wanted to hear because it was her most popular song. Her whole album had gone platinum but the single she wrote about Bu was diamond certified. She understood why. Noodle put her entire soul into that song.

As the song started, Bu's massive voice cracked through the speakers. Her body shuddered with thoughts of him talking in her ear. The arena got quiet to hear him because something about that deep, smoky southern drawl commanded attention.

"Baby... I know you probably busy and I promise I'll call you back later but I just wanted you to know I'm so proud of you. I see you doing your thing out there, not letting fear slow you down. I wish I was there to witness it in real time... I fucked up and I gotta live with this..." you could hear the chatter of the jail in his background. "I just wanted to tell you I love you and I'd chase galaxies just to find you, because loving you feels like discovering a universe I never knew I needed."

Noodle wiped her face, listening to his voice. That message got her through some tough days when all she wanted to do was crawl into his skin and listen to his heartbeat. Licking her lips, she pushed her red bedazzled microphone to her lips. "Lynn Beach!" The crowd roared. "I said, muthafuckin' Lynn Beach... my hometown... where Jacory was birthed." She looked up into the skybox that held her people. She knew Jackie was up there crying because she cried about everything that had to do with Noodle. She kissed her hand before blowing it up there. "It's some important people up there. My whole family... except my baby," she lowered her voice. The crowd yelled we love you and other terms of endearment to her.

"You ever been loved so good they bring out the best in you?" Noodle licked her lips hoping it helped her get through the emotional moment. "I ain't talkin' 'bout showing you who you could be...nah, I'm talking about lovin' you so good that the real you comes out...they love you so good it makes you feel comfortable enough to be everything you supposed to be..." The music dropped and the crowd went wild. Noodle smiled hard with tears in her eyes. "My man, my man, my man!" she yelled when pictures of her and Bu flashed across the back of the arena. All the candid images of them in their element covered the jumbotron.

The girls that got it, screamed with tears in their eyes. Noodle couldn't wait for her Bu to be free. As if they knew her heart, they started chanting *Free Bu*, over and over, creating a warmth in the stadium that burned her eyes more.

A year without her love had been a challenge but she knew there was no one else on this earth that could love her like him. Even behind bars, he made her soul feel full. On her lowest days, he comforted her with words or by having Ben drop her off at the spa, and those days were plenty. Between her budding career and running his super successful landscaping business, she barely got any sleep. It was worth it though.

"I never needed saving, I told myself that twice,
Built my walls up high, yeah, I locked up my life.
No white horse, no armor, no dreams I never drew,
But then you came along, and now I'm breaking every rule."

The crowd put their phone flashlights on to light up the arena. Noodle could only smile. If someone had told her a year ago that this was where she'd be, she would've laughed in their face, but somehow everything worked out better than she could've ever imagined.

"Bu, my Bu, you got me feeling something new,
Every step I take with you, I'm losing all my truth.
Bu (Boo), my Bu, I swore I'd never let one through,
But the way you hold me down, it's like I'm flying too.
Boo, oh Bu, my Bu."

Her voice was angelic and diverse. She could hit runs with the best of them or be on a chill vibe with the rest of them but the industry had dubbed her the sound of her generation, and she could only get better.

She sung with her eyes closed, letting her love for Bu bleed on the stage in front of the world. Her chest tightened when their shared memories flashed in her head. Noodle missed him so much, she choked on her words but the audience carried the rest of it for her, filling the empty spaces of the song with groans of sympathy.

Her knees buckled but before she fell down on the stage, she felt his arms wrapped around her. That brown sugar scent she sprayed over the beach house whenever she was in town to feel like he'd been there, cuddled her, triggering more tears.

"Get out your head, baby," he murmured into her ear as she cried so hard her body shook uncontrollably.

Everyone had their phones out, capturing the serene moment.

The two of them were so wrapped up in their own galaxy that they just swayed to her song as the instrumental played. Bu slipped the ring on her finger because everything he'd ever wanted to say to her had been said...had been felt and Noodle knew she was his, and he was hers.

The stadium lit up red and marry me flashed on every screen. "Marry me baby and I promise you the world."

"How when you already gave it to me?" she asked, still crying. Her makeup was a mess but she didn't care.

"I'll find another one then, 'cause I wanna live in every universe with you. You mine right, baby?" Bu licked her earlobe.

"Yes," Noodle jumped into his arms, placing wild kisses all over his face.

The crowd hollered more, even though they didn't hear any of that. All they knew was Noodle's Bu was home and their girl was happy.

Falling in love for them had been like chasing galaxies...

endless, breathtaking, and filled with the kind of wonder that made the universe feel small in comparison.

Forever wasn't long enough.

The End

Let's talk…

Want Paperbacks? Click the link: www.evelynlatrice.com

Follow me on IG: https://bit.ly/3UgwrLG

Join My Group: https://bit.ly/lovelustgroup

Made in the USA
Monee, IL
16 May 2025

79a180d4-beeb-450b-aee0-0b62ddad1165R01